Thrust In Your Sickle

But Watch Your Fingers

Thrust In Your Sickle

But Watch Your Fingers

Rob Eaton

First Printing: December, 1998

International Standard Book Number
0-88290-642-9

Horizon Publishers' Catalog and Order Number
1975

Printed and distributed
in the United States of America by

Horizon Publishers
& Distributors, Incorporated

Mailing Address:
P.O. Box 490
Bountiful, Utah 84011-0490

Street Address:
50 South 500 West
Bountiful, Utah 84010

Local Phone: (801) 295-9451
WATS (toll free): 1 (800) 453-0812
FAX: (801) 295-0196

E-mail: horizonp@burgoyne.com
Internet: http://www.horizonpublishers.com

Contents

Acknowledgments

I gratefully acknowledge the brutal (and therefore especially helpful) editing of my wife, Dianne, as well as her patience and support. She made the book much better, and still kept our marriage intact and happy.

I also appreciate the assistance, encouragement and constructive comments on early drafts of this book from many friends, including Paul Walker, Cathy Hanson, Rosemary Reeve, Wes Mann, Mike Niehoff, Steve Eaton, Jackson Eaton, Rebecca Eaton, and Julie Fletcher. Joel Wakefield undoubtedly would have provided many useful insights at an early stage in this project, had he not lost the first copy I gave him.

Many thanks as well to Horizon Publishers and its staff for their assistance in preparing this manuscript for publication and for being willing to publish this story. Finally, a special thanks to my father, Ed Eaton, for teaching me and inspiring me to write.

As you read this book, you will become aware that various sections are preceded by a series of three typographic symbols. Each series of symbols represents the missionary who is featured in that section.

The following legend shows which symbols relate to each missionary:

Elder Wesley Hawthorne *is preceded by*

❖ ❖ ❖

Elder Chris Roberts *is preceded by*

✦ ✦ ✦

Elder Jon Prentice *is preceded by*

✧ ✧ ✧

1
Smuggled Cd's and Smudged Glasses

As Jon Prentice stuffed his Game Boy into his suitcase, he wondered what he would miss more—kissing or music. Jon thought of the issue as kissing rather than girls because he had no intention of writing off girls altogether. Far from it—he fully planned to cultivate long-term relationships by mail with three girls he'd dated during the last few months.

J.P., as his friends sometimes called him, wanted to be sure he covered his bases. With three girls writing him, he'd get more letters, more cookies, more of whatever girls sent missionaries.

More importantly, J.P. understood that with one girl waiting for him, the odds were she'd be hanging on someone else's arm by the time he came home. With three girls, J.P. would have three times the chance of a gorgeous girlfriend waiting for him at the airport when he returned.

Of course, these long distance relationships wouldn't satisfy J.P.'s need for face-to-face socializing with the opposite sex. That need would be met by Laurels—German Laurels, to be exact. J.P. had seen how the missionaries in his home ward had used their status as intriguing newcomers and perceived spiritual giants to steal away the hearts of unsuspecting seventeen-year-olds. And the fact that the elders were off limits seemed to pique the girls' interest all the more.

Now these advantages would belong to J.P., and he had no reservations about playing them to their fullest to make the most of his two years of abstinence from kissing. Flirting in German would be a challenge, to be sure, and unshaven armpits on a woman would take some getting used to. But all in all, the cosmopolitan notion of winning the interest of a German girl or two rather excited J.P.

No, Jon Prentice had no intention of giving up girls just because he was going on a mission. But he would give up physical contact. He'd heard too many stories of elders getting sent home for minor transgressions, and J.P. did not want to get sent home. Getting sent home branded you, and J.P. couldn't live with the social fallout of that.

Like high school, a mission was a rite of passage for J.P., and the point was to have as much fun as possible without getting kicked out or sent home. Up to that line, his escapades would be something to boast about and if he later chose to get real spiritual—repent of. He would have plenty of fun—he'd have to in order to keep sane. But, as in high school, J.P.

would quickly discover what was out of bounds so he could play just inside the lines.

Titillating letters sprinkled with vague hints of marriage, flirting in a new language—these would be good, but they were no substitute for kissing. Yes, two years without kissing would be a long time.

Two years without music wouldn't be easy either. Kissing was a fabulous sensation, but the thrill didn't last very long. Music lasted for hours, and it was there when nothing else was. J.P.'s CD's pumped him up when he needed a lift, gave him company when he was down, indulged him when he was infatuated, and expressed his rage when he felt angry.

If there were a fire, the first thing J.P. would save from his room would be his CD collection. J.P. grew irritated as he glanced at the CD's his parents had bought him for his mission: *The Messiah, Hymns of Faith* by Mormon Tab, and Beethoven's odd-numbered symphonies. His parents meant well, but he'd almost rather go without than listen to this spiritually sanitized stuff.

Out of frustration J.P. tossed one of the CD's across the room and through his Nerf basketball hoop. The CD case broke open and the disc flew out. Looking at the empty CD container, J.P. had one of the flashes of brilliance that had made him a solid "B" student without spending any more time studying than dating.

He quickly grabbed one of his U2 CD's, stuck it in the *Messiah* CD container, and flipped the jacket shut. "U2 sings *The Messiah*," said J.P. to himself with a laugh. Two minutes later, J.P. had his seven favorite CD's inside the covers of the seven CD's his parents had given him. Yes, thought J.P., he would be good at this game too.

And he knew now he would definitely miss kissing more than music.

✦ ✦ ✦

As his brother's 1973 Chevy Nova chugged up the gradual incline of Ninth East Street, the knot in Chris Roberts' stomach was even tighter than when he'd driven up the same street to attend the first day of classes five months earlier. He hoped the anxiety would turn to energy and then success as quickly on his mission as it had at college. In an odd way, Chris enjoyed the tension and nervous excitement that accompanied any new adventure.

Chris's thoughts drifted to his first day of college, but he was quickly brought back to the present by his older brother. "Ok, private, the basics," barked Steve in his best drill sergeant voice. "Love the people!"

It usually took Chris between one and two seconds to figure out what his brother was doing, but once he did, he always played along. "Love the people!" repeated Chris, doing his best imitation of a private.

"Keep the rules! . . . Follow the Spirit! . . . Don't dilute!"

Even in reviewing everything he had taught Chris about missions in the last five months, Steve simply could not be conventional. He continued his litany of last-minute advice as the Nova sputtered steadily past Deseret Towers, sounding as if it ran on 7-Up.

"Be real! . . . Work hard! . . . Don't bash! . . . Cover your mouth when you cough, and don't drool!"

"Right," answered Chris, switching to his best British accent. "Don't cough while you bash and cover your mouth when you drool."

"No, no, no," corrected Steve, himself switching to a Monty Python voice and playing the straight man for once. "Cover your mouth when you cough, and don't drool."

"Aaah, right," replied Chris as they approached the last stop light on their journey. "Don't bash when you're drooling, and cover your mouth if you love the people."

Steve couldn't keep it up any more. "I'm really going to miss you, little brother," he said with a gentle shake of his head and a smile.

"I'll miss you too," answered Chris. Chris quickly glanced down at his uncomfortable new black dress shoes to avoid showing any outward sign of sentimental weakness. He was committed to acting as if his departure were no big deal. However, as the light turned green he felt himself slipping in his attempt at being emotionally nonchalant.

The Roberts brothers rode together in a rare moment of awkward silence as the Missionary Training Center came into full view. The Nova turned into the parking lot, through the February slush, and stopped behind a line of cars carrying similar cargo.

As Chris opened the door to climb out, he could actually hear the stifled weeping of a mother bidding her missionary son farewell. At the sound, Chris felt a touch of smug cynicism—just enough to stave off his own show of emotion.

Steve opened up the trunk and Chris pulled out the heaviest single suitcase he had ever carried. With great effort, Chris managed to set the suitcase down on the curb without making a thud. With even greater effort, he then turned to his brother.

"Hey, so, I'll see ya when I see ya," Chris quipped nervously, borrowing a line from some Australian movie.

"Get out of here—who are you fooling?" asked Steve incredulously. "This is a big deal." Steve pulled Chris in tight and hugged him. Without letting go, he imparted his final words of wisdom, this time in a serious tone that surprised Chris. "Don't forget—this isn't youth conference or camp or Boys' State or college. You've been called as a representative of Jesus Christ to preach his gospel. Don't let it become ordinary."

"Right. . . . Ok, so, thanks," mumbled Chris as he finally stepped back from his brother. "Thanks for everything . . . I love you." Chris turned away quickly so Steve would not see the tears forming in the corners of his eyes.

"I love you too, Bro," said Steve. As Chris lugged his suitcase toward the door of the MTC, he heard his brother chanting softly, "Brothers forever . . . brothers forever . . . brothers forever . . . ." Chris smiled despite his embarrassment.

Someone opened the door for Chris, and he pushed his suitcase inside. As the door closed, Chris could no longer hear his brother. He turned and watched as the Nova splashed its way through the parking lot's dirty snow and back out onto Ninth East Street.

❖ ❖ ❖

Wesley Hawthorne disliked few things more than uncertainty. And uncertainty was what Wesley faced as he stood at the door of the Missionary Training Center and prepared to enter. He didn't know exactly where to go once he walked through the doors, and he didn't know any of the people with whom he would spend the rest of the day or the rest of the next two years.

The only two people Wesley knew anywhere in the vicinity were his parents, and they stood immediately to either side of his rather frail five-foot, nine-inch frame. Dorothy Hawthorne, who was the only person who had ever cut Wesley's hair, clung gently to her son's elbow with one hand and wiped her eyes with a handkerchief held by the other. Winston Hawthorne patted his son rather stiffly on the back and then put his hands in his pockets. After several false starts at saying something profound, Winston sighed and pulled out three Bic pens from his breast pocket. "Here, son. You can never have enough pens." Brother Hawthorne was serious.

"Thanks, Dad," said Wesley as he accepted the gift. Wesley took a deep breath and picked up his two suitcases.

"Would you . . . would you like us to come in with you?" offered Dorothy Hawthorne eagerly between sniffles. "I understand parents can come to part of the orientation."

Part of Wesley would have welcomed the company and security, but it was only a small part. Even more than uncertainty, Wesley (who was named "Elder Hawthorne," according to his name tag) disliked looking like a little boy in need of his parents' help.

"No, Mom," he said as he set his suitcases back down and embraced her gently. "Thanks, but I can do this alone." Elder Hawthorne would miss his mother terribly, although he was eager to see if his hair still stuck up in the back when someone else cut it.

Elder Hawthorne stepped back from his mother and looked at his father. Brother Hawthorne began to hold out his hand but then stepped forward and pulled Wesley to him in a wooden embrace. Hawthorne men generally did not hug, and this quasi-hug was just tight enough to press Elder Hawthorne's glasses into his face, smudging the lenses on the upper inside corners.

"Goodbye, Dad," said Elder Hawthorne, adjusting his frames. He worried that it might be hours before he'd have a chance to clean his glasses.

"Goodbye, son," said Brother Hawthorne as he and Sister Hawthorne clung to each other's arms. The Hawthorne's waved bravely as their first and only son opened the door and struggled to get his luggage inside of the Missionary Training Center.

2
Few Are Chosen

The next few hours were a dream-like blur for Wesley—an effect enhanced by his smudged glasses. He stood in lines, received shots and packets of information, and listened to general orientation meetings. Most of the time Elder Hawthorne was surrounded by hundreds of people dressed just like him, but he felt completely alone. By late afternoon he was funneled into a room with all the new missionaries bound for German-speaking countries. Each missionary was assigned a companion and made part of a district, usually consisting of eight missionaries.

The greatest disappointment of the day was the discovery that the MTC had a gymnasium of sorts, and that Elder Hawthorne would be spending about an hour each day exercising publicly and participating in games he played poorly. Elder Hawthorne thought he had endured the last of this kind of embarrassment when he managed to get a waiver from his high school PE classes. At least missionaries won't snap wet towels, thought Wesley as he pushed his glasses back up the bridge of his nose.

The dormitory was neat and simple. Like the rest of the MTC, even the missionaries' sleeping quarters seemed like some sort of sanctuary. The whole place felt like a cross between the temple and BYU: clean, calm, proper, even reverent—while simultaneously teeming with energy and activity.

✧ ✧ ✧

The teachers had told the missionaries to sit together with their companions and districts during meals, but Jon Prentice didn't recognize any teachers in the cafeteria. J.P. did recognize a friend from California toward the front of the line, and he was glad to see a familiar face. He started toward the friend, but was shrewd enough to pause for a moment of strategic thinking. Realizing his companion, Elder Webster, was supposed to spend every minute with him for the next two months, J.P. decided it was time to make an ally.

"So talk about a head-full of rules, huh?" said J.P. to break the ice.

"What?" mumbled Elder Webster, who appeared lost in his thoughts.

"Rules. Lotsa rules, man," tried J.P. again. "Like, that's more rules in one day than I had to learn for all of high school."

"Yeah," said Elder Webster, coming out of his introspection. "Lotsa rules."

J.P. pressed forward cautiously, knowing the importance of establishing slightly rebellious friendships gradually. "Yeah, I don't think

I could remember all those rules even if I tried. Hope they don't quiz us or anything." By Elder Webster's answer, J.P. would gauge whether he had some pious seminary president for a companion or somebody who was human and would know how to have a little fun.

"Yeah, that was, you know, like a major info-dump," replied Elder Webster, himself trying to guess which answer would win him a new friend in this world of apparent clones who were strangers.

"Info-dump," laughed J.P., only somewhat genuinely. "That's good. How about rule-overload?"

The conversation deteriorated from there, spiraling into an exchange of sophomoric jokes about the quantity of rules and how it would be impossible to remember them all, much less keep them all.

Having accomplished his goal, J.P.'s next move was easy. "Hey, there's a friend of mine from college. Let's go see if we can . . . you know . . . save ourselves some time and get in line with him."

"Yeah, but—" began Elder Webster before catching himself. "I mean, sure, sounds great."

It was a small but important step, thought J.P. Heaven knew these two months could be unbearable if he'd gotten stuck with some stick in the mud.

✦ ✦ ✦

After dinner the missionaries had a few minutes to arrange their meager belongings in their rooms before heading to the classroom at seven p.m. Chris Roberts knew the missionaries weren't required to begin speaking German full-time for another three days, and he'd already had two years of high school German. This first evening class would probably be some kind of overview, thought Elder Roberts, so he slipped some seminary scripture mastery cards into his suit pocket in case he got bored.

"*Guten Abend, Geschwister*," said an enthusiastic, recently returned-missionary to each missionary as they entered the classroom. "*Ich hoisse* Elder Green."

"Right, whatever," said J.P. "My name's Jon Prentice, but my friends call me J.P."

"*Es freut mich*, Elder Prentice," responded Elder Green, with an emphasis on "Elder" and without translating any of the German phrases he'd used.

After Elder Green welcomed each of the elders and sisters, he passed out the German hymn book. "*Houte Abend singen wir das Lied auf Seite Zwei*," said the teacher with a smile, as if the missionaries could understand him. He opened his book and held up two fingers. "*Seite Zwei*." The missionaries eventually gathered that they were going to sing the hymn on page two.

"Hey teacher," declared an elder from Iowa innocently. "My book's in German."

"*Ach, so ist es,*" replied Elder Green with a nod, and one of the sisters chuckled. Elder Green then began to sing a tune the missionaries recognized as "Hope of Israel." The elders and sisters did their best to match the unknown words with the familiar notes.

After the hymn the teacher knelt, still facing inward in the circle, without resting his arms on a chair and without resting his bottom on his feet. The missionaries eyed each other and slowly assumed the same position.

For most of them, it was the first time they had knelt in prayer with anyone other than their family. Elder Roberts prayed every morning and night on his knees, but he was surprised at how taxing it was to kneel in such a straight position. He was glad Elder Webster's prayer was short.

The missionaries were still in the process of finding their seats when Elder Green, who had only recently returned from his mission, barked, "*Die Tafel, Klasse.*" He got nothing but a few mumbled responses.

He motioned emphatically with his right arm for the class to repeat his German as he pointed at the blackboard. "*Die Tafel, Klasse.*"

"*Der Tufel,*" replied many of the missionaries.

"The blackboard, *Klasse,*" said Elder Green

"The blackboard," replied J.P. in English, evoking a ripple of laughter from some of the elders.

"*Der Teppich, Klasse,*" shot Elder Green as he pointed to the carpet. Elder Green's intensity and thick neck reminded Wesley Hawthorne of his high school history teacher, who was also the varsity wrestling coach. Elder Green identified virtually every object in the room in rapid-fire succession, asking the missionaries to repeat him as he threw out each new word.

With his two years of high school German, Elder Roberts knew many but not all of the words, so he followed Elder Green without too much trouble. Then Elder Green began pointing to objects and asking individual missionaries to name them. This became more complicated, and each of the missionaries missed at least one item. Within thirty minutes, though, nearly all of the missionaries could name almost all of the objects in the room.

For the next hour and half, Elder Green taught the missionaries more useful phrases, including how to introduce themselves, how to ask how someone was doing, and how to say the basic phrases used in prayers. The pace was unrelenting, and the instruction was almost exclusively in German.

Elder Roberts forgot his scripture mastery cards and was relieved that he wasn't particularly bored. J.P. had a mild headache, but was pleased that he'd been able to make the district laugh more than once.

Wesley Hawthorne had taken only a year of high school German, and he still doubted the wisdom of a program that did not inform missionaries of the language they would speak until a couple of months before becoming missionaries. Why not give them a year's notice so they could begin to learn the language in advance rather than have it abruptly drilled into them in rapid-fire succession without any English explanation or even any written instruction?

Elder Hawthorne was visual; he knew he would forget most of the few words and phrases he had picked up in this first session. He wondered whether this whole backwards approach to linguistic training was driven by the same sort of mentality that had spawned Trek, the nightmarish youth conference experience in which Wesley had been forced to survive for two days on minimal water, a few handfuls of wheat, and a live chicken.

Elder Hawthorne's mental critique of teaching techniques that relied on artificially induced adversity was interrupted by the pleasant sound of English. "Elders and sisters, these next two months will not be easy," said Elder Green intensely but slowly. "We will work very hard to learn the language, to learn the scriptures, the discussions—to teach people the gospel. Keep the rules, speak your language. Study hard, but don't try to do it alone. The Lord has called you to preach the gospel in German, and he will help you speak it if, well, if you seek his help and acknowledge his hand. If you give it everything you have, you will see miracles happen in the next two months."

✧ ✧ ✧

"So who do you think they'll call to be our district leader," asked Elder Webster at lunch on the second day. He'd learned from the older missionaries—those who had been in the MTC for two to six weeks—that each district had a leader who was called by the branch president. Today the entire district was sitting together as instructed: Elder Roberts, his companion, Elder Jones of Iowa, J.P. and Elder Webster, Wesley Hawthorne and his companion, Elder Schley, and the two sisters in the district, Sister Snodgrass and Sister Owens.

"You mean they call one of us to be a leader over the others?" sneered J.P. "Great, like any of us really knows anything more about this stuff than anyone else."

While Sister Snodgrass explained principles of church government to J.P., Elder Roberts sized up the potential candidates. Elder Prentice was still calling himself "J.P." and had hair that seemed to be much longer than allowed by the rules. Elder Prentice's companion, Elder Webster, appeared to be following in the footsteps of his Californian companion. To Elder Roberts it was clear that these two lacked the commitment to merit serious consideration for the position.

Elder Roberts' own companion, Elder Jones, was the only one in the district with no previous German instruction and would probably have enough of a challenge just struggling to learn the language. Neither Elder Hawthorne nor Elder Schley had said much, and neither seemed like the leadership type to Elder Roberts.

Both of the sisters appeared to be spiritual stalwarts but were presumably ineligible, making Elder Roberts the most likely choice. As one with a testimony and leadership abilities, Chris Roberts had been called to lead each of the Aaronic Priesthood quorums in which he served. He suspected leading a district in the MTC would be much the same kind of challenge.

As the rest of the district speculated about who would be called and when, Elder Roberts drifted into thoughts about what he would do to inspire and motivate the missionaries in his group, if called as district leader.

❖ ❖ ❖

"Welcome to the MTC, Elder," said the smiling brother who motioned for Wesley Hawthorne to sit down next to him in the small office used for interviews each Sunday.

It was Elder Hawthorne's first Sunday in the MTC, and this tall, slender, middle-aged man with a tasteful suit, wire-rimmed glasses, and short, black, wavy hair was apparently Elder Hawthorne's branch president. Elder Hawthorne wondered why they created branches instead of wards when they had thousands of missionaries. He also wondered why it was necessary to have any sort of artificial church unit in the MTC in the first place. Were they going to have branch socials and home teaching, or maybe activation efforts for the less active missionaries? But Elder Hawthorne kept his thoughts to himself. He was not a talkative person, and he particularly dreaded interviews.

"So, why are you here?" asked President Perry after a minute of small talk. This first substantive question came rather abruptly, and it caught Elder Hawthorne off guard.

"Excuse me?"

"Why did you come on a mission?" elaborated President Perry.

"I don't know," muttered Elder Hawthorne. "The usual things, I suppose."

"Ah, a car from Dad, a girlfriend who insisted you go, general peer pressure, cultural habit, that sort of thing?"

It was a leading question, and Wesley began to agree unintentionally before catching himself. "Yes . . . I mean no, not cars or any reward from my parents or anything like that. I'm not sure exactly why I'm here. It seems like a good thing, you know, the right thing to do."

"Yes, I know," affirmed President Perry warmly. "It does seem like a good thing, and it is a good thing. How do you feel about Jesus Christ?"

"Feel? About Jesus?"

"Yes." President Perry was leaning over, his forearms resting on his knees and his hands clasped. He looked comfortable as he pried into Elder Hawthorne's heart. Wesley was anything but comfortable.

"Fine, I suppose. I mean, I believe in him, if that's what you're asking."

"What do you mean, you believe in him?" persisted President Perry.

Wesley took a moment before answering, hoping to find a response that would satisfy this priesthood interrogator and end this line of questioning. "Well, that he's the Son of God and all."

"Are you sure about this?" asked President Perry before sipping from a glass of water.

"No, I mean . . . " Something snapped inside Wesley, and he gave in to the urge to let his answers flow freely. What he then heard himself say caught him somewhat by surprise. "Well, no, I'm not sure about that. I'm not really sure about God, or Jesus, or that this is their church, or that the Book of Mormon's true. I believe these things—they make sense to me—but I'm not sure about any of them."

President Perry let this answer hang in the air for two or three seconds, and the silence was very awkward for Elder Hawthorne. He was annoyed with himself for speaking so openly with a stranger, and he was taken aback at what he had said. He'd never quite articulated this doubt to anyone before, much less a priesthood leader. In fact, he wasn't sure that he'd ever really identified the doubt to himself before. Perhaps he'd overstated his lack of testimony. Elder Hawthorne doubted even his doubts.

"I see," commented President Perry calmly, his posture unchanged. "Elder," he said, pausing until he caught Elder Hawthorne's eyes, "would you like to be sure?"

"Yes, yes I would." The damage done, Elder Hawthorne decided to open up, albeit in succinct Hawthorne style. "I, um, I'm not sure that it's honest, that it's right, you know, for me, well, for me to even be here without really knowing these things are true.

"I like certainty, I like knowing things for sure. If I'm going somewhere I want exact directions so I can't get lost. But when it comes to the things that are supposed to be, well, supposed to be the most important, you know, I just don't have certainty.

"Like in the testimony meeting we had in the branch today, several elders talked with, you know, with such conviction about how they know these things are true. I don't have that kind of conviction, and I'm not even sure they do. I sometimes wonder whether . . . whether everybody just learns the right key words and repeats them. Anyway, I don't quite know how I can go around telling people they need to change their lives and join my church when I'm not really sure of these things myself."

"I see," said President Perry again, this time sitting up and rubbing his temples gently. "You may be right about some of the missionaries repeating the magical testimony phrases out of, out of peer pressure, rather than genuine conviction. That concerns me, although it's a lot better than getting drunk because of peer pressure, I suppose." Elder Hawthorne smiled slightly at the comment, relieved to find a priesthood leader with a trace of a sense of humor.

"But some people are telling the truth, some people really mean it, when they say they're sure," continued President Perry seriously. "I am, and you can be too. Let me give you three thoughts about becoming sure.

"First, don't underestimate yourself. Think about quiet promptings and assurances of the Spirit you've felt in your life, maybe while reading the scriptures, or when you bear your testimony. Or for me, they often come when I'm singing a hymn, especially a sacrament hymn, and I actually think about the words I'm singing. These peaceful, warm feelings are what build testimonies, and we often don't recognize them because we're hoping for, well, for something grander. Remember the Lord's counsel to Oliver Cowdery in the sixth section of the Doctrine of Covenants."

Wesley knew his scriptures reasonably well, but not that well. He made a mental note to check the reference so he'd know exactly what President Perry was talking about.

"I guess that leads to my second point," continued President Perry. "Pray with faith for more knowledge, but don't expect visions necessarily or even dramatic experiences. It's true that some people have life-changing experiences that they can point to as their one-time answer to prayer. But for most of us, it doesn't work that way. We get our spiritual confirmation incrementally, a little bit at a time, not in one big, dramatic chunk.

"My third thought is not to be afraid to walk in faith, to go out on a limb a bit. Testify to the truthfulness of what you do know, and the Lord will confirm that principle and then some. Don't feel like you have to see the whole picture before you're willing to take a step. Go out on a limb and publicly acknowledge promptings of the Spirit to the Lord. When you do, I think it's like a show of good faith on your part, and the Lord often blesses that very act with another confirmation. I suspect that's going to be the biggest challenge for you, but you can do it."

Elder Hawthorne couldn't remember having such a frank, useful spiritual talk with a priesthood leader. "Thank you," he said simply.

President Perry began to stand up, but interrupted himself. "Oh, one more thing, Elder Hawthorne. I'd like you to serve as the district leader in your district. There will be a training meeting this evening for all new leaders in the MTC to explain your duties. You'll do a great job." President Perry was now standing again and offered Wesley his hand.

Elder Hawthorne was unable to resist the inertia of the moment. "Thank you," he heard himself mutter as he walked out of the room. Coming from a long line of faithful and quiet Hawthorne men who had served in comfortable obscurity as ward clerks, being called as district leader was the last thing Elder Hawthorne had expected—especially after conceding his lack of testimony. He could only assume that MTC leaders were chosen randomly.

3
A Samoan in the Sauna

After ten days, the regimen was getting to Elder Jon Prentice: up at six (or in J.P.'s case, at least by seven-thirty), gym (only three blessed days a week, unfortunately), showers, breakfast, scripture study, German out the ears for three hours, lunch, then more German with a little proselyting skills training mixed in, then dinner, then German out the nose, then bed.

The only excitement each day was finding out how many letters he'd gotten from his girlfriends and playing basketball or volleyball against Tuala, the beefy Samoan elder who'd played linebacker at BYU. He was now up to eight letters and five packages of cookies in just ten days, which was at least four more letters and two more packages than any other elder in the zone had received.

The rule was lights out at ten-thirty, but with the help of his flashlight J.P. managed to get off a letter every night to at least one of the Three Babes. "You reap what you sow," J.P. told Elder Webster, and he sowed as many letters as he could, each one mushier than the last.

"Hey Elder, six o'clock," mumbled Elder Webster in English. "Time for gym."

"I'm sick," grumbled Elder Prentice without opening his eyes.

"Yeah, right," snorted Elder Webster, who was coming to know his companion well.

"Aren't you?" asked J.P., his head still firmly imbedded in his pillow.

"What, sick?"

"Yeah, sick of this schedule, sick of this German, sick of getting up at six?" continued J.P. in English, finally opening one of his eyes.

"Sure," agreed Elder Webster.

"I thought so," responded J.P. "Remember what Elder Green said about Germans and their doctors, you know, prescribing three weeks at some spa in the mountains whenever they're feeling a little sick? Well, what we need, my boy, is a sauna—a steamy, hot, soothing sauna. But first a bit more sleep. Reset that alarm for six forty-five, climb back in bed, and please don't interrupt my precious sleep again until then." J.P. closed his eyes, rolled over, and pulled his covers tight around him. Elder Webster obeyed.

At six forty-five the construction of the sauna began. Gathering towels was easy, since most elders left them hanging over their closet doors to dry each day. With a stack of about forty towels from the first floor—they weren't stupid enough to take the ones from their own floor—J.P.

and Elder Website (as J.P. called his computer hacking companion) began stuffing the cracks under the bathroom doors and any other potential avenues of escape for the steam they would create. That took only about ten towels, so Elder Webster decided to try to build a dam across the entrance of the showers with the remaining towels.

"It's just gonna go down the drain," critiqued J.P. "If you want the water backed up, you've gotta plug the thing, like a tub." J.P. left the showers and soon returned with a pack of gum. "Here," he said as he handed his companion half the pack. "Chew like the wind."

Soon the drains were soundly plugged, the makeshift dam was erected, and ventilation was jammed. The two industrious elders then turned on all the showers full throttle as hot as they'd go, and steam filled the room. J.P. and Elder Webster relaxed in metal chairs they'd imported, swirling their toes in the rising whirlpool and generally admiring their work.

Within a few minutes the rest of the floor returned from gym. About half the elders welcomed the creation and joined in the fun. The other half headed for the showers on other floors. By the time Elder Hawthorne arrived, J.P. and two or three others were welcoming new missionaries to the sauna with stinging flicks of wet towels.

"Yo, welcome to our sauna, *Herr Distriktsleiter*," chortled J.P. as he snapped a towel five inches from Elder Hawthorne's glasses.

Elder Hawthorne generally detested the public nudity component of communal showering, in which he stood with his ordinary schoolboy frame next to people like J.P., with their fashionable stomach muscles and defined biceps.

Wesley Hawthorne had long felt that towel-snapping was a male ritual in which physically superior specimens exerted their dominance over the runts of the species—like something right out of a National Geographic special.

As his glasses began to fog over, Elder Hawthorne wondered whether as district leader he should try to do something about the mess J.P. was making. But he simply couldn't imagine himself doing anything that would be effective under the circumstances. Elder Hawthorne decided he was not cut out for this kind of babysitting leadership, so he left the home-made sauna without a word and headed downstairs with his companion in his robe for a more civil shower.

The showers one floor down were crowded with the extra elders from Elder Hawthorne's floor, so he decided to try the next floor down. To Elder Hawthorne's surprise, the showers were virtually empty on that floor, but the halls seemed to be abuzz. Just as Elder Hawthorne was turning on the shower, he heard the bathroom door open and a deep, rich, angry but controlled voice boom in broken German, "I have no towel. Where is my towel?"

Elder Hawthorne recognized Elder Tuala's voice at the same time he realized where Elder Tuala's towel was and why the showers on this floor were so empty. A slightly unrighteous smile began to spread on Elder Hawthorne's face. He turned off his shower, grabbed his robe, slipped on his steamy glasses, and stepped out into the main area of the bathroom. "Know you Elder Prentice, or 'J.P.'?" asked Elder Hawthorne innocently in German.

"Blond missionary of California?" responded Elder Tuala, whose 240-pound frame had less fat than Elder Hawthorne's 160-pound body. "Where he is?"

"I show you," said Elder Hawthorne. Soon he was leading Elder Tuala and a procession of towel-less elders to the third floor.

Buoyed by his supporting cast, Elder Hawthorne decided to try executing this thing with just a bit of a flourish. "Please wait, four or five seconds, okay?" Elder Hawthorne asked Elder Tuala in broken German. "I want . . . um, how do you say 'surprise,' Okay?" Elder Tuala smiled and nodded.

Elder Hawthorne opened the door to discover elders sliding across the wet bathroom floor, snapping towels, and singing Beach Boys' songs in the sauna showers. J.P. slid over to greet Elder Hawthorne with a tightly coiled gigantic beach towel.

"Here for some more snapping, eh Hawthorne-rims?" J.P. asked as he twirled the towel to prepare for a snap.

"Yes I am," answered Elder Hawthorne in his best imitation of an old beer commercial.

"And he friends brings," announced Elder Tuala in inverted German as he barged through the door, followed by twenty rather perturbed missionaries. "Friends who no towels have."

"Oh, hey, um, hello Tuala," stammered J.P. as he let the towel unfurl.

"I miss you about basketball today," said Elder Tuala as he walked through the bathroom and surveyed the mess.

The missionaries had not yet learned past tense, and it would be weeks before they got their prepositions straight.

"A little sick you are?" asked Elder Tuala.

"Well, yes, not feel so good," claimed J.P., now speaking German himself in the face of brute peer pressure. "But better now, yes, thank you."

"I have no towel, Elder," explained Elder Tuala slowly with both of his large hands upturned. He shrugged his shoulders. "My towel lost."

"Oh, yes, well, maybe I find your towel can," blubbered J.P., mixing his English and German.

"Maybe that my towel? See, your hand!" Elder Tuala pointed to the giant beach towel in J.P.'s hand. J.P. opened up the towel and held it out for Elder Tuala to see. "Ah, yes. My towel," he purred as he took the towel from J.P. "But my towel is wet, very wet. Wet towel is problem, no?"

J.P. could not help but nod his head in agreement. "I need dry towel," continued Elder Tuala. "You maybe have dry towel for me?"

Elder Prentice stared blankly for a moment, unsure of his next move. "Here, your towel," said Elder Webster, handing J.P. the dry towel J.P. had brought with him.

"Ah, yes, my towel," sighed J.P. as he handed the towel to Elder Tuala. J.P. smiled weakly, adding unconvincingly, "Please, you use. Make me very happy."

"Thank you," offered Elder Tuala. "My friends, they also dry towels need. Your friends have?" Soon the twenty missionaries from the first floor each held the dry towel of a missionary from the sauna as well as their own wet towels.

Some of the visiting missionaries seemed to want to exact more revenge, but Elder Tuala shepherded them slowly out of the restroom. Before he closed the door, however, he stopped to take care of one housekeeping matter.

"Oh, Elder Prentice, gum make broken. Please gum clean, okay? No want need say to teacher. One hour, gum clean, yes?"

"What?" demanded Elder Prentice.

Elder Tuala drew near to Elder Prentice. "You," he said as he gently but firmly pressed Elder Prentice's chest with one finger, and pointed to the shower with the other hand, "you clean gum. Gum make shower broken. Understand you German?"

J.P. nodded, and Elder Tuala slapped him on the back and grinned broadly as he exited the restroom. "Many thank you's, Elder Prentice."

J.P. and Elder Webster spent the next thirty minutes on their knees, cleaning the gum out of the shower drain.

"Oh well," sighed J.P. when they finished. "We needed to air dry anyway."

✦ ✦ ✦

Each Tuesday night hundreds of elders, sisters, and couples crowded into the auditorium of the MTC in Provo, Utah, to hear a General Authority—usually an apostle—impart words of wisdom, encouragement, and inspiration.

To Chris Roberts, this weekly meeting was like almost no other he had attended. For starters, simply being in a room with over two thousand full-time missionaries was electrifying. Never before and perhaps never again would Elder Roberts be surrounded by so many good people united in such a noble cause. These messengers of Jesus Christ exuded a nervous energy as they waited for their speaker and for their opportunity to be set loose on a world that desperately needed their message.

Planted each week in this fertile soil was a talk by a special witness of the Savior. The talks Elder Roberts had heard in his first four weeks at the MTC had a different edge than the sermons he heard from the

Brethren at General Conference and even BYU devotionals. They had a sense of urgency and intimacy that was exhilarating. Elder Roberts wondered whether these sessions were somewhat like Christ's sermons to the seventy before he sent them on their journeys.

The anticipation in the air tonight was markedly greater than at any of the previous weekly firesides. As Elder Roberts took his seat next to Elder Jones, Elder Hawthorne, Elder Prentice (J.P.), and the rest of the district, the auditorium seemed to be abuzz with whispered conversations.

At any given moment nearly a fifth of the missionaries were craning their necks or standing to peer toward the rear entrances to the hall. As seven-thirty passed, an increasing number of elders and sisters looked to the entrances to see if they could catch a glimpse of the arrival of the evening's speaker.

Elder Roberts' vanity prevented him from standing to watch the doors. He tried to concentrate on the fourth discussion to pass the time productively, but his efforts were futile.

Finally, at seven thirty-six, the MTC president and his wife stood, and the chorister signaled for the congregation to stand as the organist played the introduction to the hymn. The meaning of the words came vibrantly to life for Elder Roberts as the congregation sang:

> We thank thee, oh God, for a prophet
> To guide us in these latter days.
> We thank thee for sending the gospel
> To lighten our minds with its rays.
> We thank thee for every blessing
> Bestowed by thy bounteous hand.
> We feel it a pleasure to serve thee,
> And love to obey thy command.

Elder Roberts had sung these words dozens of times, but they usually flowed so smoothly off his tongue that they had rarely made their way to his heart. Now his soul swelled as he sang and, along with the entire congregation, craned his neck toward the right rear entrance to the hall.

Elder Roberts caught his first view of the Prophet as he slowly climbed the stairs to the speakers' platform, assisted by his wife. Once on the stage, the Prophet shuffled forward a few steps, still holding to his wife's arm and watching his feet. He stopped and turned toward the congregation as it came to the end of the second verse. He seemed to squint as he gazed upon the congregation, scanning it from left to right. Slowly his mouth broadened into a smile, and he waved. Then he released his grip on his wife's arm just long enough to motion with both hands for the missionaries to sit down.

For an hour the missionaries sat at the feet of the Prophet. As Elder Roberts listened intently to the Prophet's counsel, he marveled at the thought that this man truly knew the Savior and was his servant, as had been Abraham, Moses, Nephi, and Alma. The Prophet's speech was slow, and his thoughts seemed simple. Yet none of the missionaries in Elder Roberts' district would forget how the Spirit touched their hearts as they listened to the Prophet.

4
The Triple Dump

According to Elder Green, Practice and Retention—P&R in the MTC vernacular—separated the dedicated missionaries from the lukewarm ones. After almost eight hours of classes and three meals, the missionaries were put back in the classroom—without the constant guidance of a teacher—to practice and retain what they had learned during the day.

J.P. had not fallen for Elder Green's implicit challenge to use the time well and endure until nine-thirty. For two or three days after the Prophet's address, his dedication seemed to improve, but within a week he was back to his usual habits. "*Wie sagt man* 'regurgitate'?" he asked anyone who was listening.

"*Wie bitte?*" replied Sister Snodgrass.

"'Regurgitate, or vomit,' whatever, how do you say it?" repeated Elder Prentice in German.

The studious sister removed her glasses and spoke to J.P. in the same tone many of his high school teachers had used with him. "In which discussion does one use the word 'regurgitate?'"

"It's, um, one of those things I'm making up that goes along with the discussion to help people understand it better," answered J.P. in English. "You know, a metaphor."

"Do you mean a . . . " Sister Snodgrass paused, flipping through her pocket-size dictionary to find the appropriate German word. "Do you mean an analogy? There's a difference, you know."

"Yeah, yeah, whatever," mumbled J.P. as he finally resorted to his own dictionary to look up the word. For the next ninety minutes he and Elder Webster huddled together and worked with apparent intensity, looking up words and scribbling down some sort of dialogue, which they then repeated to themselves.

Finally, at nine-fifteen the surprisingly diligent elders were ready to share their creation. "Ahem, attention please," said Elder Webster in German after clearing his throat. He and Elder Prentice stood side by side at the front of the classroom. "Our analogy," J.P. said, nodding toward Sister Snodgrass.

The two elders then recited in decent German an entire scene from *Wayne's World*. It was about the only German J.P. could recite fluently when he left the MTC.

✦ ✦ ✦

After six weeks in the MTC, Elder Roberts was finally beginning to get bored. He'd read the Book of Mormon and the entire New Testament, he'd memorized every scripture reference in the discussions, and he knew the discussions far better than any other elder in his district. Perhaps his attitude showed a bit in the obligatory weekly "interview" with his "district leader," Elder Hawthorne. Elder Roberts viewed the exercise as rather unnecessary for someone like him.

While Elder Roberts found the district leaders interviews a bit contrived, Elder Hawthorne found them almost absurd. Here he sat "interviewing" a missionary who had clearly prepared his entire life for a mission and whose knowledge of German, the scriptures, and everything else in life clearly exceeded Elder Hawthorne's.

Elder Roberts even looked like the kind of missionary portrayed in church videos: his suit fit well and had no trace of polyester, the collar of his shirt was buttoned down rather than poking out, his conservatively fashionable tie was knotted symmetrically but tightly, and most remarkably, his hair seemed to fall naturally into place, even though it stopped well above his ears.

Interviewing Elder Roberts made Wesley Hawthorne feel as if he were playing house, with his father playing the role of child and himself playing the role of parent. Still, Elder Hawthorne went through the motions dutifully, asking the questions he had been trained to ask.

"Do you have any goals for the week?" It seemed an especially silly question to ask someone like Elder Roberts, who really had been a machine when it came to learning German and the discussions.

"Yeah, I was thinking I'd start reading the Book of Mormon in German," sighed Elder Roberts in English. (All interviews were held in English.)

Elder Hawthorne just shook his head in admiration. He was still struggling to master the basics of this new language; he couldn't imagine trying to read scripture in it.

"How's your companionship?"

"It's fine, I guess," answered Elder Roberts. "Elder Jones is a good guy, but we're not really able to talk much because of his difficulty with the language. Sometimes I wonder how much more I might learn if I had a companion who could push me."

A thought entered Elder Hawthorne's head, which he initially resisted, since sharing it might make it appear that he thought he had something to offer Elder Roberts. But the thought persisted.

Elder Hawthorne mustered his courage and gave it a try. "You know, I've been thinking, your German really is, well, it's incredible. And you're way ahead of the rest of the district in, um, in learning the discussions. Maybe, you know, maybe for these last couple of weeks you might, well, you could have, or I mean, you could consider having, um, a goal of helping your companion with his German. He really is struggling with it, you know, and I think if you acted, like, as his personal tutor maybe, well, you know, that could help him a lot. I mean, it's just something to think about. That's all I'm saying."

Elder Hawthorne's suggestion subtly implied that perhaps Elder Roberts should have been doing more all along, that he may have been a bit too focused on himself. At least that's how Elder Roberts took it, and he found himself pouring instinctively over his memories of the last few weeks to build a defense.

Elder Roberts had worked with his companion during P&R and during all the language exercises that each companionship was asked to perform together. Sure, he'd mostly read his scriptures and memorized his discussions while waiting in line for meals or waiting for meetings to begin, but he was just trying to use his time well.

Still, to refuse Elder Hawthorne's suggestion outright would demonstrate an obvious lack of humility, so Elder Roberts half-heartedly went along with the suggestion. "That's a good thought," he forced himself to say to his district leader. "I'll see what I can do."

As the interview concluded, Elder Hawthorne said a silent prayer and breathed a sigh of relief. He had sensed that Elder Roberts was bristling at his suggestion, and the tension, although slight, had been almost unbearable for him. Hawthorne men were not cut out to lead, he decided.

✧ ✧ ✧

"Elder Prentice, three letters for you," said Elder Hawthorne as he handed J.P. his daily mail at lunch time.

"That makes thirty-seven," said J.P. in English as he ripped open the letters from his girlfriends. "But no cookies today. Darn."

"He must be paying them," said Sister Snodgrass, who had difficulty understanding what any girl could see in Elder Prentice.

J.P. managed to open one of the letters with one hand while continuing to stuff himself with the other. Suddenly he dropped his fork and grabbed the letter with both hands. "Oh no, oh no, oh no," moaned J.P. "What was I thinking? How could I have been so careless?"

"What is it?" asked his companion.

"The letters. I must have mixed up the letters," J.P. said in a panic. "Oh please, let it be only two and not three." J.P. tossed aside the first letter and tore open the second.

Elder Webster grabbed the letter his companion had already opened and discarded. "'Dear J.P.,'" read Elder Webster aloud. "'Who is Alicia? I hope she is more forgiving than me. Your former friend, Gina.'"

"No!" howled J.P. "Alicia got Cindy's, not Gina's. I'm doomed. All three sunk in a single week."

"'Dear J.P.,'" read Elder Webster, opening the third letter. "'Don't ever write me again, you lying dog. May your lips forever be infested with cold sores, Cindy.'"

The entire district erupted into laughter at J.P.'s expense. "No more cookies, no more cookies," muttered J.P. to himself.

"I guess you reap what you sow," consoled Elder Webster.

✦ ✦ ✦

The last Sunday in the MTC for Elders Roberts, Hawthorne, and Prentice and their comrades was also the first in the month. As usual, testimony meeting featured a parade of elders who were soon to depart.

To Elder Roberts' surprise, his companion, Elder Jones was among the first to reach the pulpit. Elder Roberts didn't recall Elder Jones volunteering to say anything during the nine weeks they'd been together constantly.

"This has been hard for me, this MTC stuff," began Elder Jones with an Iowa farmer's drawl. "I never been very good in school, or that kinda stuff, so spending all day in a classroom, well, it's been hard. For the first few weeks, I couldn't understand anything we was being taught in class. Thought maybe I oughta go home. Nothin' was workin'. I tried, but I just couldn't learn German."

Elder Jones' lips began to quiver uncontrollably, and he paused to wipe his nose. J.P. rolled his eyes.

"Then about three weeks ago I remembered something our teacher, Elder Green, said on the first night. He told us we couldn't do it alone, that we needed the Lord's help. So I prayed and prayed every night that the Lord would help me. I never prayed like that before, not for anything.

"And then a few days later, well, all of a sudden my companion . . . Elder Roberts . . . he stops reading his scriptures in line and starts talking to me in German all the time. For the last few weeks he's been . . . like a constant tutor."

Elder Jones lips began quivering again, so he bit his bottom lip for a moment before choking out the rest of his testimony. "I just wanna thank Elder Roberts for helping me. And I wanna thank Heavenly Father. He answered my prayer. In the name of thy Son, Jesus Christ. Amen."

At some point Elder Roberts had realized that Elder Hawthorne's suggestion was certainly inspired. From then on he had worked intensely with Elder Jones during every spare minute. He hadn't had time to get very far in the Book of Mormon in German, but wondered how much he really would have gained from such an exercise at this point anyway. Elder Roberts caught Elder Hawthorne's eye, and he nodded slightly to his district leader.

Never one to pass up an opportunity to entertain, J.P. strode confidently up to the podium to try his hand. He couldn't say that he shared in any of the sentiments that were apparently making the other missionaries gush, but he figured hearing his own voice was better than listening to another missionary weep publicly.

"Hey, so I guess it's about time to fly," he began with one hand resting on the podium and the other shoved casually into his pocket. "I just wanna thank you guys . . . and gals . . ." he said with a glance toward Sister Snodgrass and Owens, who undoubtedly disapproved of the use of both "guys" and "gals" to describe missionaries. "I just wanna thank you for being so cool and helping me out with cookies and stuff after I got dear Johned three times in the same day."

The reference to the "triple dump," as it had become known, brought hoots of laughter from Elder Prentice's friends.

"The only people who gave him cookies were elders who were paying to listen to one of his CD's," whispered Elder Webster to the missionary next to him.

"Anyway, I'm psyched to get outta this place and check out Europe, but I'm gonna miss you. Some of you actually kind of grew on me. And for those of you who still have a few weeks left here, let me tell ya, it goes fast so don't panic. . . . Anyway, I know the Church is true, and that we have a prophet and stuff. I didn't always show it by the way I acted, but I know this is where we're supposed to be right now. Anyway, I guess that's all. So take care, in the name of Jesus Christ. Amen." J.P. brushed back his hair with one hand as he returned to his seat.

Two missionaries from other districts bore their testimonies before Elder Roberts decided to take his turn. "I'm grateful for what I've learned here, and for what some of you have taught me. I know through the power of the Holy Ghost that God lives, that Jesus Christ is his Son, and that this is their work and their church. I know now more than ever that this church is led on earth by a prophet of God. I also know that . . . that the Lord inspires . . . all those he calls. In the name of Jesus Christ. Amen."

With five minutes to go, each member of the district except Elder Hawthorne had borne his or her testimony. Elder Hawthorne began rocking back and forth ever so slightly as he fought conflicting inner urges. Finally, he gave in to the Spirit that prompted him to stand, and he made his way to the stand.

"I'm . . . uh . . . I'm not very good at bearing testimonies," confessed Elder Hawthorne, mostly looking at the wire running out of the podium microphone. He grasped the edge of the podium with his left hand and played with the base of the microphone with the other. "This is a good place. It feels good here."

Elder Hawthorne hesitated, hating the thought of calling a feeling the Spirit if it wasn't really the Spirit, but also remembering President Perry's counsel. "I believe I have felt the Spirit here. I believe I felt the Spirit when the Prophet spoke. I believe I felt the Spirit when I read about the Savior in Third Nephi."

As he spoke, Elder Hawthorne felt a surge of confidence and surety. He stopped, smiled, and then looked out at the congregation. "And I like how it feels. Thank you for being my friends. In the name of Jesus Christ. Amen."

President Perry grabbed Elder Hawthorne lightly by the arm as he returned to his seat. "Thanks, Elder," he said as he squeezed Elder Hawthorne's arm.

"Thank you," answered Elder Hawthorne. "They should promote you to bishop."

✧ ✧ ✧

Although he was the tallest player in the game at six-foot-four, Elder Tuala was very mobile and preferred to play guard. At a flat six foot, J.P. gave up four inches and forty pounds, but he was half a step quicker than the BYU linebacker who had taken a sabbatical to serve a mission.

There was only a minute left before gym ended, and J.P.'s team was ahead six to five in a game to seven. J.P. had the ball and decided it was time to use one of his patented inside moves against Tuala. It was his last day in gym and would be his last chance.

J.P. crouched low and held the ball on his hip away from his Samoan nemesis. He faked left and then cut right, pushing hard off his pivot foot and slicing through the middle of the lane. Unable to get past Tuala completely, J.P. came to a two-footed jump stop in the heart of the key, with Tuala between him and the hoop.

J.P. bent his knees and then jerked his head and the ball upward, faking a jump shot. Elder Tuala bit, thrusting his entire frame what seemed like two feet into the air.

For many ball players, this wouldn't have helped much because J.P. had used his dribble. But J.P. finished the move he'd used dozens of times over the years by taking a large crossover step just to the right of Tuala with his left foot, and gently tossing the ball off the backboard and through the hoop with a baby right-handed hook as he jumped into the air off of his left foot.

"Traveling!" shouted at least two of Tuala's teammates. This reaction to J.P.'s move was common among less experienced players. J.P. began to show the move in slow motion to prove that he had taken only the permitted step and a half, but he was interrupted by Tuala.

"No, he just took a step and a half," injected Elder Tuala in English, which was permitted during gym. "Nice move, Elder." Elder Tuala put his arm around J.P. as they headed toward the drinking fountain.

"Thanks," said J.P. as he wiped the sweat from his eyes. "That last shot helped make up for the three that you blocked."

Elder Tuala laughed. "You know, you're a talented boy."

J.P. might have bristled at being referred to as a boy by someone else, but Elder Tuala could call him whatever he wanted.

"Thanks. I played some high school ball."

"Not just basketball," explained Elder Tuala as J.P. drew a long drink of water from the fountain. "I've been watching you. You don't work hard, but you've got a lot of talent. You've got a gift for making people laugh, and people will follow you, even in the wrong direction."

J.P. decided no response was appropriate.

"If you decide to become a real missionary, you could do a lot of good. The Lord needs you, and so do his children. Think about it." He offered his giant hand to Elder Prentice and squeezed for three or four seconds, as if to emphasize his message. "May the Lord bless you, Elder. And may every defender hold back against you as much as I did." Elder Tuala slapped J.P. on the back, then grabbed his sweats and walked away.

5
The Difference Between Adults and Children

As he waited for his interview, Jon Prentice knew enough to speak his language with the missionaries in the mission home, who seemed to be some sort of mission leaders. Not having spoken much German in the MTC, his wasn't very good, but he managed to convey the question he'd had for weeks: When would he get to drive on the Autobahn? All four experienced missionaries laughed.

"Can you say bicycle?" answered one of the elders in German. "It's a much more useful word for missionaries in this mission than Autobahn."

"What? No cars?" asked J.P. eagerly, forgetting in his great disappointment to show the kind of restraint that is essential to being cool.

"Not unless you're an assistant or a secretary to the president," answered another older missionary.

"The president has secretaries?" asked J.P. "And they get cars?"

"Yes, the president has two secretaries," responded a short, skinny elder with wire-framed glasses. "And they drive a van to pick up new missionaries."

"Whoa, I missed out," J.P. blurted out in English. "You two were the only ones there picking us up."

"We are the secretaries," said the husky companion of the bespectacled elder.

"And we speak German here, Elder Prentice," said a tall, slender elder with black hair that looked good cut short. "Soon you'll forget about the Autobahn and think only of the people." The missionary, whose name tag read Elder Jensen, somehow said this without sounding self-righteous to J.P.

"Yes, but you have car, no?" pressed J.P. Elder Jensen nodded. "Easy saying so, then, no think for Autobahn." The assistants and secretaries laughed, partly at Elder Prentice's comment and partly at the zest with which he spoke despite his broken German. Elder Prentice, of course, would have no idea how humorous his German was until months later.

✦ ✦ ✦

"Elder Roberts, your turn," said Elder Webster, his tired expression not really giving any hint of how his interview had gone.

Chris Roberts had looked forward to this interview for some time—he always looked forward to interviews. They were a chance for people to get know each other, and people usually liked what they found out about Chris Roberts, which is perhaps why he enjoyed interviews so much. And this was no ordinary interview. It was Elder Roberts' first interview with the man who Chris assumed was destined to have a tremendous influence on his life for the next two years and even beyond.

"Come on in, Elder," said President Cook, motioning toward the empty chair next to his own.

The office was cluttered with mission memorabilia, souvenirs given to the president by German saints as a token of their gratitude for the service he had rendered. Hanging prominently from the wall above the president's large oak desk was the captain's wheel of an old ship.

Elder Roberts sat down next to the mission president in one of the two hardback chairs that had been placed in the middle of the office. President Cook sat in the other, his lanky frame overflowing from the chair's limited confines. He appeared to be in his mid-sixties, which Chris thought was somehow odd for a tall person, but he supposed even tall people eventually got older.

Except for a few obstinate strands of hair, President Cook was completely bald on top. A cluster of lines converged softly at the corners of his eyes, and he looked as if he needed more sleep. But while the president looked as though he'd been working hard for a long time, there was an intensity in his eyes that suggested he had the energy and drive to continue working hard indefinitely.

President Cook's suit, shirt, tie, and shoes were not those of an executive, but of someone who dressed up only for church. They were adequate, but not dapper. All in all, President Cook looked like someone who'd spent his life getting things done rather than talking or reading about getting things done.

"Well Elder, it's good to have you here," said President Cook, shaking Elder Roberts' hand firmly and warmly. The president's hand was large, the skin rough.

"Thanks, President. It's good to be here," Chris replied sincerely. For years he had yearned to enter the mission field as one called of the Lord to preach the gospel. Maybe that would come up in the interview, he thought almost subconsciously.

"Now there are just a few things I want to discuss with you while I've got a chance," began the president without hesitation.

Chris was a bit surprised at how quickly President Cook was getting into the meat of the interview, and he wondered if more small talk would follow their discussion.

"Three things. Don't flirt with women or girls in any way. Do as President Kimball directed. Lock your heart and throw away the key while you're on your mission. A missionary who transgresses can do irreparable damage to the work. If you're in an area where a woman—

an investigator, a member, a sister, I don't care who she is—takes an active interest in you, just call me. Don't wait until problems develop. Let me know and I'll transfer you right out of there. We don't want to have to deal with any of those kinds of problems in this mission."

Elder Roberts fully planned on being obedient to this rule and every other, but President Cook spoke with such directness and authority that he felt guilty anyway.

President Cook's voice was serious and efficient as he continued his monologue. "Second, don't view life through rose colored glasses here, or you'll run into lots of trouble. I don't mean to say that life on a mission can't be wonderful or that you won't see a lot of success—if you work hard you will see a lot of success. But we've had a lot of problems with some missionaries who've gotten pretty depressed because they hadn't anticipated how much work and adversity goes along with being on a mission. . . ."

President Cook paused to wipe the perspiration from his face with both hands, starting with the heels of his hands near his eyebrows and slowly pulling them down to his chin as if drying a car with a chamois. "Finally, Elder, don't worry about getting called to leadership positions."

As he made this last point, President Cook's eyes locked onto Elder Roberts so that Elder Roberts didn't dare to look away.

"We don't worry about that in this mission. Callings and leadership positions are not necessarily a reflection of righteousness or spiritual success."

President Cook's posture then became more relaxed. He clapped his hands softly together, as if to indicate he had said what he had to say.

"Any questions?" he queried in an almost jolly manner.

Elder Roberts was still puzzling over what had happened when he heard himself say, "No, not really."

"It's good to have you here, Elder," said President Cook as he slapped Elder Roberts on the back. "May the Lord bless you."

That's it? Elder Roberts thought as President Cook showed him out of the office. Doesn't he want to know about my background? My family? What I majored in at college or what my interests are? Doesn't he want to tell me how glad he is that I've made the right choice and decided to come on a mission? Or that he's sure I'll make a great contribution to this mission? Isn't he going to ask how well I did in the MTC with the discussions and the language? How about my testimony—doesn't he want to hear my testimony? Apparently this mission president hadn't read those books that say the interviewer should mostly listen in an interview, Elder Roberts mused.

* * *

The next morning after breakfast all the missionaries filed into the mission home's conference room and sat down around the long rectangular table. After about forty-five minutes of details about mission life and mission policy from the assistants, President Cook came in wearing his dark blue, pinstriped suit. He smiled warmly at this latest batch of missionaries, whose faces conveyed a mixture of anxiety and eagerness.

"Did you sleep well last night?" he asked the group in general. "I hope you did, because just a few hours from now you'll be on your way to work in your golden city." (The missionaries soon learned in this mission the word "golden" was used instead of "greenie" to describe new missionaries and their first city.)

President Cook told the elders how much they would love their first city and how he still remembered his. After a few minutes of reveling in his own mission memories, President Cook paused and gulped down a few swallows of water. Before continuing, he looked around the room and let his eyes rest briefly on each of the new missionaries he'd been sent.

"You know, elders and sisters, most of your lives, everything has been centered on you. At home, at school, in mutual, even in the MTC—everyone has worked to make you happy. That's the difference between an adult and a child. Adults worry mostly about the well-being of others, while children worry mostly about themselves. There are a lot of people my age and older who are still essentially children. Serving a mission will make you adults. You'll learn to start forgetting about yourselves and think more about others. At least I hope you do."

President Cook paused for another swallow of water before continuing. "You know, elders and sisters, you only get one shot at this mission, one bite at the apple. You'll look back on it for the rest of your life, but you'll never get a chance to do this mission again, to do it over. It's my job to . . . I'm here to . . . to help make sure that when you go home, you go home without any regrets.

"You all know the phrase from the Doctrine and Covenants about thrusting in your sickle with all your might. Well, I'd like to read a variation, a twist on that, from Section 6 verse 3. I want you to think about this at the outset of your missions. 'Whoso desireth to reap, let him thrust in his sickle with his might, and reap while the day lasts. . . .'

"Elders and Sisters, your missions won't last forever. Reap while the day lasts, give it all you've got for this short period of your life. Thrust in your sickle with all your might, but watch your fingers," President Cook said with a wink.

"Seriously, if you give it everything you have, you'll go home without regrets. That's my prayer, that you'll do just that. In the name of Jesus Christ. Amen."

At the conclusion of the president's remarks, the golden's received their assignments.

"Elder Roberts, you're headed to Goettingen," said Elder Jensen. "You'll love it. It was my golden city. And your companion, Elder Thomas, is a great missionary. You'll learn a lot from him."

Wesley Hawthorne soon learned that his first city would be Luebeck, but that meant nothing to him. With his distaste for uncertainty, Elder Hawthorne quickly extracted all the information he could from the other assistant, Elder Oman. He learned that it was a beautiful city on the northern coast of Germany, and that it could get very wet there. The branch was also small, but the branch president was very energetic and supportive of missionary work.

"With the right missionaries in that town, the work could really take off," suggested Elder Oman.

"Elder Prentice, my friend," said the other assistant with a knowing grin as he slapped J.P. on the back. "I understand that your German is very good for at least one sketch from Wayne's World. I hope your new companion, Elder Greisel, shares your sense of humor, because you'll get to use whatever German you know quite a bit with him. I'm afraid poor Elder Greisel's English is even worse than your German—he's from Austria. May the Lord bless you both in Braunschweig," concluded Elder Jensen with another slap on the back.

6
Panic Caught on Film

On the train to Braunschweig, reality began to settle in on Jon Prentice slowly and painfully. He had played the game well in the MTC, he thought, but somehow he had not reckoned with the fact that he would end up in a country where everyone spoke another language.

Elder Prentice knew that he'd no longer have a built-in audience of seven for his antics, but he'd assumed he'd at least have someone like Elder Webster to kill time with. Now he was on a train filled with people who couldn't understand him, heading toward a strange city with a foreign companion he'd never before met. For once in his life, J.P. felt unsure of himself.

❖ ❖ ❖

Wesley Hawthorne had felt great uneasiness as he entered the MTC and as he boarded the plane for Germany, but those were only minor bouts of anxiety compared to what he experienced on the train to Luebeck, his first city. Now Elder Hawthorne was alone, except for hordes of German strangers who accompanied him on the train.

Although Elder Hawthorne's German was much better than J.P.'s, he was even more worried than Elder Prentice about his inability to communicate with these people. Just looking at the people on the train with him, Elder Hawthorne sensed their Germanness. Even when they weren't talking, Elder Hawthorne could almost hear them thinking in German. They could communicate with each other easily, intelligently, effortlessly, while Elder Hawthorne would be communicating on the level of a young child.

Trying to learn a new language in a foreign land might not be so bad if he weren't expected to convert people in the new language, thought Elder Hawthorne. Now that it was immediately before him, the combination of proselyting in German was truly overwhelming—not that Elder Hawthorne had ever felt anything nearing confidence in his missionary skills. He had never even been able to sell a Scout-a-Rama ticket to anyone but his uncle. How would he survive two years of invading people's lives to discuss religion in a new language?

Elder Hawthorne closed his eyes and tried to stop thinking. Soon he was enjoying a deep slumber induced by jet lag.

❖ ❖ ❖

Elder Hawthorne awoke some time later when he heard passengers in his cabin grabbing their luggage. He felt the train grind to a halt. An announcer's voice repeated something over the PA system, but it was in

German and Elder Hawthorne was still coming to his senses, so he couldn't quite make it out."Where, um . . . where we are?" he stuttered urgently in German to a grey-haired woman sitting across from him.

She smiled at the pitiable American and said several words in German, one of which sounded like Luebeck.

"Luebeck? Are we in Luebeck?" repeated Elder Hawthorne, now in a panic.

"*Ja wohl!*" affirmed the woman. "*Machen Sie schnell!*" Elder Hawthorne understood this much German from the movies, and he scrambled to pull down his two bulging suitcases from the overhead luggage storage racks. Each suitcase weighed nearly as much as Elder Hawthorne, and he almost clipped the elderly woman with each of them as they plummeted to the floor, their fall virtually unbroken by Elder Hawthorne's feeble attempt to stop them.

The German voice on the PA system again issued some sort of warning. While Elder Hawthorne couldn't understand the meaning of the words, the tone sounded suspiciously like the voice of an attendant calling for the last boarding of a flight.

Elder Hawthorne scrambled to squeeze himself and his luggage through the cabin door and into the narrow hall that connected the cabins and led to the exit. Unfortunately, the corridor was quickly filling with passengers who were boarding.

Elder Hawthorne pressed himself and his luggage as close as possible to the outside wall of the passageway, repeating "Excuse please, excuse please" as he valiantly but futilely fought through the incoming stream of passengers toward the exit.

He was still ten feet away from the door when the whistle blew and the train lurched forward. As the train slowly pulled out of the station, a clean-cut young man in a blue suit caught Elder Hawthorne's eye. It was Elder Smith, and he was looking in every direction. Elder Hawthorne rapped hard on the window just in time to catch his dismayed companion's attention.

Elder Smith himself appeared to panic initially, but quickly regained his composure and decided to enjoy the moment. His face broadened into a grin as he trotted alongside the train while fumbling through an over-the-shoulder bag that looked like a cross between a purse and an athletic bag.

In a flash, Elder Smith produced a small camera from his bag, stopped, squared, and snapped a picture that gloriously captured Elder Hawthorne's panicked expression as the train sped away from Luebeck. It was a picture that would be circulated at virtually every zone conference in the mission for the next thirteen months.

Once his companion was out of view, Elder Hawthorne collapsed in despair, using one of his suitcases as a stool. He remained there until a ticket taker stopped and spewed forth German at him.

"Luebeck," mumbled Elder Hawthorne. "Um, . . . I want Luebeck. . . ."

The train employee's face softened, and he let out another stream of German, apparently in an attempt to comfort Elder Hawthorne or explain what he should do next. Elder Hawthorne returned only a blank a stare. "Um, English, you understand?" asked the man.

"Yes," admitted Elder Hawthorne, more humiliated than grateful. "I understand English."

"Next stop, you out," explained the helpful official with animated gestures to get across his point. "Big chart, look for Luebeck. See for time, then Gleis, um, you know, Gleis?"

"Track," answered Elder Hawthorne.

"Yes, track. So, you look Luebeck, then time, then track. You go to track, then on train. Ask people if Luebeck train, okay?"

"*Ja*," responded Elder Hawthorne, somewhat less dejected. "*Danke schoen*."

"Are you tourist?" asked the employee in German, very slowly.

"*Nein. Ich bin Missionar*," offered Elder Hawthorne timidly.

"A missionary?" said the puzzled official in German. "Where are you going? Africa?"

"No, here, Germany," apologized Elder Hawthorne.

"Here?" repeated the ticket taker with a laugh. "But we already Christians!"

Elder Hawthorne was ready for this conversation to be over. He was ready to be somewhere he could call home, perhaps soaking in a warm bath. He tried to think of some way to explain why he was in Germany as a missionary without offending the man. "I am, um, I speak with people, only peoples who with me speak want to, over my church."

"What church?"

"Um, my church is The Church of Jesus Christ of Latter-day Saints," replied Elder Hawthorne, bracing himself for the helpful stranger's response.

He did not understand most of the official's words, but sensed the employee was amused at the notion of missionaries proselyting in Germany. As he moved to the next cabin he slapped Elder Hawthorne on the back and wished him luck.

I'll need it, thought Elder Hawthorne.

✦ ✦ ✦

Elder Roberts was too excited to sleep on the four-hour train ride from Hamburg to Goettingen. As he gazed out the window at the pastoral countryside, his head spun with visions of missionary miracles he hoped to perform. He was realistic enough to know that he would not baptize thousands or even hundreds in this land, but he was not one to let others impose limitations on him.

He would work as hard at being a missionary as he had at being a student and a baseball player. His German was already remarkable for someone just coming out of the MTC, and Elder Roberts planned to hone it to perfection in the coming months.

His scriptural knowledge surpassed that of many returned missionaries. With the help of morning scripture study, Elder Roberts planned to memorize every reference and passage that he might ever need in his arsenal of scriptural evidence. He fully intended to do everything listed in the white handbook to become a successful missionary.

7
JW's and Geometric Proofs

At the train station, Elder Roberts was greeted by Elder Thomas, a trim missionary a few inches taller than himself. Clad in a blue polyester suit that could have been purchased only in Utah, Elder Thomas wore his sandy blond hair unabashedly short and his forward thruster shoes without apology. He appeared completely comfortable dressed as a missionary.

Elder Roberts immediately liked the natural air of confidence Elder Thomas exuded as he navigated the companionship comfortably through the train station, which seemed so daunting to Elder Roberts. To his surprise, in front of the station, Elder Thomas hailed a cab.

"This is not typical," explained Elder Thomas as they climbed into the cab, or at least that was what Elder Roberts guessed the word "typisch" meant. "It's a Goettingen tradition to take the golden to the apartment in a taxi. Elder Oman did it for me, so now it's my turn." Elder Roberts was relieved to be able to generally understand his companion's German.

"I've got something special for you tonight—a discussion with a Jehovah's Witness and some tracting."

The moment of truth was near. Elder Roberts knew tracting would take up much of his time for the next twenty-two months. And he knew he was supposed to be able to say that these two years were the best of his life. He had not quite figured out how both of these statements could be true at the same time. The mere mention of the word "tracting" had made his heart sink. He hoped his face didn't show it.

"We'll see what they taught you in the MTC," grinned Elder Thomas as the cab pulled up in front of the missionaries' apartment building.

The elders lugged Elder Roberts' suitcase up two flights of stairs. At the top, Elder Thomas unlocked the door, pushed it ajar, and waved Elder Roberts inside as he declared, "Welcome to Ginsterweg."

Elder Roberts learned that the apartment was located on a street named Ginsterweg, and his companion poetically referred to their residence by its street name, as if their apartment were a quaint British estate.

"Hey, this isn't half bad," said Elder Roberts as he surveyed his new home. The apartment was small but clean and modern. A kitchen served as the front hall, opening into a single room with two makeshift beds and two meager desks. A narrow passageway led from the kitchen to a sink, toilet and shower.

"It's not much, but it's clean, warm, private. And it's got a good shower," explained Elder Thomas with pride. "President Cook made sure we don't have any dumps left in the mission." Elder Thomas gave Elder Roberts the grand tour, which lasted about two minutes.

"Why don't you go ahead and unpack your stuff while I get lunch ready. We don't have any drawers or anything, but we do have a closet. The rest you can just organize in your suitcase."

Elder Roberts unpacked his things while Elder Thomas prepared the first of many original meals the new missionary would enjoy, compliments of his companion's cooking. This one was called "Thomas Delight" and appeared to contain potatoes, cheese, pineapple, and a few ingredients Elder Roberts couldn't identify precisely. All in all, it beat Top Ramen.

At exactly five p.m., Elder Thomas declared it was time to go "on the work." The elders knelt in prayer and within minutes were knocking on doors.

Elder Thomas insisted that his new companion take the lead at every other door. Elder Roberts' approaches were, of necessity, quite simple. But the people apparently understood his German, although they occasionally asked him to repeat himself. And to his delight, Elder Roberts was able to understand enough of what people said to him to make a reasoned guess at the complete meaning of their end of the conversation.

Of course, what people communicated to him was mostly that for one reason or another, they weren't interested in talking with the missionaries. The rejection was not enjoyable, but Elder Roberts found tracting much less painful now than when he had gone out occasionally with the missionaries in his ward at home. Here there was no chance of running into the girl from his high school biology class on whom he'd had a secret crush. And if people were swearing at him, Elder Roberts couldn't really tell. He just nodded his head and smiled.

At eight p.m., Elder Thomas and Elder Roberts arrived at the Brundt home for their first discussion. Herr Brundt was about thirty-five, and his mother was about sixty. They were, as Elder Thomas had promised, Jehovah's Witnesses.

"Do you mind if we begin with a word of prayer?" asked Elder Thomas after a few minutes of small talk.

"Not at all," replied Herr Brundt. "As long as you pray to Jehovah, of course." Herr Brundt smiled.

Elder Roberts looked at Elder Thomas to see how he would handle this one. After ten minutes of coming at the issue unsuccessfully from several angles, Elder Thomas finally gave up. "Why don't you offer the prayer?" Elder Thomas suggested.

"Good idea," said the man, whose mother looked on proudly.

During the prayer, which was addressed to Jehovah, Elder Roberts debated whether to say "amen" at the prayer's conclusion. Jesus taught that we should pray to his Father, thought Elder Roberts, and Jehovah was the Son. But was it a sin to pray to the Son? Or was it all right to assent to Herr Brundt's prayer as long as Elder Roberts knew in his own mind he was offering the prayer to the Father? Or, perhaps because Herr Brundt thought Jehovah was the Father, and everyone really intended the prayer to go to the Father, agreeing to the prayer would be permissible.

Elder Roberts was startled when Elder Thomas cleared his throat and began the discussion. Elder Roberts opened his eyes and discovered the prayer was over and his dilemma behind him.

The discussion went reasonably well; the man and his mother listened to what the missionaries had to say. Elder Roberts was excited that he was able to participate. He taught his concepts, and the people seemed to understand his German without too much difficulty.

Elder Roberts was even able to use his scriptural knowledge in attempting to answer some questions. He felt much like he had after driving a car for the first time and not running into anything.

"Not bad for a first discussion, Elder," said Elder Thomas as he and Elder Roberts rode their bikes back to the apartment after the discussion. "In fact, that was pretty darn good for a golden on his first day."

"Thanks," replied Elder Roberts. "You teach well," he added, and it was true. The assistant had been right.

"But this Jehovah thing is a problem," said Elder Thomas. "And it's your job to solve it. I'm assigning you to use that scriptural knowledge of yours to break through this barrier. When we teach them next time, I want you to use the Bible to show Herr Brundt and his smiling mother that Jehovah is Jesus Christ. You up for it?"

The wheels in Elder Roberts' mind were already turning. "I'll do my best." He was flattered that his senior companion had enough confidence in him to give him such an assignment.

Elder Thomas and Elder Roberts arrived back at the apartment at nine thirty-five. It had been a long day with no dinner—a mission custom—and Elder Thomas had pushed him hard on the bikes and up the stairs while tracting. Elder Roberts' body was still running on Mountain Standard Time, where it was five thirty-five a.m. He was exhausted.

"Here," said Elder Thomas as he opened the door, took off his coat and grabbed a loaf of bread practically in one motion. "Have a piece of bread and some Nutella. It's great stuff."

Elder Roberts examined the jar of creamy substance that looked like chocolate peanut butter. It was different, but it beat the heck out of fish eyes, lamb's head, and some of the other exotic international foods he had heard returned missionaries talk about.

Elder Roberts said a silent prayer of thanks that he hadn't been sent somewhere with strange food. After a couple of pieces of bread and

Nutella, Elder Roberts quickly undressed, said his prayers, and slipped into bed. His toes dangled over the edge of what appeared to be a converted couch. Soon he was sleeping as soundly as he ever had on any mattress.

❖ ❖ ❖

"Morning Elder," croaked Elder Hawthorne's trainer, Elder Smith. "Welcome to Day Two of life in the real mission field."

"Huh?" said Elder Hawthorne. He forced his eyes open slightly, but his mind was still immersed in a dream. In his dream, Elder Hawthorne had for some reason put his two suitcases in the overhead storage space of the airplane usually reserved for carry-on luggage, and he was scrambling to get them down without hitting anyone.

Once he managed to pull down the bulging bags he got them stuck in the narrow aisle between the seats. Before he was able to get out of the plane, the sliding door was shut and the pilot's voice intoned, "Next stop, the Ukraine."

After the plane took off again, the pilot came back to comfort Elder Hawthorne. The pilot was polite enough, but he spoke with an affected sincerity as he repeatedly asked Elder Hawthorne to explain why "Mormon" meant more good in Hebrew.

"It's five fifty-five," rasped Elder Smith. "Time to get up."

Elder Hawthorne rubbed his eyes and his dream began to fade. But he still felt like there was a stack of heavy bricks on the back of his neck, keeping him down. Elder Hawthorne's half-conscious mind raced to find a way to explain why it wasn't really five fifty-five and why he didn't really have to get up. Finally he propped himself up on one elbow and opened one eye.

Elder Smith promptly slipped into his best Al Michaels imitation and provided some color commentary. "The golden is down but not out. He's lifting his head, the focus is returning to his eyes," continued Elder Smith, bouncing his voice on each syllable. "What's this? He's getting up! The golden is getting up! We are witnessing history in the making, ladies and gentlemen. Only his first day in the mission field, and he's getting up on time!"

Elder Hawthorne felt as if his head were a huge magnet and the bed was made of steel, but he finally managed to bring himself fully upright.

"Great. Now let's try shifting to the kneeling position for comp prayer."

Elder Hawthorne gladly collapsed his body to the bed and dangled his knees on the floor, resting his head on his hands only a couple of inches from his pillow.

When they were done, Elder Smith joked, "If I were you, I'd wait a while to say my personal prayer. You look like your head might get stuck in the pillow if you do any more praying now."

Elder Hawthorne took Elder Smith's sound advice and found his way to the shower. To his relief, the shower actually had hot water and water pressure, and it had no cockroaches, spiders, or raccoon-sized rodents. Elder Hawthorne wasn't sure if the returned missionary stories he'd heard about such detestable showers were from less fortunate parts of the world or were simply missionary hyperbole. But his shower was warm and cockroach-free, and Elder Hawthorne was glad.

After a soothing shower, Elder Hawthorne studied his scriptures for thirty minutes and his German for thirty minutes. Both took on an air of more immediate importance now that he had the chance to use what he learned within hours of studying it.

Elder Hawthorne had difficulty shaking his jet lag, and on more than one occasion he dozed off with his face in a book. Each time this happened he was awakened by a flying pair of dirty socks and some friendly taunting from his trainer.

Finally it was time for breakfast. Elder Hawthorne had visions of smooth, creamy European yogurt dancing in his head, but he soon learned breakfast in the field was quite different than Sister Cook's sumptuous mission home breakfast.

Elder Smith pulled an unmarked jar of a white, goopy substance that looked like generic Miracle Whip from what Elder Hawthorne later learned was a yogurt cooker. His senior companion poured one third of the jar into one bowl and one third of the jar into another. He then poured in milk with the remaining third, put the lid back on, and placed the reconstituted goop back in the cooker.

"Eat up, Elder," said Elder Smith with a straight face. "I like mine with hoffies and a little jam," he added as he poured in some oatmeal and scooped in gelatin-like imitation strawberry jam.

"The hoffies really make it stick to your ribs. It'll last you all morning." Elder Hawthorne watched in silence as his companion stirred his homemade yogurt. It was not a pleasant sight.

"That looks like barf," said Elder Hawthorne, bewildered.

"Ah, but it isn't," replied Elder Smith, unfazed. "In fact, it's quite good," he continued with his mouth now full. "Although, it may be an acquired taste. I can't remember."

"Doesn't oatmeal have to be cooked?" pressed Elder Hawthorne.

"I don't think so," said Elder Smith, still on his first bite. "This is a time-honored recipe, almost as old as the yogurt starter itself."

Elder Hawthorne was afraid to ask, but he couldn't help himself. "What do you do with the rest of this yogurt goop stuff?"

"This 'yogurt goop stuff,'" explained Elder Smith, "is starter. We always leave one third of the yogurt, add milk, cook it, and boom, more yogurt. It's got something to do with bacteria growing." He took another large bite of the strange concoction.

"And just how just how far back does the genealogy of this bacteria-infested stuff go?" demanded Elder Hawthorne.

"Well, it was here when Elder Simms arrived in the apartment, and he was still using it when I got here." Elder Smith paused for another bite, and then continued with a sense of pride. "I guess it's been perpetuating itself for at least 11 months. It may even get better with time. Kind of like fine wine, I suppose."

Elder Hawthorne felt sick. He made himself two pieces of toast with Nutella and passed on the evolutionary yogurt. He was coming to realize that the MTC food that had been the butt of so many jokes and so much mockery for the last two months, would be—with the exception of an occasional meal in members' homes—the best food he would eat on his mission.

✦ ✦ ✦

Elder Roberts had spent a portion of scripture study every morning working up his scriptural strategy for convincing the Familie Brundt that Jehovah was actually Jesus Christ. When he was finished, he was proud of his outline, which resembled a geometric proof. Like any good proof, it began with subtle, seemingly unobjectionable premises and eventually wound its way to inescapable conclusions.

Finally the evening arrived for the second discussion with the Brundt's. Before attempting to have a prayer, Elder Thomas decided to resolve the Jehovah issue. "I'd like to begin by having my companion discuss Jehovah a little," he said as he turned and nodded to Elder Roberts. The junior companion noticed that Herr Brundt picked up his green Bible and held it firmly in both hands.

Elder Roberts' German wasn't smooth, but it was good enough to lead Herr Brundt and his mother on the short scriptural expedition he had prepared.

"Herr Brundt, could you please read Isaiah forty-four, verse six? Thank you."

Herr Brundt reticently complied. "Thus saith the Lord the King of Israel, and his redeemer the Lord of hosts; I am the first, and I am the last; and beside me there is no God."

"That's right, no God but Jehovah," interjected Frau Brundt. "Jehovah only."

"So this scripture . . . it is about Jehovah, yes?" asked Elder Roberts, just to verify their agreement with the premise.

"Surely," nodded Herr Brundt, still eyeing Elder Roberts carefully.

"Frau Brundt, could you please read now Isaiah forty-three, eleven?" continued Elder Roberts.

Frau Brundt read from her own green copy of the Bible. "I, even I, am the Lord; and beside me there is no savior." She looked up at Elder Roberts and said "*Na, und?*"—a German phrase that, roughly translated, means "So?"

"You agree, this scripture also about Jehovah?" asked Elder Roberts.

"Yes, I suppose," said Frau Brundt warily.

"Herr Brundt, could you read now please on Revelation twenty-two, thirteen?"

"I am Alpha and Omega, the beginning and the end, the first and the last." Herr Brundt did not look up after reading this verse, but instead scrutinized the rest of the page somewhat frantically.

"You agree, this scripture, like scripture in Isaiah, is also about Jehovah?" asked Elder Roberts. Out of the corner of his eye, he caught a glimpse of a smiling Elder Thomas, who now understood where Elder Roberts was taking the Brundt's.

"I, uh, . . . I suppose," stuttered Herr Brundt. "I mean, it sounds like it's also about Jehovah."

"Now read please verse sixteen," asked Elder Roberts, trying to contain his excitement. He'd always heard that it was impossible to convince Jehovah's Witnesses of anything, and yet he seemed to be on the verge of doing so.

"Jesus," mumbled Herr Brundt. "It's about Jesus . . . ." His voice trailed off in dismay.

Frau Brundt flipped to Revelation twenty-two, sixteen, to read the reference for herself. "I Jesus have sent mine angel to testify unto you these things in the churches. . . ." She too now began searching the chapter to find some explanation for this scriptural oddity.

Elder Roberts had them on the ropes and he knew it. It was time for his knockout punch. "Finally," began Elder Roberts, using a German word he had learned the day before, "I read Zechariah twelve, ten." Elder Roberts read the first few lines of the verse and then came to the punch line: ". . . and they shall look upon me whom they have pierced, and they shall mourn for him, as one mourneth for his only son. . . ." Elder Roberts glanced to his side to his gloating senior companion, and their eyes conveyed a mental high five to each other.

"Wait a moment," said the matriarch of the Brundt home. "Let me read that scripture for myself." And she did, out of her green copy of the Bible. "Aha, just as I thought. Your Bible has it wrong!"

"Excuse me?" answered Elder Thomas.

"Here, listen," said Frau Brundt, having regained her composure. "And they shall look upon *him* whom they have pierced. . . .' You see, your Mormon Bible has it wrong," declared Frau Brundt, before shutting her Bible for emphasis.

"Excuse me," injected Elder Thomas incredulously, ready for the fray. "This is no Mormon Bible. It's a Luther Bible, translated by Martin Luther and used by most Germans."

"Well I'm afraid we're not 'most Germans,'" answered Herr Brundt, coming to his debating senses again. "We're Jehovah's Witnesses, and we use a uniquely accurate translation of the Bible."

Elder Roberts decided to move off the issue of Bible translations and back to Jehovah, so he pursued another route: the "I Am" scriptures of Exodus three, fourteen and John eight, fifty-eight. Forty-five minutes and much heated discussion later, Elder Thomas and Elder Roberts left after a prayer to Jehovah by Frau Brundt asking him to show these two young Americans the error of their ways.

As they climbed on their bikes and headed to Ginsterweg, the elders rehashed the discussion.

"I thought we had them for a minute there," said Elder Roberts in a rare bit of English.

"Me too. But then, that woman came swooping in with her Green Dragon," said the senior companion, referring to the translation of the Bible used by the Jehovah's Witnesses.

"Next time I'll get a copy of their Bible and check their translations in advance," mused Elder Roberts. "If I had only known, I could have stopped at the Revelation scripture."

All the way back to the apartment, throughout the preparation for bed, and even after their prayers, the post-discussion analysis continued, with each missionary coming up with rebuttals they could have used for the Brundts' arguments. Finally they drifted off into unsatisfying sleep.

8
The Pedestrian Zone

"This is it," declared Elder Smith with pride. "*Die Fussgaengerzone.* No cars allowed—only people. They shop, they walk, they talk. It was built for street contacting, Elder."

Elder Smith paused and drew in a deep breath. He released it slowly, relishing the briny spring air.

Elder Hawthorne couldn't tell whether his companion actually looked forward to street contacting or was simply putting on a good show for his golden.

There was no question about how Elder Hawthorne felt. His heart sank as he surveyed the cobblestone square surrounded by quaint, century-old shops and a majestic cathedral. People were indeed shopping, walking, and talking. But they appeared to be talking mostly with friends, not unknown foreigners wearing suits and asking invasive questions about religion.

Elder Hawthorne's stomach muscles tightened involuntarily as he tried to imagine himself stopping complete strangers to ask what they knew about the Church. The tracting they had done together during their first week was difficult enough, but at least the pace of rejection was rather slow, since most people weren't home or simply chose not to open their doors for the missionaries. But this, this was open spiritual combat with no shields and no excuses—other than fear—for not being constantly engaged in conversations with the people.

"So how you this do?" asked Elder Hawthorne nervously in German.

"We stick and spin," said Elder Smith in English as he dismounted from his bike and locked it up. "It's mental. No pain, no gain."

Elder Hawthorne was still sitting on his bike. "Huh?"

"C'mon, Elder," encouraged Elder Smith. "Just do it."

"You're asking me to stop strangers cold to discuss religion, and all the instruction I get is trite sports phrases?" demanded Elder Hawthorne in English. His rare use of English outside the apartment caught his companion's attention.

Elder Smith hesitated for a moment as he considered his companion's point. Then he locked up Elder Hawthorne's bike and started toward the people. "Yup," he said as he walked away. "Nike paid somebody a lot of money to think that up, you know."

Elder Hawthorne followed reluctantly. "No they not did," Elder Hawthorne shouted, speaking in German again. "They steals it from President Kimball."

The first three people Elder Smith approached brushed him off without acknowledgment. But the fourth one stopped without hesitation.

"My companion and I are speaking with people today about good and evil," began Elder Smith, who almost never used the same approach twice. "A lot of people these days seem to scoff at the idea of there being good and evil, right and wrong. What do you think, mein Herr? Is there such a thing as good and evil?"

"Oh, there is most definitely good and evil, most definitely. And let me tell you this," continued the older German gentleman, who poked Elder Smith in the chest as he spoke. "I'll tell you who's evil. It's those Communists. People think they're not a threat any more, but they're out there, waiting for their chance. And I'm not going to give it to them, no sir."

The man did not stop for air. By Elder Hawthorne's estimation, he understood only about twenty percent of the one-sided conversation, but he thought the man was saying something about a secret formula he had developed that would make him invisible to the Communists.

At last Elder Smith interrupted. "You know, my companion here is very interested in this sort of thing. He studied political science at an American university." Elder Smith slapped Elder Hawthorne on the back and whispered in English, "He's all yours."

After another three or four minutes of listening to the man, Elder Hawthorne determined that the gentleman needed more help distinguishing fantasy from reality than he needed discerning evil from good. But the prospect of approaching someone else was daunting, so Elder Hawthorne nodded his head politely for another ten minutes.

Eventually Elder Hawthorne tired of getting poked in his chest by a man who seemed to be saying something about Communists trying to control his brain waves through his electric blanket. The time had come for the missionary to take the plunge, to try contacting someone himself. But first he had to somehow end his conversation with the anti-Communist Don Quixote.

"Want you with us to church come Sunday?" blurted Elder Hawthorne in his golden German, interrupting the man in mid-sentence.

The man was startled. "Members our church no smoke, no drink alcohol or coffee, also pay ten percent our money to church. Church beginning nine a.m., three hours is."

The gentleman mumbled something about how foreigners were often Communists and went on his way.

Finally freed from the cognitively impaired old man, Elder Hawthorne took in the scene around him. Elder Smith stood about twenty feet away, confidently gesticulating to emphasize a point as he spoke with a young couple.

Between Elder Smith and Elder Hawthorne were several people, none of whom Elder Hawthorne knew. He tried to pick a person to approach, but he had a hard time focusing in on individuals before they had walked by. He made two or three false starts, only to return awkwardly to the place where he had been standing. He felt as if he were at his first church dance.

Eventually a pipe-smoking gentleman walked into view at a slower pace. Elder Hawthorne swallowed hard and headed straight for the man. "Um, excuse please," he began timidly.

"What?" snorted the man without removing his pipe. He glared at Elder Hawthorne like a gruff principal eyeing a delinquent teenager.

"Um, uh," Elder Hawthorne stuttered. He could think of nothing to say. "Know you where a restroom is?" asked Elder Hawthorne.

The man continued to look suspiciously at the golden. After a long pause he took out his pipe and pointed behind Elder Hawthorne. "Right behind you. Good day." The missionary took a quick trip to the restroom to avoid further embarrassment.

With his bladder empty, Elder Hawthorne returned with renewed resolve to open his mouth and share the gospel. This time he quickly stepped in front of a younger man walking at a brisk pace. "Excuse please," he said with as much confidence as possible. "Believe you in God?"

"Whether I do or not is none of your business," sneered the man as he brushed the elder aside.

Wounded but not beaten, Elder Hawthorne stopped an older couple who seemed to be out on a Saturday walk. "Excuse please, but believe you in God?" he asked bluntly.

The woman quickened her pace, clutched her husband's arm tightly and muttered something indecipherable as she passed. Elder Hawthorne was not enjoying himself.

Next, he let a few more people pass before taking another crack at "GQ-ing," missionary slang for asking the "golden question." He soon spotted a bespectacled man in his late twenties sitting on a bench reading a book. Elder Hawthorne thought he remembered a scene like this from *Saturday's Warrior*. He walked over to the man with the most hope of the morning.

"Interesting book?" asked Elder Hawthorne as he sat down next to the man, hoping to appear nonchalant.

The man looked up slowly. "I'm sorry," he said deliberately as he lowered his book. "Do I know you?"

"No. I am Elder Hawthorne. And you is?"

"I am in the middle of reading a book. I find your interruption rude."

Elder Hawthorne didn't recognize all of the man's words, but he did recognize "rude," and it stung. But he remembered the scene from *Saturday's Warrior*, so he pressed on. "I'm sorry. I don't believe . . . I don't think . . . I . . . um . . . don't want rude to be. But I want talk with you about where we from came."

"And I would not like to talk with you about where we came from. From your accent and your broken German, I assume we come from very different places. And I find your persistence even more rude than your initial interruption." The man closed his book and walked away.

Elder Hawthorne did not like street contacting—not at all.

✧ ✧ ✧

During his first two months together with Elder Greisel, J.P. spent virtually every minute that the missionaries were in the apartment with his headset on listening to his CD's. In the MTC his CD's had been a great novelty, a treasure he enjoyed showing to those missionaries he knew would appreciate them.

But here in the heart of Germany—thousands of miles away from Menlo Park, California, and at least a train ride away from any American missionaries—here Elder Prentice needed his seven CD's more than ever. They created a personal retreat from the strange new world in which he suddenly found himself, his only connection to the pleasant familiar world from which he'd come.

J.P.'s high school friends would hardly have recognized his demeanor. If the president meant to break J.P.'s spirit, he'd succeeded.

J.P. could neither communicate nor have fun with his Austrian companion. His only hope had been the *Wayne's World* routine he'd memorized in German. Unfortunately, it seemed that *Wayne's World* had not made its way to Austria, because Elder Greisel was completely baffled by the dialogue.

Nor did Elder Greisel appreciate any of J.P.'s other attempts at humor. He was a missionary machine who had no time for anything extraneous to "the work"—words he occasionally attempted to pronounce in English with unintentionally humorous results.

More than anything, Elder Greisel tracted, and Elder Prentice had no apparent choice but to tract too. They rarely visited members' homes, and when they did, the visits were short and official—nothing like the evening-long ping-pong tournaments that elders in the States had told him about.

The Braunschweig companionship also didn't teach much, and they had no investigators in their pool who were past the second discussion. Elder Prentice wondered whether this was the result of Elder Greisel's style at the doors and in discussions. For the Austrian senior companion, all questions from investigators seemed a nuisance, and any doubts were presumed disingenuous excuses for wicked living. He never varied a word from the discussions, which he considered sufficient to address all essential spiritual matters.

"Our job," Elder Greisel instructed his golden once, "is to lay down the word of God as stated in the discussions. It is then up to the people to accept it. I have absolutely no intention of getting defensive about the gospel or getting overly concerned with those who reject it. Once I have presented the message, I have fulfilled my duty." J.P. couldn't understand at least half of the words his companion used, but from Elder Greisel's tone he was able to fully grasp the gist of his companion's philosophy.

After a few futile attempts at small talk in between doors early in the companionship, Elder Prentice had given up on communicating with his companion except when absolutely necessary. They spoke less with each other in an entire day than most members speak before church in the chapel.

The silence and loneliness that accompanied his plunge into introversion were unwelcome novelties in J.P.'s life. Throughout his youth J.P. had a carload of friends at his disposal almost constantly. Now six days a week passed without J.P. seeing anyone whom he considered a friend, even in the loose American sense of the word.

If his mission president had hoped to force Elder Prentice to learn German by putting him with Elder Greisel, he had failed. J.P. held his mission president and the Lord responsible for his misfortune, and he countered by putting as little effort as possible into the entire endeavor, particularly the language.

J.P. was amazed at how well he could survive knowing hardly any German. He memorized two different two-sentence approaches for the doors, and they proved sufficient; most people closed the door before he finished the two sentences. When someone responded in a more substantive or positive way, Elder Greisel simply took over the conversation.

In discussions, in a similar manner, J.P. managed to get by, roughly memorizing the even-numbered concepts from the first two discussions. His presentation of those concepts was by no means fluent, but he got across the main points. Elder Greisel handled everything else in his steamroller teaching style, which ensured that they would never get to a third discussion.

"I have learned something in my first two months in Germany," wrote J.P. to a friend who was still at home. "Returned missionaries are lying about two things: that missions are the best two years of their lives, and that missions go fast."

J.P. admitted to his friend that he was miserable, and that the last two months had felt more like two years. He could only come up with two reasons returned missionaries perpetrate the fiction. "First, peer pressure to act like a spiritual giant is overwhelming. Second, like going through initiation for an athletic team or a fraternity, you continue the tradition once you've put in your suffering. If you're too honest about how bad it is, you won't get to enjoy watching others go through the same misery."

✦ ✦ ✦

When the time for June transfers came and went, Chris could hardly believe two months had already passed. Elder Thomas had become a better friend than perhaps any other friend he had.

In just eight weeks, according to his calculations, Elder Roberts and his companion had taught one hundred, fifty-eight discussions to sixty-seven different people. Their investigators had included theology students, widows, a young couple from Poland, a large Islamic family from Morocco, three refugees from Nigeria, and other Germans of assorted ages and religious backgrounds.

After the second discussion at the Brundt's, Elder Roberts had been caught off guard scripturally only once. A cerebral, agnostic architect who knew the Bible surprisingly well had scoffed when Elder Roberts explained that Lehi was a descendant of Joseph who lived in Jerusalem.

"Yes, that's a very interesting story," the architect had commented patronizingly. "Of course, there's one problem. Neither Ephraim nor Manasseh had an inheritance in Jerusalem, did they?"

Elder Roberts had never heard this argument before, and he didn't discover an adequate response in the Old Testament until the next morning. The architect didn't answer his door when Elder Thomas and his companion returned, so Elder Roberts wrote a note with his belated answer to the man's question and stuck it under the door. It wasn't nearly as gratifying as having a definitive rebuttal on the spot.

Not surprisingly, the theology students were the most intellectually challenging. No two students seemed to have the same set of beliefs, which made finding areas of consensus upon which to build rather difficult. Still, Elder Roberts enjoyed the task.

One student would believe only in the writings of Paul and the next would reject Paul's epistles altogether. Each used a different translation of the Bible, and Elder Roberts began collecting translations and searching them to see which versions interpreted the discussion scripture references most accurately.

Unfortunately, none of the investigators seemed to be making real progress towards baptism. The Brundt's had simply been unable to accept the Book of Mormon, despite Ezekiel thirty-seven, fourteen through seventeen, *Ancient America Speaks*, and Elder Roberts' discussion of word print studies. More than once, Elder Roberts wished that some of the excellent scholarly research he'd read about the Book of Mormon had been printed in German.

"Still, under the circumstances," Chris wrote his brother, "I feel things are going extremely well."

9
Confounding Children of Hell

Elder Hawthorne had a lot of time to think as he tracted in Treppenhaueser, the seven and eight-story apartment buildings with two or three apartments on each floor opening into a common stairwell. Ten weeks into his mission, he was feeling fine about the gospel, except the part that made every member feel obligated to preach the gospel to every creature on earth, including those clearly disinterested in the message.

If it weren't for this problem and a couple of other minor doctrines that Elder Hawthorne would refine—if given the chance—everything would be just fine. I'd even go on a mission gladly, he thought as he pressed to keep up with Elder Smith's steady climbing. But a mission would consist only of visiting the homes of referrals the missionaries would receive from members and visitors' centers around the globe.

Yes, thought Elder Hawthorne, television would be ideal. Just have great minds create spiritually powerful videos, transmit them to television sets throughout the world, have interested people call the eight hundred number, and then let missionaries spend all their time teaching these people and other people who show up on their own at church.

Presently, Elder Hawthorne's life was complicated by the fact that the Church had not yet adopted this enlightened approach to missionary work. Instead, it insisted that he spend approximately six to ten hours a day disturbing people who clearly had no interest in speaking with him about anything, much less religion.

In fact, it was not at all clear to Elder Hawthorne that missionaries did more good than harm under the current approach. He could count at least a couple of people a day who had taken great personal offense at the fact the missionaries had the audacity to disturb their peace.

One man in Elder Hawthorne's second week had threatened to call the police simply because the missionaries had knocked on his door. The golden had since lived in almost continual fear that he would get chastised or even arrested for tracting. For someone who experienced vicarious anxiety of major proportions when watching scenes in movies in which private detectives searched other people's houses, such fear of getting into trouble was not easy to bear.

"Your turn," said Elder Smith to his golden as they reached the seventh floor.

Elder Hawthorne drew a deep breath, mostly to make up the oxygen debt he had just incurred. He knocked three times just loudly enough so the resident would hear him, but not so loudly that the resident would feel compelled to answer the door.

He waited five seconds and then began to drift toward the next door. Elder Smith interrupted his companion's early exit with six sharp raps on the door.

"I'd hate for this person to miss their chance to hear the gospel because the TV was turned up too loud," explained the senior companion.

The sound of footsteps cut off the missionaries' brief discussion. Elder Hawthorne subconsciously retracted his toes in his shoes, as he did before each door approach, always fearing that behind each door was a person angrier than the last one. The door opened quickly about eighteen inches to reveal the rugged face of an older German man—Herr Krueger—if the name plate next to the door was accurate.

"Yes, what is it?" he demanded.

When Elder Hawthorne felt pressure, he stumbled over his German all the more. "We, um, we is, I mean, we are missionaries from The Church of Jesus Christ of Latter-day Saints, and we have a message for you. Do you . . ."

"Lutheran," interrupted Herr Krueger cryptically. "I have no interest."

That was good enough for Elder Hawthorne, so he did nothing to prevent the man from closing the door. But just before Herr Krueger could close the door completely, Elder Smith took one last shot. "Excuse me, sir, but do you believe in the resurrection?"

Herr Krueger opened the door slightly wider than he had initially, and Elder Hawthorne was sure his companion was in for some verbal abuse.

"I wish I did, young man. My wife died three months ago, and I have no hope of seeing her again."

"May we come in?" pressed Elder Smith boldly. "We have a message that will bring you hope."

To Elder Hawthorne's astonishment, the cantankerous old man acceded to Elder Smith's request and waved the missionaries in.

✧ ✧ ✧

As transfer time neared, Elder Prentice actually began to pray fervently, perhaps for the first time in his life. His prayers were focused, intense, and sincere; he wanted a new companion.

He knew that a transfer would not necessarily be the answer to all his problems, but it was certainly worth a shot. Based on the missionaries he'd met in the MTC and at district and zone meetings, his odds of getting a better companion out of any trade were quite good.

Elder Prentice was also unsure of the propriety of asking the Lord for something like a new companion, but he decided he'd take his chances on that front as well. As J.P. saw it, he didn't have much to lose, since he was probably not doing very well in the Lord's eyes so far anyway.

This realization gave J.P. another idea, and he immediately incorporated it into his prayers. If he got a new companion, he promised, he would work hard to become a better missionary.

✧ ✧ ✧

Each day as they returned to the apartment for lunch, J.P. took it upon himself to check the mailbox. He and Elder Greisel usually ate lunch at about one or one-thirty, but today Elder Prentice had insisted that he was starving, so the elders pulled in for lunch at twelve-thirty.

Of course, both elders knew the real reason for taking an early lunch. It was Wednesday of transfer week, the day transfer letters arrived. Today Elder Greisel rushed to the mailboxes along with his companion, and J.P. wondered whether the Austrian missionary had been praying for a transfer too. If so, it would be the first time they had worked unitedly with prayer and faith.

J.P. fumbled with the mail key in his excitement. Finally he managed to turn the key and open the tiny metal door, revealing two envelopes. J.P. felt his heart pounding rapidly in its cage as Elder Greisel grabbed the letters out of the box. Then J.P.'s eye caught the mission letterhead on a legal size envelope.

"Yes!" shouted J.P. as he clenched his fist, bent his knees and pulled his elbow into his body in a classic American jock gesture. Elder Greisel contained himself only slightly better as he tore open the envelope from the mission president.

Both elders quickly scanned the text of the two-page letter. "What does it say, Elder?" asked Elder Greisel, who had great difficulty reading English.

J.P. practically whimpered his broken German response. "Money . . . more money, month, more money on the month get we . . . ." J.P.'s voice trailed off. Any other day such a letter about an adjustment in the monthly allowance would have been great news.

"Another month," sighed Elder Greisel, clearly disappointed.

As an afterthought J.P. flipped to the second page of the letter. It was actually a second letter addressed to Elder Prentice. J.P. scanned it quickly before finding the magic words.

"Bremerhaven! I'm going to Bremerhaven!" Elder Greisel grabbed the letter and examined it for himself while J.P. did another victory dance.

In his biggest display of emotion in their entire four months together, Elder Greisel smiled and nodded after scrutinizing the letter.

"Yes you are," he said slowly in English. The two missionaries who had hardly spoken in four months then enjoyed their most amicable lunch in weeks.

✦ ✦ ✦

Elder Roberts knew his companionship with Elder Thomas was too good to last. In August the capable senior companion was transferred to Hamburg to serve as district leader. Elder Thomas was replaced as senior companion by Elder McKinstry, who had spent the first year of his mission in Hamburg, apparently without seeing much success.

Elder Roberts soon learned that Elder McKinstry was very humble and soft-spoken, unusually so for someone with his level of intelligence. A National Merit scholar, Elder McKinstry came equipped with plenty of intellectual horsepower. However, most of it seemed to be in the physical sciences and did not spill over into the sort of improvisational skills required for door approaches, GQ-ing, and teaching. Elder McKinstry was certainly not the dynamic debater that Elder Thomas was.

Nor did he have the same sense of faith and confidence Elder Thomas exuded. This became apparent at their first district meeting together when the district leader, Elder Seitz, had asked Elder Prentice and Elder McKinstry to demonstrate a baptismal challenge. Elder Seitz played the investigator.

"So, um, what do we know about you?" asked Elder McKinstry apprehensively.

"Well, I don't know, let's just say I'm a typical investigator you feel prompted to challenge to baptism," said Elder Seitz.

"Okay. All right. Let's see," fumbled Elder McKinstry. Finally he plunged into the memorized dialogue, which flowed quite smoothly until he came to the point where he was supposed to ask the investigator to be baptized.

"Would you . . . um . . . well . . . we're not asking you to do anything you don't want to do, but would you consider praying about these things to see if they're true, and . . . well . . . if you find out they're true would you consider getting baptized? I mean, if you knew they were true?"

It was not like any baptismal challenge Elder Thomas had ever issued. Given Elder McKinstry's timidity, Elder Roberts found himself taking on much more responsibility in the companionship than he had as a golden with Elder Thomas.

The second major change was one in teaching style. While Elder Roberts had initially enjoyed the challenge of trying to build on whatever common ground the missionaries shared with their investigators, after four months, he became increasingly annoyed with the logical inconsistencies in the beliefs of the people he taught. His greatest frustration was reserved for the University of Goettingen theology students, who seemed more concerned about nuclear destruction than spiritual destruction.

Several of these budding ministers insisted that those portions of the New Testament testifying of Christ's literal resurrection had been added in decades after the fact by overzealous disciples. Elder Roberts met few theologians—or Goettinger's generally—who believed in the literal resurrection of Jesus Christ.

The second Saturday afternoon following the transfer, Chris decided he'd had enough. He and Elder McKinstry had spent the morning GQ-ing in the pedestrian zone, engaging anyone in religious conversation who would stop. Elder Roberts had encountered a self-proclaimed gay Christian, who said, "I think the most important commandment Jesus gave is to love one another, I mean really love one another."

Then there was a Lutheran adult Sunday School teacher who believed that Christ was not physically resurrected ". . . but he certainly lives on symbolically in our minds . . ." and the usual slew of Northern Germans—nominally Lutheran—who firmly believed in being Lutheran because that meant they didn't have to firmly believe in anything at all.

That afternoon, as Elder Roberts and Elder McKinstry tracted, Elder Roberts' frustration with the contradictions inherent in these positions reached a boiling point. Elder Roberts had restrained himself from countering these comments, but perhaps it was time to give these pseudo-religious, enlightened people a dose of his high school debating prowess.

Yes, Chris decided, it's time to reason persuasively and forcefully like Paul, to call people to repentance like Abinadi, to speak candidly like Captain Moroni.

What was that line he had read recently from Captain Moroni? "I perceive that thou art a child of hell. . . ." Maybe that was just the hardhitting response that would have jolted someone into repentance this morning. What if he inserted "intellectual?"

Elder Roberts liked the sound of the line already—"an intellectual child of hell." He was searching his mind for the German word for "intellectual" when the door opened.

Behind it was a typically bearded, casually dressed Greenpeace type. Like many young Goettinger's, he was easily engaged in conversation. Eventually the man allowed the missionaries to come in, and they worked their way into the first discussion.

Much like a parent annoyed by past behavior awaits an excuse to discipline a child, Elder Roberts sat on the edge of his chair, waiting for the investigator to make a mistake in logic. But the German disappointed him, mostly listening and asking a few clarifying questions as the elders taught.

However, when Elder McKinstry finally discussed the physical resurrection of the Savior, Elder Roberts saw his chance coming. Elder

McKinstry asked the investigator how he felt about the Savior and his physical resurrection.

The investigator's response was predictable. "Well, I appreciate what Jesus taught, but the notion of somebody being physically resurrected is just too much for me to believe."

Here's yet another German who believes that Christ lived but denies he lives today, thought Chris. How is it that they can believe what the New Testament records about the Savior's life while rejecting what the New Testament documents about Christ's death and resurrection? Is the Bible like a smorgasbord, with readers free to sample some of the Gospels, have a few extra helpings of Paul's epistles, and then just pass on the subject of the Resurrection?

Elder Roberts wondered whether smorgasbord was a German word too, but decided to leave this line out of his argument, since he wasn't sure. Instead, he would begin his response by reading the passage from Luke twenty-four that unequivocally proves the Savior's physical resurrection. Then he would expose the silliness of selective belief in the New Testament.

But before Elder Roberts could jump in with his rebuttal argument, Elder McKinstry surprised him with an answer of his own. "You know, Herr Schindler, your response is very understandable. I assume that like the rest of us, you have never seen a resurrected being." Herr Schindler cracked a smile and nodded.

Elder McKinstry continued. "To imagine someone who is dead living again with an immortal body is, well, it's almost too much to believe, really." Elder Roberts wondered where his companion was going with this one.

"In fact, your reaction to the notion of Jesus being physically resurrected is very similar to how the apostles responded." Herr Schindler cocked his head slightly, intrigued by the comparison.

"Although the Savior had foretold his resurrection to the apostles on more than one occasion, they, too, found it difficult to believe that he was physically resurrected—and he appeared to them personally."

Elder McKinstry turned to Luke twenty-four as he spoke. "They thought he was a ghost, so Christ invited them to feel him so they would know he had flesh and bones. Here. Read verse forty," said Elder McKinstry as he handed his Bible to Herr Schindler.

Herr Schindler read how the original apostles still could not believe Jesus was physically resurrected, even after touching him, and how the Savior ate a piece of cooked fish to finally convince them.

Although Elder Roberts had read this story many times on his mission, he was amazed, more than ever this time, at how slow the apostles were to believe, despite having the resurrected Savior before their eyes. Elder Roberts then watched with interest as the investigator responded warmly to Elder McKinstry's use of the same scripture Elder Roberts had planned to invoke in a very different way.

"Nice touch," said Elder Roberts to his companion afterward.

"Thank you. I learned it on a split with a district leader in Hamburg," explained Elder McKinstry in grammatically correct but plodding German. "He always emphasized using the scriptures as a tool rather than a weapon."

10
Snuffing Out Old Habits

"Welcome to the Bremerhaven Wohnung," J.P.'s new companion said in English and a smidgen of German, as he opened the door to J.P.'s new home.

Elder Lafferty immediately walked to the kitchen and proudly opened the cupboard. Pointing to a large container of Skippy Peanut Butter, he boasted, "We've got more peanut butter than any other city in the mission."

J.P. hadn't really noticed the absence of peanut butter from his diet until Elder Lafferty mentioned the substance, but now that he thought about it, he suddenly craved it.

Moving to the bathroom, J.P.'s new senior companion produced American-made toothpaste and toilet paper. "The members of the American military branch have access to almost everything you miss about home, and they keep us generously supplied," explained the shorter elder with a distinct Texas twang.

Elder Lafferty had a slight build, sparse light brown hair, a receding hairline and a clearly visible bald spot. He didn't look like a jock, but he also didn't sound or act anything like Elder Greisel—a fact that was much more significant to J.P. at the moment, after having spent four months with the "spiritual exterminator," as he'd come to call his machine-like golden trainer with the Arnold Schwarzenegger accent.

"Do we . . . um . . . work much with the American branch?" asked J.P. hopefully.

"Much?" parroted Elder Lafferty with a Ross Perot smile. "We're supposed to split our time fifty-fifty. But I generally like to spend my time where I'm most welcome, and that tends to be in the American branch—with members."

"Can't argue with that," concurred J.P. as he surveyed the small apartment. A large lasso was draped over his companion's bed, a calendar and a piece of paper stating "267 Days Left" hung over the desk, and a full length poster of Ty Detmer hung from the wall. Squarely in the middle of an otherwise immaculate study desk was a framed, glossy eight-by-ten photograph of a semi-attractive brunette in a dreamy, pseudo-glamorous pose.

"That's Heather," explained Elder Lafferty. "Gotta picture of your girl?"

"Um, well, which one?"

"So, no girlfriend, huh?"

"Not anymore," confessed J.P. "I had three, but I kinda blew it in the MTC with a postal mistake. I got my letters mixed up."

Elder Lafferty doubled over in laughter for a full thirty seconds. J.P. decided to change the subject. Pointing to the Ty Detmer poster, he asked, "Say, do any of the American members have, well, any kind of access to American sports on TV or anything?" It was September, and J.P. was about to spend his first football season outside of the United States.

"Video—of everything," answered Elder Lafferty definitively. "We generally watch thirty minutes or so of some great old BYU game or a 49ers' game from the Young era—you know, the Lord's teams—every time we go to our ward mission leader's house for our weekly meeting. He's great. Says he figures happy missionaries are the best. There's no need for us to walk around like spiritual zombies. Heck, in the old days, like sixty years ago, they even used to let missionaries dance and stuff and they still did the work okay."

"Sounds like my kind of ward mission leader," said J.P. And my kind of approach to missionary life, he thought to himself. Finally things were getting back on track—back to the way he had envisioned his mission would be.

* * *

Because Herr Krueger's main interest had been in the afterlife, Elder Smith had chosen to begin with a full discussion about the plan of salvation rather than the usual first discussion. The discussion had gone reasonably well, and Herr Krueger had agreed to let the missionaries come back for another visit.

Herr Krueger had greeted the missionaries warmly when they arrived for their second discussion. He had actually prepared some cookies and herbal tea (without caffeine) for his guests, which they enjoyed before beginning the discussion. The retired widower had then stunned the missionaries when they began discussing modern-day prophets.

"Just as God revealed his will to prophets in ancient times," Elder Smith had explained, "he has spoken to prophets in our day."

"Joseph Smith . . . 1820 . . . in the state of New York in the United States," interjected Herr Krueger. Noticing the astonished looks on the faces of his young teachers, Herr Krueger explained, "I read those brochures you left with me, yes I did."

Despite the missionaries' best efforts at committing people to read, most people didn't, especially after only one discussion. "Very interesting," continued Herr Krueger, "very interesting."

At the elders' invitation Herr Krueger attended church the next Sunday. Never before had Elder Hawthorne's hopes for an investigator been so high, and never before had he felt so much anxiety during church meetings.

"Please," Elder Hawthorne half-thought to himself and half-prayed, "please don't let there be any more talks about plants and animals resurrecting. And please don't let the ward choir sing. If it does, please let Brother Gruen be sick."

Elder Hawthorne witnessed the entire three-hour block of meetings through the eyes of a newcomer, and it was a painful experience. He noticed every flaw in logic and every inadequacy in presentation during the three meetings. More than once Elder Hawthorne found himself wishing that if the Church didn't use full-time, trained ministers, bishops would at least call only on the more reasonable, articulate members to speak in sacrament meeting.

After priesthood meeting, Elder Hawthorne decided he'd better explain to Herr Krueger the thinking behind having a lay clergy. "I am sorry," Elder Hawthorne began his apologetic explanation. "In our church . . ."

"In your church," interrupted Herr Krueger as he placed a hand firmly on the shoulder of his young American friend, "in your church God is among us."

Elder Smith decided his junior companion should have the opportunity to challenge Herr Krueger to baptism at the next discussion. Elder Hawthorne had given the baptismal challenge only three times in his first four months, and this was the first one he had any real hope would be understood, much less accepted.

"Oh, I was baptized as a baby, thank you," each of the first two investigators had responded to Elder Hawthorne's challenge. Herr Krueger was beginning to look golden, but Elder Hawthorne now knew enough about missionary work to know that no conversion was automatic.

The day of the discussion the elders fasted. As the moment in the discussion for the baptismal challenge drew near, Elder Hawthorne's heart pounded audibly. He said a silent prayer to seek the Lord's guidance and the affirming presence of the Spirit. He was so immersed in his prayer that Elder Smith had to cue him twice to begin the challenge.

Elder Hawthorne swallowed hard. It was not easy to ask a sixty-seven-year-old man to join a church that he'd never heard of three weeks ago, even if he had read the brochures and liked the meetings.

Beginning the challenge felt almost like jumping from the high dive for the first time. "Brother Krueger, could you read please Second Nephi, thirty-one, ten?"

Herr Krueger dutifully complied. "And he said unto the children of men: Follow thou me. Wherefore, my beloved brethren, can we follow Jesus save we shall be willing to keep the commandments of the Father?"

"What do you think, Brother Krueger?" asked Elder Hawthorne almost rhetorically. "Can we follow Jesus without keeping the commandments of the Father?"

"No, of course not," answered Herr Krueger quickly and calmly.

"Are you willing to keep the commandments of the Father?" Elder Hawthorne felt a rush of adrenaline and a surge of what could have been the Spirit as he asked the question.

"Do his commandments include not using snuff?"

The question about the only tobacco product created exclusively for consumption through the nose caught both missionaries off guard, although they had been concerned about whether Herr Krueger would be able to give up his unsightly habit. But they wouldn't mention the Word of Wisdom for another two discussions, and none of the brochures included it. Consequently, neither elder had anticipated Herr Krueger even knowing about the issue yet.

Elder Hawthorne looked to his senior companion for help out of the jam, but Elder Smith simply returned his trainee's glance with a nod that let Elder Hawthorne know he was expected to field this question himself.

To his surprise Elder Hawthorne answered before he thought he was ready, and for the remainder of the baptismal challenge he felt almost as if he were listening to someone else speak when the words were coming out of his mouth.

"Yes, we talk about the commandments on other discussion, but no tobacco a commandment is." Elder Hawthorne's German was improving, but as with all new foreign-speaking missionaries, there was still a marked difference between his extemporaneous German and his memorized German.

"Let me guess. It's something the Lord revealed to that Joseph Smith," speculated Herr Krueger.

"Yes. How you know about tobacco commandment?" asked Elder Hawthorne out of curiosity.

"Just a feeling, a suspicion, I guess," granted Herr Krueger with a shrug.

"I believe that feeling come from the Spirit," offered Elder Hawthorne in a statement that was quite bold for him. Then he looked Herr Krueger squarely in the eyes and asked, "Are you willing to keep the commandments of the Father, Brother Krueger?"

"*Ja*," answered Herr Krueger deliberately. "*Ja wohl.*"

Elder Hawthorne's next question was not called for by the discussion outline—it was not called for until two discussions later—but it rolled off Elder Hawthorne's tongue (in broken German) anyway. "Will you no more tobacco use too?"

Herr Krueger looked offended. "You just said it was one of the commandments, didn't you?" he asked rhetorically. The elders nodded. "Then I'll stop using snuff. In fact, here," Herr Krueger continued, proving his point by pushing himself out of his chair and walking toward the kitchen.

"I may as well get the stuff out of my house." He returned in a moment with a bag full of canisters containing the uncommon inhalant. "Forty-nine years I've used this stuff," sighed the older man with the red nose wistfully as he gazed into the bag for a moment. Then he abruptly handed the bag to the missionaries. "Take it away."

Free of the bag, Herr Krueger looked at the floor for a moment, pulled a well-used handkerchief from his pocket and blew his nose to get the last vestiges of snuff out of his life.

"Anything else," demanded Herr Krueger. "Any other commandments?"

Elder Hawthorne paused to reflect on this question for a moment, but decided against further elaboration of any of the remaining commandments. He continued with the baptismal challenge as outlined.

"Yes. Could you read verses eleven and twelve please? Thank you."

"And the Father said: Repent ye, repent ye, and be baptized in the name of my Beloved Son. And also, the voice of the Son came unto me, saying: He that is baptized in my name, to him will the Father give the Holy Ghost, like unto me; wherefore, follow me, and do the things which ye have seen me do." Herr Krueger looked up expectantly after finishing the verses.

"Brother Krueger, will you keep the commandments of the Father and repent and be baptized?" Elder Hawthorne felt such warmth and peace when he finally asked the question that he was actually surprised when Herr Krueger hesitated momentarily before responding.

"By immersion?" asked Herr Krueger. He had apparently been reading his brochures again.

"Yes, by immersion," confirmed Elder Hawthorne.

"Will other people be getting baptized at the same time?" Coming from a man who had just given up a life-long vice, this question puzzled Elder Hawthorne.

"Quite possibly," interjected Elder Smith optimistically.

"Could I go last? I have a bad leg and I'd hate to make the water dirty if someone else were to use it after me."

Elder Hawthorne literally wanted to hug the man. He was so overwhelmed that he forgot to respond to Herr Krueger's comment. Elder Smith finally stepped in.

"I think we can arrange for that," he said, as if he'd need to pull some strings. "Congratulations, Bruder Krueger. You've just made the most important decision in your life."

11
Batting Averages and Baptism Rates

Elder McKinstry and Elder Roberts were seeing unprecedented success teaching discussions. One week they taught twenty-three discussions, and they were averaging between fifteen and twenty a week. From what Elder Roberts could glean from other missionaries, these numbers were fantastic for Germany.

Yet they weren't baptizing. This fact vexed Elder Roberts, but didn't seem to bother Elder McKinstry much. Elder McKinstry had still not baptized, and he'd been out thirteen months.

One morning during personal scripture study, Elder Roberts read Ammon's explanation of the success he and his brothers experienced among the Lamanites. Elder Roberts read Alma twenty-six, twenty-two aloud to Elder McKinstry: "Yea, he that repenteth and exerciseth faith, and bringeth forth good works, and prayeth continually without ceasing—unto such it is given to know the mysteries of God; yea, unto such it shall be given to reveal things which never have been revealed; yea, and it shall be given unto such to bring thousands of souls unto repentance, even as it has been given unto us to bring these our brethren to repentance."

"So, what about this, Elder?" asked Elder Roberts, hitting the page with the back of his hand for emphasis. "Why aren't we baptizing thousands of souls? Why aren't we baptizing any souls? Is it because we're not exercising enough faith, not praying enough, not pure enough?" Elder Roberts continued, pacing in their small room.

"I don't know," said Elder McKinstry from his bed, where he sat Indian style with his scriptures on his lap, choking down a banana. "Try telling that to Noah, Mormon, and Moroni. For that matter, do you know of any missionaries in this century who have baptized thousands? There must have been righteous missionaries who haven't baptized many people, much less thousands of souls." Elder McKinstry rested his case and contentedly finished off his banana with a third bite.

Elder Roberts didn't have a quick comeback for this argument. Unable to address his companion's question, he decided to ignore it and go back on the offensive himself. "Are you telling me you don't think the number of people you baptize has anything to do with the amount of faith and prayer you exercise? I mean, what do you do with this scripture?"

"I don't know," Elder McKinstry replied, his mouth still full of banana. "I won't say they've got nothing to do with each other. But for me, there are just too many good missionaries, too many prophets who never converted a soul to be worried about not baptizing. I'm just here to plant the seeds. I can't control what people choose to do with the seeds. If some of the seeds grow, great. If not, I've still done my job."

"Well I want to harvest," said Elder Roberts, somewhat jokingly but impatiently. "How about we send you down the street to plant the seeds and I'll follow about fifteen minutes later to harvest?"

Elder McKinstry laughed. "How about we stop this philosophical discussion and get ready for the work, or we won't get any planting or harvesting done," said the senior companion.

However, as the days and weeks wore on without a baptism, Elder Roberts couldn't shake the nagging feeling that he was failing as a missionary—no matter how many discussions he was teaching. He'd never heard anyone ask a returned missionary how many discussions he'd taught. People only asked about baptisms, and Elder Roberts had none. He was keeping the commandments and the rules and working hard, but he was still getting shut out. It didn't seem right, especially when some missionaries who didn't keep the rules were baptizing.

The next week at zone conference, Elder Roberts spilled his feelings to President Cook during their interview. "I'm just not baptizing," Elder Roberts said. "What more do I need to do to baptize? Is Elder McKinstry right? Is it good enough to plant seeds?"

For what seemed like a full minute, President Cook said nothing. He looked at Elder Roberts as if the missionary were still talking. Just when Elder Roberts was about to say something—anything—to break the silence, President Cook asked, "What was your grade point average in high school?"

The question caught Elder Roberts off guard, but the answer was apparently deeply ingrained in Elder Roberts' psyche because it rolled off his tongue as if on automatic pilot. "Three point nine seven."

"How about your first semester at BYU?"

"Three point nine three," Elder Roberts responded.

"Your batting average your senior year of high school?"

"Two ninety-seven."

"What'd you get on your ACT?"

"Thirty-one."

"How many discussions did you teach last week?"

"Nineteen," said Elder Roberts with a trace of pride. He was beginning to enjoy this opportunity to finally share some of this information with his mission president, although he was having a hard time seeing where this was leading.

"What's the most discussions you've taught in a week?"

"Twenty-three," replied Elder Roberts without needing any time for reflection. Perhaps the president was sizing up his potential so he could assure him that success would come, just as it had in these other areas. Yes, sort of like a batting slump, thought Elder Roberts. "Just hit through it," his high school coach would have told him.

President Cook paused again. "Elder, does this series of questions seem at all odd to you?"

"I suppose . . . well . . . yes, sort of," he mumbled, once again confused about where this was all leading.

"I should hope so," said the president firmly but not too sharply. "Elder, these people you're teaching, they're sons and daughters of our Heavenly Father. They're not baseballs to be hit, tests to be aced, potential notches for your belt. Preaching the gospel of Jesus Christ is fundamentally different than anything else you've ever done. Forgive my frankness, Elder, but as missionaries we're not building our own spiritual resumés, we're trying to save other people's souls."

The president's words cut straight to Elder Roberts' heart. When they pierced through, a flood of emotions gushed out, including guilt and a trace of resentment. Ironically, the sinking feeling in his stomach was similar to the emotion he experienced when he received a disappointing test result.

"Elder Roberts, you're a great missionary, and I wish I had more like you. You keep the rules, you work hard, your testimony is strong, your German and scriptural knowledge are great. But it takes more to reach these people than good skills. It takes love, genuine love."

President Cook put a hand on Elder Roberts' shoulder and squeezed it. "Lose yourself, Elder. Some missionaries I've got to tell to work more on their goals. And I know that I ask you all to track certain activities on your weekly report so I can see how you're doing. But what you personally need is to lose track of the numbers. Do you have any idea how many people I baptized on my mission?"

Elder Roberts reflected on past zone conferences for a moment, but couldn't recall the president mentioning a number. "No, I guess I don't."

"Neither do I," said President Cook. "I can tell you about each person, each life, but I've never stopped to translate the lives into numbers and add them up."

This revelation was shocking to Elder Roberts. The thought of not knowing how many people you baptized on your mission was almost incomprehensible, almost like . . . like not knowing your batting average. He blushed at the connection his mind had subconsciously made. The president had pegged him.

"Keep working hard, Elder Roberts," the president continued. "But do it for the people's sake, not yours. Be concerned that they're not getting baptized, not that you're not baptizing. Nothing you do can guarantee that people will choose to come to Christ, but when you're driven by the kind of love Ammon had, when you can't bear the thought of souls perishing, then you'll be a powerful tool in the Lord's hands."

President Cook stood up and hugged Elder Roberts, as he did with all the elders at the end of their interviews. "I love ya, Elder."

The first couple of times this practice had seemed strange to Elder Roberts. But as the president squeezed him, Elder Roberts felt a warmth and peacefulness that began to heal the wound he'd sustained when he was reprimanded moments earlier.

✦ ✦ ✦

On the train, returning from zone conference, Elder McKinstry and Elder Roberts discussed their interviews with the president.

"So, I asked President Cook how he explained Alma twenty-six and the lack of success of Mormon and others," began Elder McKinstry.

"What'd he say?" asked Elder Roberts. He was eager to hear how President Cook had explained this one.

"He said he couldn't explain it completely. He was sure that Mormon and other prophets who hadn't converted thousands of souls had exercised as much faith as Ammon, so he thought maybe it was a timing thing. You know, like the people were just too hard then."

Elder McKinstry continued. "So I said, 'Yeah, kind of like the people in Germany in the last days. Some of the punkers here even sound like the Lamanites that Enos described.' And then the president, he says, 'Don't sell these people or yourself short.' He said people have their free agency, and it's possible that people won't respond even to the most righteous prophet or dedicated missionary, but that I still had a long ways to go before I was on Mormon's level.

"He said maybe Ammon's formula didn't guarantee baptisms, but that the more I prayed and the more faith I exercised, the more likely I was to be instrumental in bringing souls to Christ. He asked me if I was praying continually and how I exercised faith, and then he reminded me of the pain of Mormon and other prophets when people didn't respond to their teachings. I guess I got slammed."

Elder Roberts reflected on his companion's words for several seconds. Finally, he said, "Me too."

"Really?" replied a surprised Elder McKinstry, straightening up. However, he seemed pleased by the news. "But you do work with faith, and you're taking it hard that we're not getting through to people better."

Nodding, Elder Roberts continued, "But I suppose I'm taking it hard for the wrong reasons."

"Oh," said Elder McKinstry. "I guess that's true." His grin showed he'd made the comment without malice.

"Thanks. So anyway, I need to work on showing more love, less on self-interest."

"I'll give you some of my love and lack of self-interest for some of your drive and faith," joked Elder McKinstry as he slid back down into his seat, preparing for a nap.

The senior companion pulled his overcoat up around his neck and had just closed his eyes when Elder Roberts hit him lightly over the head with a triple.

"It's a deal," said Elder Roberts. "Wake up and study the scriptures with me. Let's talk about getting your calling and election made sure."

"I've got a better idea," retorted Elder McKinstry as he reached into his bag and pulled out the list of people in the missionaries' teaching pool. "Let's talk about how we can get Herr Ammerman to church."

✧ ✧ ✧

There were times during his first week in Bremerhaven that J.P. felt such gratitude that he thanked the Lord and fleetingly remembered the promise he'd made in his hour of despair. But as the sense of desperation lifted, so did the resolve to change.

Of course, it wasn't as if he were forgetting the promise altogether. With Elder Greisel, he'd pretty much turned off his heart completely. What few teaching opportunities the companionship had were all in German, and since he couldn't speak German, there was nothing J.P. could do to contribute beyond reciting his even-numbered principles. But in Bremerhaven, more than half of the missionaries' discussions were in English with American servicemen and their families. To Elder Prentice's surprise, he rather enjoyed trying to explain principles of the gospel to people—at least those who were interested in learning about it.

By virtue of having been raised in the Church, J.P. figured he had sat through about thirty-seven lessons on each basic principle of the gospel, and some of it had actually sunk in. Generally, it made sense to J.P., even if he didn't feel deeply about it in any spiritual way. And when someone else attacked it, or when he compared it to other religions, J.P. could even get downright defensive about the Church.

J.P. spent his mornings learning the discussions in English; reviewing a bit of German (Elder Lafferty's was actually tolerable, so he helped J.P. out some); writing letters to friends; reviewing the scripture references from the discussions; and learning to use the lasso.

Elder Lafferty had cleared a path in the little apartment from one corner to the bedpost, which they used as their target. After J.P. finally got down the basic motion, the two elders had contests, with Elder Lafferty using his left hand to even things out. He still prevailed, but J.P. never lost a game on the Game Boy.

"So, Lafferty," mused J.P. one morning as the missionaries ate peanut butter and jelly sandwiches for breakfast and practiced lassoing the bedpost. "Do ya' ever, you know, wonder whether we'd see more success if we did things differently?"

The senior companion was perplexed by J.P.'s question. "Whadya mean?"

"Well, you know, do you think it makes any difference whether you keep all the rules?" J.P. needed some reassuring.

"Heck no, E.P." answered Lafferty, using the initials for Elder Prentice. "Look at me. I've baptized three people so far, and that's more than some district leaders. We just work smart, that's all, making sure we don't run faster than we got strength. You see, people who are gonna join the Church are gonna join the Church, whether we work until eight-thirty or nine-thirty at night."

"Yeah, I suppose you're right," reflected J.P.

"Of course I am," insisted the Texan. "Now put in one a them CD's a yours and lemme show you this trick I been working on." Strains of Pearl Jam soon filled the air along with Elder Lafferty's lasso loops.

✧ ✧ ✧

For three months—three wonderful months—J.P. and Lafferty "worked smart" together. Elder Prentice became quite proficient with a lasso, Elder Lafferty mastered the Game Boy, and together they even taught and baptized an American serviceman. Most important of all, J.P. managed to drum up two correspondence relationships with past flames. Having partially remedied his MTC error, J.P. now had his mission going precisely as planned.

12
The Transfer Board

"How's it going, Elder?" President Cook asked Elder Roberts during the monthly interview at the October zone conference.

"Actually, quite well," replied Elder Roberts honestly.

"You feeling comfortable with the language?" queried the president.

Elder Roberts thought for a second about how to answer. His German was quite good, especially for someone out only eight months, but he didn't want to boast. "I'm happy with the progress I'm making."

"It sounds great in your testimony," commented the president. Testimonies at zone conferences were always borne in German. "And I assume you've had your discussions down for months." Elder Roberts nodded. "Elder McKinstry says great things about you. Says you're the best companion he's had, including all his senior companions."

Elder Roberts was pleased to learn of Elder McKinstry's comment, but also slightly embarrassed. He looked down at the floor, not quite sure how to handle the compliment.

"How's the work going?"

"We've been blessed," said Elder Roberts succinctly. In the last two months, Elder Roberts and Elder McKinstry had seen three of their investigators join the Church, including two very strong converts. "I hope we're getting better as we go," he added. For the last three months he had dispensed with most of his scriptural proofs. Instead, he had been encouraging investigators to learn the truthfulness of the missionaries' teachings themselves by reading the Book of Mormon and asking God if it was true.

"Well," continued President Cook as a he let out a sigh, "I suppose it's time you got a new challenge."

Elder Roberts looked up and waited with anticipation for President Cook to complete the thought. But he didn't. "The Lord loves you Elder, and so do I." The president stood up and embraced Elder Roberts. The interview was over.

On the train back from zone conference, Elder Roberts tried hard not to think about his interview with President Cook. But the harder he tried, the more he thought about it. And Elder McKinstry didn't help any.

"So how'd your interview go?" his companion asked with apparent innocence.

"Fine," said Elder Roberts, doing his best not to divulge any details.

Elder McKinstry knew his companion well by now. "That's the shortest answer I've ever heard you give to anything," he said with a smile. "And you won't be able to keep it that short, no matter how hard you try. It will eat at you, fester within you like sin," Elder McKinstry was beginning an uncharacteristic roll, like a Baptist preacher, "until you finally free yourself and spill your soul to your companion."

Elder McKinstry's German had always been grammatically precise, and over the three months he'd been with Elder Roberts it was becoming increasingly smooth.

"Man, your German's sounding good," said Elder Roberts, trying to divert his companion with a sincere compliment.

"That was pretty good, wasn't it?" Elder McKinstry smiled with satisfaction. "But you're getting off the subject. What did the president say in your interview?"

"You know, the usual." He was futilely trying to keep his interview private. But he knew his companion was right: he would eventually tell all. He made one last, weak effort to avoid disclosing his tidbit of news that their companionship might be coming to an end. "What makes you think anything interesting was said?"

"Oh, I have my sources," replied Elder McKinstry, feigning knowledge.

"Really?" Elder Roberts assumed his companion was bluffing, but his curiosity had been piqued.

"I predict that next week you'll be transferred to Kiel and made a district leader," said Elder McKinstry boldly.

Elder Roberts was surprised and a bit pleased by Elder McKinstry's prediction. Although he had been fighting off the thought, he couldn't help but wonder what President Cook had meant with his "new challenge" comment. Of course, in all probability the president would simply make Elder Roberts a senior companion somewhere. But Elder Roberts' mind often raced vainly out of control, so Elder McKinstry's comment was not the first time he had thought of the possibility that he might become a district leader sometime soon.

"I'm not even a senior companion yet," objected Elder Roberts. "And how could you possibly know something like that?"

"For one thing," answered Elder McKinstry, "President Cook all but told me I'd be losing you come transfer time. I was telling him how much I enjoyed working with you, and he says, `I hope you enjoy this companionship while you can.' Then he asks me a bunch of specific questions about you and your skills and stuff. Look, Elder, he already knows you're senior companion material. Anybody can see that. He's got bigger plans for you, my friend."

These comments bolstered Elder Roberts' suspicions, but he still tried to resist the notion that he might become a district leader so soon. "Get serious," he said, jokingly translating the English colloquialism directly into German. "President Cook is not going to make some junior companion a district leader somewhere."

"He's done it before," retorted Elder McKinstry smugly. "Elder Stone in Hamburg went senior and district leader at the same time when he was seven months out, and you're an even better missionary than he is. In fact, I've wondered why the president hasn't made you a senior sooner. Now I think he was just waiting for the right spot to open up for you. And Elder Wolfert's going home this month. That means the district leader slot in Kiel is open." Elder McKinstry was becoming more convinced of his speculation as he spoke.

"Well, the president did say something to me about being ready for a new challenge," conceded Elder Roberts.

"*Also, bitte schoen,*" declared Elder McKinstry like a true German. Literally translated, the phrase meant something like, "Then you're welcome." Figuratively, the phrase meant something more like, "So there," or, "My point exactly." The Germans used this phrase frequently, even after comments that had not proved their point at all. "Yeah, I can see it now. Young Elder Roberts leading the Kiel district. Hey, when you're a leader, remember one thing. Be real. All right?"

Over Elder Roberts' objections, Elder McKinstry spent the rest of the train ride giving his junior companion advice on how to lead his new district.

* * *

"You got your board ready, E.P.?" asked Elder Lafferty. It was one-thirty, and the senior companion had declared the companionship in need of an extended lunch break on this rainy October afternoon, two days before November transfers were announced.

The elders' overcoats, jackets, pants, and white shirts were draped over anything immobile in the apartment, drying out from the morning's bike ride. Every Wednesday morning Elder Lafferty loved to bike the fifteen kilometers that separated the apartment from a charming little outlying village to check on three very lukewarm contacts who were never home in the morning and hadn't actually spoken with any missionary in over six months.

"Mine's ready. We gonna look at each other's before we finalize them, or are we gonna do it blind again?" asked J.P., sheltering a three-by-three piece of cardboard from his companion.

"What the heck, let's take a look," said the Texan as he rolled off his bed and pulled out his own piece of cardboard from underneath his bed. "As long as you don't just change all yours to match mine after lookin' at 'em."

"Dream on," countered J.P. as the missionaries placed their cardboard side by side on the desk. They were transfer boards, complete with different colored pins attaching a piece of paper representing each companionship and city in the mission.

The two missionaries used their creations every month to predict who would get transferred where. Most transfers were impossible to predict, but they could make some educated guesses about leadership positions and whether or not certain companionships would be broken up.

Elder Lafferty and J.P. started the contest their first month together, and at their latest count, eighteen missionaries would be participating in the contest this month. They did bet a milkshake between them, but they limited all wagers to companionships to make sure their enterprise wasn't detected by the president.

"What about Kiel? Elder Wolfert is going home, so there's a district leader slot open. Who do you have joining the elite ranks of leaders this month?" asked Elder Lafferty disdainfully.

"A dark horse," said Elder Prentice, who was finally starting to develop his own network of information sources at district meetings and zone conferences. "Elder Roberts, from my MTC district. He's only been out eight months, and he's a junior, but I hear he's hot. He was a real machine in the MTC, and he's not a bad guy."

"Maybe," answered the senior companion. "But I think the president will go for experience. Elder Johnson's been around for a long time, and this may be his last shot at a leadership position before he goes home. He gets my vote."

"We'll see," said J.P. "Hey, what do you got for our companionship? You think I'll go senior somewhere?" He was joking, and Elder Lafferty knew it.

"Yeah, maybe, like if we decide to open a new city in Florida or something. I hear the president likes to have senior companions who can at least give a talk in German, you know?"

"Hey, I can," spouted J.P. "I can do four whole scenes from Wayne's World in German now."

"Nope, doesn't count. 'Fraid you're stuck here with me in English-speakin' heaven." J.P. could only hope his companion was right.

✦ ✦ ✦

Generally, missionaries in the Germany Hamburg mission learned of transfers by mail on Wednesday. However, when an elder was transferred into a leadership position, he always received a call on Tuesday night from the president. Elder Roberts tried not to focus on this fact, but it was difficult with the steady ribbing he was getting from his companion. At each ring of the phone, Elder McKinstry shouted gleefully, "That must be the president! I'll get it!"

But none of the calls had been from the president, and Elder Roberts was beginning to feel embarrassed at having even begun to believe his companion might have been right in his wild prediction.

Then, at ten-fifteen, the phone rang one last time. Elder McKinstry answered: "Hello, this is Elder McKinstry from The Church of Jesus Christ of Latter-day Saints speaking. . . . Hello, President!"

Elder McKinstry's face lit up brightly at his recognition of the president's voice. "Just a moment, let me get Elder Roberts. . . . What?" The grin left Elder McKinstry's face almost as quickly as it had come. "Um, well, yes, of course, President. Kiel?" Elder McKinstry conversed with the president for two or three minutes, with his end of the conversation consisting mostly of the audible equivalent of nodding.

Finally, Elder McKinstry spoke again: "Well, thank you for the opportunity, President. I'm, uh, I'm very surprised. . . . By the way, may I be so bold as to ask who Elder Roberts' new companion will be?"

As Elder McKinstry listened, the grin returned to his face. "You don't say? . . . Yes, I agree. I'll pass that thought along to Elder Roberts. Thanks again, President. Good night." He hung up the phone and collapsed on his bed.

"Well, so much for your sources, eh?" jumped in Elder Roberts without hesitation. He was excited for his companion and ashamed of himself for having thought or cared about becoming a district leader. "Congratulations on becoming the new district leader of Kiel," said Elder Roberts genuinely. He knew this would be a great opportunity for Elder McKinstry.

"Wow," sighed Elder McKinstry, looking dazed. "How about that?" he said, mostly to himself. "I think I need some pudding." Elder McKinstry stumbled toward the kitchen and began mixing up the snack in which he frequently found solace.

"So, um, who's my new companion?" asked Elder Roberts innocently.

"Huh?" mumbled Elder McKinstry.

"My new comp?" persisted Elder Roberts.

"Oh, yeah, your new companion," responded Elder McKinstry, coming out of his daze. "You're getting a slacker. The president's sending you a slacker senior companion. Can you believe it?"

Elder Roberts could not. He had thought he would at least become a senior companion with this transfer. Not only was he remaining a junior companion, but he was apparently getting one of the elders endearingly called slackers in the Germany Hamburg Mission—missionaries who didn't work very hard and weren't very obedient, missionaries more interested in passing their time painlessly than in sacrificing to bring souls unto Christ.

Many of the missionaries he'd seen in his ward at home would have been eminently qualified for the title of slacker. They were quick to attend ward socials, start water fights, and flirt with the young women. They were slow to leave members' homes, wake up or go tracting.

Getting a slacker for a companion had been one of Elder Roberts' worst nightmares, and he was immensely pleased that he'd been spared the trial so far. He'd come on a mission to serve the Lord, and he had no use for someone who might hold him back with his lack of commitment.

A slacker senior companion would be a much greater challenge than a slacker junior. If Elder Roberts were senior, he could pretty much drag his companion on the work. But as a junior, he would have to be much more creative and careful in dealing with his new companion's lack of commitment. The wheels in his mind began spinning with ideas and fears.

"His name is Elder Lehmann, and he's not your typical slacker," said Elder McKinstry as he mixed the chocolate powder into a bowl of milk. "I split with him once in Flensburg. This guy is 23 years old, and he's already graduated from college . . . from Stanford. His German is impeccable. His parents were born in Germany and taught him German as a kid. And he knows the scriptures better than any other elder I know, with the possible exception of you."

"So what's the deal?" This hardly sounded like a description of a slacker.

"If you ask me, he's a little too smart for his own good," continued Elder McKinstry matter-of-factly. "He picks and chooses the rules he'll keep, the books he reads, the order in which he'll teach the discussions, everything. If he wants to do something, he will. If he doesn't, he won't." Elder McKinstry shrugged his shoulders as he poured the pudding into two tall glasses.

Elder Roberts laughed to himself for a moment as he reflected on what passed for being a slacker in the Germany Hamburg Mission. He was proud to be in a mission where a missionary calling home passed for scandalous news.

"So this is the challenge President Cook had in mind for me?"

"Looks like it. I'm just glad it's you instead of me," said Elder McKinstry. "I think my new job will be a lot easier." Almost as soon as he said this, he abruptly took a swig of the unchilled pudding.

"Elder, what am I going to do? I'm not the district leader type. I have no idea how to lead a district."

"Fortunately for you," said Elder Roberts, "I've got some great advice on how to be a good leader." With a laugh, he put his putting in the refrigerator to chill. As Elder McKinstry unflinchingly finished off his pudding shake, Elder Roberts repeated back all the advice Elder McKinstry had given him the previous week.

❖ ❖ ❖

For someone with as much disdain for uncertainty as Elder Hawthorne, it was remarkable how little attention he paid to transfers. Perhaps he put them as far out of mind as possible, precisely because he knew he would be tormented by the impending possibility of change each month if he allowed himself to dwell on the subject. When he stopped to reflect, as he did on rare occasions, he knew that he and Elder Smith had probably been companions longer than any other companionship in the mission.

Still, Elder Hawthorne was somehow surprised when transfer notices came and he learned that his new senior companion would be Elder Greisel. He didn't have any particular expectations, but he knew Elder Smith, and he could live with him.

Elder Greisel meant change, and Elder Hawthorne saw no need for change. In fact, Elder Greisel was unknown change, because neither he nor Elder Smith knew anything about Elder Greisel, except that he was Austrian and had been out over a year. While Elder Smith packed, Elder Hawthorne got down to business and began worrying about life with his new companion, who thought in a language Elder Hawthorne had not mastered completely.

✧ ✧ ✧

"A drum roll please," announced Lafferty as he held back his companion from the mailbox. J.P. did his best to create a drum roll with his fingers on the metal mailboxes. "The moment of truth for the month of October has arrived."

Elder Lafferty turned the key and flipped open the box with a dramatic flair. Empty. The box was completely empty. It was one of the few times either elder celebrated receiving no mail.

"Dude!" exclaimed Elder Prentice as he slapped his companion's uplifted hand. "Safe for another month. This calls for a Snickers milkshake." Inside the apartment the two Americans celebrated their good fortune with greasy cheeseburgers, milkshakes with chunks of stale Snickers bars, and a two-hour lunch.

13
Telestial Companions

Three days after transfer Wednesday, Elder Roberts said a very warm farewell to another companion he had grown to love. Sitting in the train station on a chilly November morning, waiting for Elder Lehmann's arrival, Elder Roberts began to contemplate how he would deal with the challenge his new companion was certain to be.

As he stared blankly at the pages of his Book of Mormon, Elder Roberts prayed for guidance without closing his eyes. His mind drifted back to his brother's missionary journals. At first he could only vaguely recall that his brother, Steve, had encountered a similar situation with a lackadaisical senior companion.

Elder Roberts struggled to remember more exactly what he had learned from Steve's journal, but the details remained foggy. Then he offered another short but intense plea for the Lord's help. Like a picture coming into focus, the memory of his brother's words began to become more clear.

Steve's senior companion had spent hours sleeping in the apartment while the companionship should have been working. Steve stewed indignantly while diligently studying his scriptures and discussions. His resentment toward his companion mounted with each violation of the rules and each minute of missed work.

As the days passed, Steve found the influence of the Spirit waning in his life. This angered him all the more. Steve blamed the Spirit's departure on his companion, who was standing in the way of Steve's obedience to the mission rules.

Steve confronted his companion sharply on two or three occasions, but his companion's commitment to a noncommittal attitude only intensified with each rebuke. After three or four weeks, they rarely spoke to each other. They did some tracting and teaching, but the Spirit did not accompany them. Their teaching pool dried up, and tracting was sheer drudgery.

Oddly enough, Steve soon found himself subconsciously resenting the Lord for placing him in this predicament. "I came to serve the Lord," Steve had complained in his journal, "and now I'm stuck in this companionship. I'm helpless. Nothing I can do makes a difference," he'd written.

The darkness was almost palpable as Elder Roberts read those pages in his brother's journal. Then one morning, at about eleven o'clock, when he and his companion should have been out working, Steve read Moroni, chapter seven. He struggled mightily as he read, initially fighting off the promptings of the Spirit that told him he needed to repent.

However, Steve finally succumbed to the Spirit, and admitted to himself and the Lord that he was falling short of charity's challenging imperative to bear all things and suffer long. For thirty minutes, he prayed, seeking the Father's help with all the energy of his heart, pleading that his heart be filled with love for his companion. He repented of the hateful feelings that were festering inside, and asked the Lord for forgiveness.

From that day on, Steve tried to see the good in his companion. Still he could not condone much of what his companion did, but he became less preoccupied with his companion's lack of commitment. They began talking again, and the Spirit slowly returned to their companionship.

Steve's companion was transferred a week after he changed his own attitude. He wrote in his journal that he deeply regretted not coming to his spiritual realization sooner.

Elder Roberts was amazed at the clarity with which he'd been able to remember his brother's experience. He thanked the Lord for the view and for his brother, who had so carefully recorded his feelings and observations.

Elder Roberts had once read a quote from Garrison Keilor, one of his favorite writers, saying that no matter how hard we try, we cannot really benefit from the experience of others. We're destined to learn our lessons through our own painful experience. Elder Roberts firmly believed the famous author had missed the mark with this one, and he vowed to prove him wrong with this companionship. His brother's hard-earned insights would not be lost on Elder Roberts.

✦ ✦ ✦

During their first morning together, Elder Roberts studied his scriptures while Elder Lehmann devoured *The Great Divorce* by C.S. Lewis. Chris himself was a budding fan of C.S. Lewis, but missionaries were supposed to read only the standard works and five other approved books. None of Lewis's books was on the list.

When the time came for companion scripture study, Elder Lehmann jettisoned the outlined topic in favor of one of his own. "This morning, Elder, let's begin to try to reconcile the dichotomous view of the afterlife preached by Book of Mormon prophets with the more complex scheme enunciated by the Lord through Joseph Smith in Doctrine and Covenants, seventy-six."

"The di-what?" asked Elder Roberts.

"Dichotomous—a dichotomy. It means, 'consisting of two opposite or opposing parts,'" answered Elder Lehmann patiently. "You know, heaven and hell, left and right, black and white, that sort of thing. On the surface, at least, that's a very different post-earth arrangement than the three degrees of glory—potentially with infinite sub-degrees—along with a dumping bin for an unspecified number of true villains."

Elder Roberts swallowed hard and went along for the ride. He had decided that whenever he could in good conscience, he would indulge his companion. Actually, the scripture study proved fascinating, even though it was not the recommended topic for the day. Often it left Elder Roberts with several perplexing questions. The more difficult test came at nine-thirty, when it was time to go out on the work.

"Where ya goin', Elder?" asked Elder Lehmann from the kitchen. Elder Roberts had his on coat and was hovering near the door.

Remember, don't be self-righteous, thought Chris to himself. "I'm, uh, I was just getting ready to go out on the work."

Elder Lehmann was not, which was apparent from the apron he wore. "Oh. You know, I thought I'd make some bread this morning instead. We can give some loaves to our investigators. I find that a better use of time than morning tracting. No one's ever home then, anyway, Chris."

Elder Roberts nodded his head and took a deep breath as he returned to the desk. This kind of disobedience to the rules by Elder Lehmann made it impossible for Elder Roberts to obey the rules. Still, he remembered his brother's experience, so he prayed for love for his companion and for direction in dealing with the challenge.

When the elders finally went tracting at eleven-thirty that morning, Elder Roberts had a plan. An older woman answered Elder Roberts' first door. "Good morning, we're representatives of The Church of Jesus Christ of Latter-day Saints," the junior companion began.

"And I'm Lutheran, thank you," said the woman as she began to close the door.

"So you believe that you resurrected physically will be after you die?" persisted Elder Roberts.

"Excuse me?" asked the woman, the door not quite closed.

"Well, you said you're Lutheran, so you, you must believe that you live on after death, you know, with a resurrected body."

"No, not necessarily," replied the woman. "That's quite another matter. I don't know what I believe about life after death."

"But that's a fairly significant matter, isn't it?"

"I suppose, but right now I'm cleaning my oven, and that's even more important at the moment."

Elder Roberts knew he couldn't interrupt a German woman's household chores. "We understand. We'd like to come back, to come and share with you a message some time. How about tomorrow morning at nine-thirty?"

Out of the corner of his eye, Elder Roberts thought he saw a somewhat startled look on his companion's face.

"Tomorrow? Yes, well . . . all right. Tomorrow at nine-thirty. *Auf wiedersehen*," she said and closed the door.

On each of his doors Elder Roberts tried to set an appointment for nine-thirty. Between doors, he prayed for the Lord's help. By the end of the day the missionaries had scheduled nine-thirty appointments for the next four days.

"That was quite a clever trick you pulled, setting up those morning appointments," said Elder Lehmann that evening as he flossed his teeth.

"Thanks," replied Elder Roberts, trying to sound good-natured rather than smug.

Elder Lehmann dropped the subject. They were never late getting out of the apartment again.

❖ ❖ ❖

Wesley Hawthorne and Elder Smith had taught Herr Starke the first three discussions before Elder Greisel arrived in Luebeck. The two Americans had established a genuine rapport with this young graduate student in their first three visits.

Herr Starke was full of earnest doubts, but he seemed to listen with an open heart and mind as the elders patiently responded to each of his concerns. As a result, the missionaries had not been able to complete an entire discussion during any of their visits, but they felt they were making some real progress.

Upon Elder Greisel's arrival, he reviewed the companionship's weekly evaluation sheet and noticed that Herr Starke had not yet been challenged to baptism. "We will challenge him at our next appointment," declared Elder Greisel dispassionately.

"I'm, uh . . . I'm not sure that a good idea is," suggested Elder Hawthorne in German, the only language in which the companions could communicate. "Herr Starke, he is coming more slowly—good, but slow."

"I appreciate your thoughts, but the mission program says all investigators are to be challenged by the third discussion, and I intend to adhere to it."

And adhere to it he did. On their next visit—Elder Greisel's first—Wesley was still trying to explain to a slightly bewildered Herr Starke where Elder Smith had gone and why Elder Greisel was there when his senior companion interrupted. "As missionaries, we are sometimes transferred. We are about the Lord's work, and we do as directed. We are here to give you the Lord's direction for you. Please read Second Nephi, thirty-one, ten." The missionary said this in the same detached, confident monotone with which he had instructed Elder Hawthorne to make breakfast for the companionship that morning.

Herr Starke shot Wesley a look of muted astonishment before slowly picking up his Book of Mormon and reading the reference.

"Herr Starke, we cannot follow Jesus without keeping the Father's commandments, can we?" Elder Greisel's question was apparently intended to be rhetorical, because he began to ask Herr Starke to read verses eleven and twelve without waiting for a reply.

"I'm sorry," interrupted Herr Starke. "Greisel—is that your name?—did you want me to answer that question?"

"Elder Greisel is my name," corrected the Austrian. "You may answer the question if you like, although there is clearly only one answer."

"Is that so?" asked Herr Starke, who was probably five or six years older than the missionaries. Elder Hawthorne was not surprised at Herr Starke's response, although it was not the kind of point over which he usually argued.

"Yes," affirmed Elder Greisel. "I just read from the Book of Mormon that we must keep the commandments of the Father in order to follow Jesus."

"I'm not sure yet what I think of your Book of Mormon," said Herr Starke as he leaned back in his chair and folded his arms.

"Well, then you must find out," answered Elder Greisel mechanically. "I'm sure Elder Smith and Elder Hawthorne have explained how you do that," he stated with what Elder Hawthorne perceived to be a bit of a sneer. "You simply read the book and then ask God with faith and in the name of Jesus Christ if it is true. Then he will confirm its truthfulness to you through the power of the Holy Ghost." Opening his own Book of Mormon, Elder Greisel ended the unscheduled detour in his baptismal challenge by reading verses eleven and twelve himself.

"Herr Starke, Jesus and the Father expect you to be baptized," intoned Elder Greisel. "They have commanded you to be baptized. Will you obey that commandment?"

Herr Starke initially said nothing. He uncrossed his arms, placed a hand on each thigh to brace himself as he leaned forward, opened his mouth, and then simply shook his head with a slight laugh of disbelief. Finally, Herr Starke spoke slowly and only to Elder Greisel. "Herr Greisel, I am in the process of trying to determine what God's will is for me. When I discover what it is, I intend to fulfill it. At the moment, I must confess that I find you a rather unlikely messenger of God's will for me."

Elder Greisel did not appear to take offense at the slight. In fact, he did not even acknowledge Herr Starke's comments. Instead, he plunged right into the memorized dialogue of the next principle in the authorized discussions.

As the elders left Herr Starke's apartment at the end of what was only nominally a discussion, Herr Starke shook Elder Hawthorne's hand warmly. "If you speak with Elder Smith, please tell him I miss him." Elder Greisel was already halfway out the door, so Wesley whispered "me too" before leaving his favorite investigator's home.

"How do you feel about the discussion with Herr Starke?" asked Elder Hawthorne at companionship inventory that Sunday night. In most companionships, companionship inventory was a time when missionaries filled out their weekly evaluation form, discussed their investigators, set goals, and generally talked about how things were going. In this companionship, there was little discussion of anything extraneous to the actual numbers required by the form.

"Feel?" responded Elder Greisel, as if repeating a new word. "I feel fine about the discussion. We completed an entire discussion, as we should during each visit, and we challenged him to baptism, which should have happened a discussion earlier."

Wesley tried to think of an appropriately soft answer to his senior companion's implicit criticism, but gave up. "Do you think it much good did?"

"I doubt it," replied Elder Greisel unemotionally. "For most people, Elder, what we do and say makes little difference, because most people are set in their ways. Most people are not the elect of God. For those people, our job is to share the message so that our garments will be clean, free from their sins. The rest of our job is to find the elect of God. There aren't very many of them, but when we find them, they require no persuasion. We simply deliver the message, and they seize upon it. I've only found two people so far on my mission who are elect."

Two people who joined the Church despite you, thought Elder Hawthorne. Twenty-four hours a day with this companion was sure to be the greatest spiritual challenge of Wesley's life.

✧ ✧ ✧

The two amigos, as Elder Lafferty and J.P. had taken to calling themselves for no particular reason, had found one of the elect. In one of his few cynical moments, President Cook called such converts "missionary-proof."

The new contact was an American soldier by the name of Jason Hancock, and he had read the Book of Mormon from cover-to-cover within three weeks of receiving it from the missionaries. He was baptized one week later on December first by a member and confirmed by Elder Lafferty. Jason's conversion simply reinforced the two amigos belief that they could be perfectly effective missionaries without having to be religious zealots.

14
Uwe

Companion scripture study with Elder Lehmann was never boring. Among other things in the first three weeks, Elder Lehmann and Elder Roberts had analyzed how it was that people baptized before the atonement were able to receive an actual remission of sins; whether Jacob two and Doctrine and Covenants one thirty-two were consistent on the subject of plural marriage; and whether it was just for God to curse or bless a person's descendants based on that particular person's conduct.

In each of these discussions—which often raged on throughout the day as the missionaries traveled between appointments and doors—Elder Roberts felt pressed to defend what he saw as the official church position. Much of the time Elder Roberts was able to respond successfully to Elder Lehmann's needling questions by using reason and scriptures. But he also encountered a novelty for him—questions he simply could not answer on an intellectual level.

Elder Roberts prided himself in the strength of his testimony, so he was surprised to find that some of these questions remained with him for days, festering like unsolved math problems.

One night Chris sought answers to these riddles in prayer. He knew that there was a reasonable answer for each of these questions that had been troubling him, and that the Lord gave wisdom through prayer to those who sought it.

Instead of receiving a revelation of insightful answers with which he could enlighten his companion, a simple thought came into his mind. "It's true. The gospel is true. You'll understand more of the details with time, but for now just remember that it's true."

Initially, this answer was not particularly useful to Elder Roberts. It did nothing to douse the flames of Elder Lehmann's skepticism. To the contrary, it fanned them. Elder Roberts was embarrassed at first to admit that he stood by a conclusion he could not explain. But with time he came to embrace this I-may-not-know-the-answer-to-all-things-but-I-know-God-loves-his-children approach to dealing with Elder Lehmann's I'm-so-clever-I-see-the-inconsistencies-in-scripture observations. And today, Elder Roberts was going to take the offensive.

"Is it my turn to pick a companion study topic?" asked Elder Roberts after three weeks of sometimes stimulating, but often disconcerting companion scripture study topics chosen by Elder Lehmann.

"Sure," allowed Elder Lehmann, caught a bit off guard.

"Great," said Elder Roberts as he pulled out his scriptures. "Then today we're studying the virtue of obeying God's commandments even when we don't completely understand them." He'd been mentally preparing this study session for the past three weeks.

"What? You can't be serious. I'd hardly expect someone as intelligent as yourself to advocate blind obedience."

"Aahh. An excellent fallacy to—what is your word?—debunk? Yes, debunking this fallacy will be our starting point," said Elder Roberts, evoking an appreciative chuckle from Elder Lehmann.

During the past three weeks Chris had established a decent enough relationship with Elder Lehmann. And his companion had come to respect Elder Roberts' intellect, although it was clear that they differed in their approach to the gospel and to mission rules. Elder Roberts had indulged his senior companion enough that the elder missionary knew that for once, the younger one had earned the right to run with his topic.

Elder Roberts began with the exchange between Adam and the angel about why Adam was offering sacrifices. "Adam wasn't obeying blindly because he knew that the commandment to offer sacrifices came from God. But he was obeying without understanding the purpose of the commandment, the rationale behind the commandment."

"And he was better off when he knew the purpose behind it," interjected Elder Lehmann. "Several General Authorities have said we need to get spiritual confirmation for ourselves of each component of the gospel rather than just blindly believing. We need to understand the why's, not just the what's."

"I'm not saying we shouldn't try to understand the why's," answered Elder Roberts. "I am saying we should obey while we're trying to understand the why's instead of insisting on understanding the why's before we obey. The thing we need to know is whether a commandment is from God. Once we understand that, we should obey it even if we don't have a clue about why God gave it."

To demonstrate his point Elder Roberts turned first to the story of Naaman, the leprous Syrian military leader who journeyed to Israel to be healed by the prophet Elisha. After hesitating, Naaman was finally persuaded by his servant to heed the prophet's directive to wash himself seven times in the river Jordan, and he was healed.

"The prophet didn't give any explanation about why or how washing himself seven times in the waters of the river Jordan would cure him. He just told him to do it. If Naaman had insisted on understanding how that bizarre act would cure him before he did it, he would never have been healed."

Elder Lehmann was impressed with the fervor of his junior companion's presentation, so he allowed him to continue without interruption.

Elder Roberts turned next to the story of the poisonous serpents that were sent among the children of Israel during the Exodus.

"All they had to do to be saved was look to the brass serpent. They didn't need to understand how it worked, or even exactly why it worked. If they looked to God's serpent, they lived. If they didn't, they died."

"Yes, but the whole point of that exercise was to teach the children of Israel about the atonement," asserted Elder Lehmann as he paced the small apartment, which he often did when companion scripture study became intense. "If they looked to the serpent and lived, but didn't strive to find out what God was trying to teach, then they missed the whole point."

"But the only ones who had the chance to think about the message—to strive to understand the why behind the commandment—were the ones who obeyed," explained Elder Roberts. "I agree. The people who were best off were those who obeyed and tried to figure out why they had been given the command. But they had to obey first, even if they didn't already understand why."

"Actually, as I think about it," continued Elder Roberts, "the principle with the atonement is really the same. None of us can comprehend exactly how it works, exactly how the Savior was able to take our sins upon him by suffering in Gethsemane and on the cross. It's good to try, but it's not essential. What is essential is that we believe in Jesus Christ and keep his commandments."

Elder Lehmann rubbed his chin thoughtfully before giving his final critique. "I'm still not sure you've sold me on your thesis. I think there are too many scriptures and too many comments by modern prophets—along with too many examples of people who have mistakenly done horrible things in the name of God because they didn't question enough—just too much for me to give up questioning. But you do make some good points. You did a good job for leading your first companionship scripture study. Sorry I haven't asked sooner whether you had any subjects you wanted to discuss. Anything else you want to get off your chest while we're on this subject?"

Elder Roberts thought for a moment. "As a matter of fact, there is one more related point. I think it's dangerous to assume certain commandments don't apply to us, or that since we understand the reason behind them we can ignore them when they don't seem to apply."

"And your supporting scripture on this one," speculated Elder Lehmann, "is undoubtedly the rather morbid story in which the aged prophet Samuel literally hacks a non-Israelite king to pieces as a gory object lesson for the technically disobedient Saul."

"No, but I'd like to hear it," said Elder Roberts, who was amazed at his companion's gifted tongue and almost total recall of the scriptures. Elder Lehmann recounted in remarkable detail—albeit with a slightly caustic tone—the whole episode. It did demonstrate Chris's point wonderfully.

King Saul had been directed by the Lord through Samuel to kill all the people and their flocks in a particular battle, but he had spared their king and some of the best animals, purportedly to offer sacrifices. It didn't seem like a bad idea, but it wasn't what the Lord commanded, and as a result of Saul's disobedience, his seed lost the opportunity to rule over Israel.

"And I suppose your application of this whole not-so-subtle lesson is that I should stop calling you by your first name and reading *The New York Times*?" mused Elder Lehmann when he completed the story.

Elder Roberts saw no reason to hide the ball. "If the shoe fits . . ."

"All right, tomorrow we'll study this great essay on Liahona Mormons and Iron Rod Mormons," suggested Elder Lehmann. "For today, suffice it to say that you're an Iron Rod Mormon, which is fine for you, and I'm a Liahona Mormon, which should be fine for me."

"So you're saying the Spirit prompts you to call me by my first name and read the newspaper?" asked Elder Roberts incredulously.

"No, no, I'm not suggesting that," replied Elder Lehmann, who actually seemed to be slightly at a loss for a response. "I . . . well, it just seems that a rigid approach works better for some people than others. I mean surely you don't think the Lord revealed to the Prophet everything that's in the white handbook," said Elder Lehmann, referring to the rule book for missionaries published by the Church. The senior companion had gotten his legs underneath him again. "The thought of revelation on such a trivial subject seems almost sacrilegious."

"No, I'm not saying that I think the white handbook was revealed like a section of the Doctrine and Covenants or something," conceded Elder Roberts. "But I have had a spiritual confirmation that the Prophet is ordained of God, and if he puts something in a book like this, then I'm willing to do it. For all I know, every word may have been inspired. Even if it weren't—even if it were fine with the Lord if some of the rules were written completely differently—I think we're blessed if we obey them. That's all."

"Okay, okay," resigned Elder Lehmann as he knotted his tie. "Would it make you happy if I called you Elder Roberts instead of Chris?"

"Sure," replied Elder Roberts, hoping that he hadn't come on too strongly.

"Ok, I'll do it if you'll stop referring to me as your senior companion. I hate this hierarchical stuff."

"It's a deal," agreed Elder Roberts. As he shook hands jokingly with his companion, he suspected he hadn't really changed Elder Lehmann's thinking, but he hoped Elder Lehmann at least understood his thinking better.

✧ ✧ ✧

"I've got a service opportunity for you, elders," the district leader told J.P. and Elder Olson, who had replaced Lafferty at the December transfer. To Elder Prentice's relief, Elder Olson was no more pious than Elder Lafferty, and the two continued to "work smart," as J.P. had come to characterize his approach to missionary work.

"Whatcha got?" asked Elder Olson as he worked over a substantial piece of Double Bubble. The missionaries were allowed and even encouraged to spend up to four hours a week performing service, which was a welcome relief from proselyting. Unfortunately, the service was supposed to be for nonmembers, and it was often difficult to discover opportunities. Consequently, Elder Lafferty and J.P. had applied the service label rather loosely to their activities on past reports.

"Got a widowed woman the sisters in Bremerhaven are teaching," began the district leader during his weekly companionship interview with the elders. "She's got an adult son with a bad case of cerebral palsy, and she's developed a bad back. He needs to be cleaned every week, and she can't lift him any more. I told the sisters to tell this woman, Sister Kressmann, that we had two able-bodied young men who would show up every Friday morning at nine-thirty to help her out."

"Cleaned?" blurted out J.P. "As in bathed?"

"Yup," confirmed the district leader. "Sister Kressmann lives a bit out of your area—about a thirty-minute bike ride—but I figured you two wouldn't mind," added the district leader, who knew perfectly well what kind of missionaries he had on his hands.

Initially, it seemed to J.P. that the only good part about this service opportunity would be the thirty-minute bike ride. And even that wasn't nearly as good a deal in January as it would have been in June.

The next Friday after district meeting Elder Olson and J.P. arrived at the Kressmann apartment at nine forty-five and reluctantly knocked on the door. They heard a general clamor inside, and after almost a full minute, they were greeted at the door by a woman in her mid-fifties. She looked as if life was getting the best of her. The missionaries introduced themselves, and she quickly showed them in with a sigh of relief.

"Welcome to my apartment," said Frau Kressmann, too exhausted to be embarrassed about her home, which was a veritable zoo.

J.P. and Elder Olson had been told only about one adult son with Cerebral Palsy, but J.P. counted three people in wheelchairs and two more children with thick, Special Ed glasses and tilted heads. All but one child were huddled around a small television that blared loudly in the corner of the apartment. The nonconforming child was chasing two dogs, which barked loudly in protest. An unkempt cat sat curled up in the lap of one of the wheelchair drivers.

The apartment reeked of a repugnant combination of aromas J.P. could not precisely identify. He felt sick.

Frau Kressmann walked over to one of the wheelchair residents and placed her hands lovingly on his shoulders. Because J.P. still understood very little German, he did not understand much of what she said, but he gathered that the invalid was her son, Uwe.

Apparently the others were children she took in from the state to make ends meet. Uwe smiled as his mother spoke, and when she stopped, he uttered "good day" in speech almost as broken as J.P.'s German. Frau Kressmann then turned and headed down a narrow hall and motioned for the missionaries to follow her.

"I guess we're gettin' right into this," whispered Elder Olson to J.P. in English. "She says for us to follow her to the bathroom and to bring Uwe. You push him."

"Why me?" objected J.P. "You're the senior companion."

"That's right, and I say you push him."

J.P. reluctantly complied. When he and his cargo arrived, Frau Kressmann was giving further instructions to Elder Olson. She smiled at both missionaries before leaving and expressing her thanks.

"So what do we do?" asked J.P. with a nervousness that bordered on irritation.

"Well, comp, she says we undress him, then put him in the tub and let her know when he's ready for his bath. You really oughta try picking up German one of these first months."

"I'll put it on my to-do list," replied J.P. He sized up Uwe, who hung his head and said nothing. J.P. stood motionless with his hands on his hips and looked back at his companion.

Elder Olson returned the look of apprehension. "Whew," he sighed, shaking his head. "Well, let's do it."

Elder Olson began the awkward process by trying to remove Uwe's shirt. After few seconds J.P. feebly joined in. Uwe raised his hands to just above his shoulders, still looking at the floor.

J.P. was surprised at how rigid Uwe's arms were, apparently frozen at a ninety-degree angle at the elbow. J.P. inadvertently touched Uwe's clammy skin in removing his undershirt, and his own flesh flinched at the strange, unpleasant sensation.

After a couple of minutes, the elders succeeded in pulling off the shirt and the undershirt, revealing some sort of monitor that was crudely taped to Uwe's chest. They paused to size up the remainder of their task.

"How do we get his pants off?" asked J.P.

"We're gonna have to lift him. You get behind him and lift up under his arms, and I'll do the dirty work."

J.P. wasn't sure which job was worse, so he took his place behind his new service project. He took a couple of breaths, hesitated, and then reached clumsily over the back of the chair, underneath each of Uwe's arms, and joined his hands in front of Uwe's chest. He tried to touch Uwe as little as possible as he raised him up in a move that resembled the Heimlich maneuver in slow motion.

"Aaachh!" cried out Uwe in pain.

"Put him down!" shouted Elder Olson, but J.P. had already let go at the sound of Uwe's yelp, causing a second, but milder shriek.

"Here, lemme try," offered the senior companion, and the two missionaries traded places. Elder Olson tried an approach from the front that involved more body contact but was apparently easier on Uwe, who was silent as the missionary lifted him so that his bottom no longer rested in the chair.

Elder Prentice fumbled with Uwe's belt and fly button. "Hurry up, would you, man?" complained Elder Olson. Finally J.P. loosened the pants and managed to pull them off Uwe's hips, unleashing a rank urine-based stench.

"C'mon, ya gotta get the underpants too," directed Elder Olson through clenched teeth.

"I'll take tracting any day," muttered J.P. to distract himself as he peeled Uwe's damp briefs off the man's deformed legs, using only the thumb and the forefinger of each hand. After tossing the yellow-stained underwear into the corner, J.P. stood between Uwe's legs, placed a hand under each of Uwe's knees and lifted, while Elder Olson carried his end of the load by hooking his hands under Uwe's arms. The missionaries both grunted as they struggled to place Uwe into the tub without dropping him, and they barely succeeded.

"*Mensch*, how did that woman ever get him in here alone, even with a good back?" asked J.P.

"Don't know," agreed Elder Olson as he wiped his brow with his shirt sleeve. "I'll get Frau Kressmann."

In a moment the older missionary returned with a befuddled look.

"Where's the lady?" asked J.P. anxiously.

Elder Olson shook his head. "One of the kids out there had an accident. She asked if we would bathe him for her—said it would be a big help."

"Are you kidding?" demanded J.P. "I'll wait, thank you."

Elder Olson ignored his junior companion. He wasn't the zealous type, but he wouldn't turn his back on a person in need, even if the task was distasteful. He rolled up his sleeves and surveyed the tub.

"Let's see, how do I do this?" he asked himself aloud in English.

"I . . . I can . . . talk, you know . . . but only . . . only in German," offered Uwe, still looking down.

"Oh, I'm sorry," said Elder Olson genuinely in German. For the next fifteen minutes Uwe told the missionaries in halting German how to bathe him. After watching his companion clean Uwe alone for a couple of minutes, J.P. begrudgingly decided to join in. He used a sponge and did rinsing only, keeping as much space as possible between his hand and Uwe's naked, crippled body. Bathing another man—especially one who reeked of urine—was not exactly J.P.'s preferred mode of service.

As J.P. was trying to rinse Uwe's torso without touching him, Uwe suddenly lifted his hand out of the water and slapped it back down on the surface, splashing J.P. in the face. Uwe laughed wildly at his trick, and after a couple of seconds so did Elder Olson.

J.P. was irritated only for a moment, before deciding to return the favor, splashing Uwe in the face. Uwe squealed with delight.

After forty-five minutes, the two missionaries had finally bathed Uwe, shampooed his hair, dried him, and gotten him dressed in clean clothes. Frau Kressmann thanked the elders profusely as they left.

From his wheelchair parked again in front of the television, Uwe said hopefully, "I'll . . . see you . . . next week."

15
Sins on Shoulders

When Elder Roberts received a transfer letter in January informing him he would serve as senior companion in Rendsburg, his emotions were only slightly mixed. If the president had viewed a companionship with Elder Lehmann as an appropriate challenge for Elder Roberts, Chris didn't know whether terminating the companionship after just two months signaled success or failure on Chris's part.

With the help of his brother's journal insights, Elder Roberts had pushed himself to establish a reasonably good working relationship with his maverick senior companion, keeping his own feelings of resentment and frustration largely in check. But while Elder Lehmann seemed to be making some progress toward keeping mission rules more completely, he still routinely and openly flaunted many of them.

Elder Roberts wondered whether President Cook had hoped he might be able to bring the cynical senior companion around. If so, he had let the president down. Maybe he could have done more to help convert his companion.

But whatever the reason for the transfer, Elder Roberts breathed a sigh of relief. He had not been entirely successful in extinguishing feelings of resentment toward his companion for his failure to do what had been asked of them. And he was tiring of the struggle to muzzle those feelings.

Perhaps more than anything, Elder Roberts yearned to be free of feeling that he was constantly obligated to defend every mission rule and every point of church doctrine—not against attacks from investigators, but against constant questioning from his own companion. At times his discussions with his Stanford-educated senior companion were invigorating, but more often, they were spiritually exhausting. Chris was ready for a break.

And as much as he loved the members in Goettingen—especially the two that he and Elder McKinstry had baptized—he felt that he was ready for a new beginning, a clean slate, and the opportunity to be a senior.

He had imagined he might set a record for going senior early in his mission, given his missionary skills. Not going senior until his eleventh month out was almost an embarrassment to Elder Roberts, even though he knew he was still the first in his district to do so. He was ready to see what he could do as the leader of a companionship.

✧ ✧ ✧

It was with mixed emotions that J.P. returned to the Kressmann apartment the next Friday morning. He dreaded the smells and the task, yet a small part of him inexplicably seemed to look forward to coming back.

Frau Kressmann greeted the missionaries warmly and again directed them to the bathroom. As Elder Prentice struggled to navigate the wheelchair down the narrow hallway to the bathroom, Uwe stuttered, "What . . . what . . . what is your name?"

"*Ich heisse* Elder Prentice," replied J.P.

"Are you . . . are you . . . American?" asked Uwe. Uwe spoke with such difficulty that it pained J.P. just to listen.

"Yes," admitted Elder Prentice. "How know you?"

"I . . . I may be . . . in a wheelchair," answered Uwe, "and I . . . may talk slowly, . . . but I'm not . . . stupid." Elder Olson roared at Uwe's dig at his companion.

After the third week, the missionaries began reading a chapter from the Book of Mormon with the motley family after bathing Uwe. On the fourth Friday, Elder Prentice asked why they hadn't come to church yet.

"Oh, I'd love to," replied Frau Kressmann, "but there's just no way I can with all these kids."

Elder Prentice shot his senior a companion a glance, and Elder Olson seemed to read his mind. "You know," said Elder Olson, "we go to church Sundays two times, because a German congregation there is and an American servicemen congregation. We could stay with your childrens, then you and Uwe to church if go, yes?"

"The roof . . . will fall in . . . if my mother, if my mother . . . walks into a church," teased Uwe.

J.P. wanted to tease Uwe back, but his German wasn't good enough for him to say what he thought in English. After returning her son's kidding, Frau Kressmann gratefully accepted Elder Olson's offer.

✦ ✦ ✦

Elder Roberts spent more time tracting his first day in Rendsburg than he did his last seven days in Goettingen combined. With no appointments for the day, the missionaries tracted without interruption or success. It rained all day.

Located in the northern tip of Germany, Rendsburg was sandwiched between two cold seas. Being a Seattle native, Elder Roberts didn't expect to be bothered by the wet weather the locals called *nasskalt*, or "wet-cold." But by the end of the first day of riding through relentless rain, Elder Roberts realized he hadn't spent many days in Seattle riding his bike or walking in the rain all day.

Of course, in Goettingen Chris would have been teaching for much of the day. Success there, at least in terms of finding people to teach, had come much more easily. The city had a venerable tradition of outstanding missionaries like Elder Thomas and Elder Oman who had helped create an inertia that carried new missionaries in the right direction.

Rendsburg, on the other hand, had a long line of elders whose greatest distinction was in not getting sent home. Elder Johnston, whom Elder Roberts was replacing as senior companion, had spent much of his last month in Rendsburg (and the mission field) souping up his bike, saying goodbye to members who were glad he was leaving, and learning Hebrew by mail. Despite the diligent efforts of Elder Johnston's humble but earnest young companion, Elder Averett, there was not much of an investigator pool in Rendsburg.

Finding new potential converts looked like it would be a slow and an arduous process. Unlike the students, professors, and professionals of Goettingen, the toughened workers of this damp, northern German city were quite disinterested in what they perceived to be irrelevant philosophical questions.

After tracting for three weeks straight in the January rain, the Rendsburg elders were finally blessed with a balmy Saturday. Having been trained by one of the best street-contacting missionaries in the mission, Elder Roberts decided the time had come to show Elder Averett what he'd learned in Goettingen. Elder Averett had never been GQ-ing.

As they approached the pedestrian zone on their bikes, Elder Roberts felt the same sort of knot in his stomach that he felt before a big game or debating match. People were no more likely to reject the missionaries on the street than they were behind their doors. But in street contacting, the people came as fast and steadily as a missionary had the nerve to approach them.

There were no stretches of sidewalk between buildings, no apartments on end without anyone home. While tracting in the morning, the missionaries sometimes encountered only three or four people in an hour. During an hour of street contacting in the city center on a Saturday morning, a diligent missionary could talk to thirty or forty people. As the number of contacts increased dramatically, so did the number of rejections.

For a moment Chris hesitated. Many missionaries never did street contacting. Certainly Elder Averett would not object to another morning of watching people peek through their peepholes without answering their doors.

Elder Roberts missed having Elder Thomas to spur him on. Having Elder Thomas by his side had been sort of like having a coach to help push you when conditioning. Now he had the responsibility for pushing the companionship. He swallowed hard, said a prayer to himself, and dismounted his trusty bike with the fat tires. He would carry on the Goettingen tradition.

Elder Averett and Elder Roberts approached the first few people together. Chris was somewhat concerned about his companion, who wasn't much of a talker. In fact, at many points during his door approaches there were awkward silences as Elder Averett groped for words. But Elder Averett seemed to do reasonably well as he and Elder Roberts spoke with the first few people, although he showed none of the creativity or cleverness of an Elder Thomas or Elder Lehmann. After four or five encounters, Chris suggested they work individually as he and his Goettingen companions had.

Elder Roberts watched for his companion's reaction, remembering the anxiety he'd felt the first time Elder Thomas had made him GQ someone alone. But Elder Averett's face showed no reluctance as he stepped away to make his first solo approach.

Elder Averett stepped squarely in front of a large lumberjack of a German, whose frame dwarfed Elder Averett's short, stocky figure. The man stopped, and soon he was deep in conversation with the quiet American from Blanding, Utah. Elder Roberts was glad Elder Averett's first encounter was a positive one.

For the next hour, the companions remained within eyesight of each other but doubled their efforts by working alone. Finally, when neither of them had a conversation going, they paused a moment for a rest.

"So how'd it go, Elder?" asked Elder Roberts. He had engaged several people in discussions and had obtained two referrals himself.

"All right," said Elder Averett without expression.

"Anybody chew you out?" asked Elder Roberts.

"Just a couple of people," he replied smiling.

"So, any luck?" asked the senior companion, trying to be patient.

"Yeah, I got some referrals," was the answer.

"How many?" asked Elder Roberts, pleasantly surprised.

"Six. And two appointments," the junior companion finally smiled.

"How did you do that?" asked Elder Roberts, not even attempting to hide his dismay.

"I don't know," said Elder Averett humbly. "Prayer, I guess."

So much for the nifty tricks I learned in Goettingen, thought Elder Roberts.

❖ ❖ ❖

Herr Starke had canceled the missionaries' last two appointments, so Elder Hawthorne was pleasantly surprised to receive a phone call from the man who had been his most promising investigator. Unfortunately, Herr Starke was belatedly forced to serve his mandatory stint in the German military, so he would not be able to continue the discussions with the missionaries. However, he did want to see them one last time before he left.

True to form, Elder Greisel saw no need for deviating from the principles outlined in the next discussion—responsibilities of membership in the Church. It mattered nothing to him that the discussion was intended to assist investigators in making the transition to membership and that Herr Starke was nowhere near that himself. Herr Starke patiently endured about ten minutes of Elder Greisel's canned presentation before finally interrupting.

"Greisel . . ."

"Elder Greisel," corrected the Austrian elder.

"Yes, as you wish, Elder Greisel, this presentation you've prepared for tonight seems much better suited for someone whom you have, shall I say, more successfully proselytized. For just this last discussion, would you mind perhaps discussing some questions and concerns I have?"

"But—" began Elder Greisel.

Wesley glared at his senior companion with such intensity that for once Elder Greisel acceded to his junior companion's wishes.

"Fine," he said, folding his arms and leaning to the back of his chair.

For the next forty-five minutes Herr Starke asked questions about the Book of Mormon, about Jesus Christ, about personal revelation, and about the concept of commandments.

The discussion meandered, rather than steamrolled, and Elder Hawthorne did most of the talking, while Elder Greisel sulked. The senior companion said almost nothing until nine o'clock.

"We must go now," the senior companion announced definitively and abruptly.

"All right," said Herr Starke with resignation. But then a spark returned to his eye. "Say, there's just one more thing. I don't know if you'd be interested, but I might give you a bit of feedback on your teaching, if you don't mind. I mean, I thought you might like some input on how you come across."

Elder Greisel was reluctant, since he'd never been instructed to seek such feedback and it was already nine o'clock. But he hesitated, and Elder Hawthorne seized the opportunity.

"Yes, we that appreciate would."

"All right then," began Herr Starke as he adjusted his bottom in the chair, warming up to his task. "Now, no offense is intended by this, you understand? I'm just giving you helpful feedback."

Elder Hawthorne tried not to grin.

"Let me begin with my American friend, Hawthorne. Your German is not at all bad for someone who's been here only a few months. But don't let up; you still have much work to do. If you keep improving, though, like you have since you've been teaching me, you'll soon be speaking fluently."

Wesley nodded, not knowing how else to respond.

"I appreciate your flexibility, your willingness to answer my questions. And sometimes when you speak about something you seem to feel deeply, I can sense the strength of your conviction. I think that is good.

Don't be afraid to speak boldly, even if you think others disagree with you."

Herr Starke shifted in his seat as he looked toward Elder Greisel. "Greisel, er, Elder Greisel, you too speak with great . . . great certainty. But you convey this certainty—how shall I say it?—without any real sense of, well, concern. It's as if you just dump it out on me, if you know what I mean.

"When you give your prepared presentation, I feel as if you are more interested in finishing the presentation than you are in convincing me or answering my questions. I still don't know whether I believe Jesus actually lived, or whether you are his representatives. But if he did live, I imagine he taught more like Elder Hawthorne."

Elder Greisel sat stonily in silence.

"Well," said Herr Starke, slapping his hands on his thighs. "I'm afraid I've said too much. But I do most appreciate the sacrifice both of you have made to be here, and I wish you both well."

In his more honest and petty moments, Wesley would look back on this evening as one of the highlights of his mission.

✦ ✦ ✦

"By the way, the Familie Schmidt has invited us over for dinner Sunday afternoon," said Elder Averett as he and Elder Roberts rode through the February rain, which was not much more pleasant than the January rain.

"Oh," replied Elder Roberts, wondering why his companion was telling him this.

"They, um, they're used to the missionaries staying a long time for dinner," said Elder Averett awkwardly. "It's kind of hard to get away. Not that Elder Johnston ever tried."

"Like how long?" queried Elder Roberts.

"Oh, maybe two, three, four hours," answered Elder Averett. The white handbook said missionaries generally should not stay more than an hour. Elder Averett was a man of few words, but Elder Roberts assumed the situation had frustrated Elder Averett, or he wouldn't have mentioned it.

"Well, let's see if we can change that."

"How?" asked Elder Averett, who wondered how even good missionaries could shorten a visit with the Familie Schmidt.

"What time is dinner?" asked Chris

"Two o'clock."

Just then Elder Roberts noticed a young man with long hair walking on the side of the street without a hat. Elder Roberts slowed down his bike and decided to try an unconventional approach.

"How come you're not wearing a hat?" Elder Roberts asked, unsure where the question would lead, but hoping something would come to him.

Somewhat startled, the man with the wet, stringy hair replied, "I don't mind the rain. I kind of like it."

"Don't people think you're kind of crazy, though?" asked Chris lightly.

"Maybe," said the man without stopping.

"Doesn't that bother you?"

"What?" asked the man, drawing smoke from his cigarette that somehow managed to keep burning in the rain.

"That people think you're a little strange for not wearing a hat?"

"No. Do some people think you're crazy for riding bikes around in shiny blue suits in the rain and speaking to strangers with an American accent?" asked the slender smoker, turning the tables on Elder Roberts.

"Yes, some people think we're crazy." answered Elder Roberts. "And we're religious fanatics too. Did I forget to mention that?"

"Yes, you did," answered the slender smoker. "So that explains the matching short haircuts. What are you guys—really? Are you with the CIA or something?"

"Yes," said Elder Averett to Chris's amazement. "We're with the new CIA bike patrol."

"That's good . . . the CIA bike patrol," said the man to himself with a chuckle. "I like that."

"Actually, we're missionaries from The Church of Jesus Christ of Latter-day Saints," said Elder Roberts in a slightly more serious tone. "A lot of people think we're a little crazy. We spend two years of our lives, without pay, talking to people who are mostly not interested in what we have to say."

"So why do you do it? Maybe you should take a hint," suggested the man casually as he dropped what was left of his cigarette and crushed it with the toe of his boot.

"It's too important," added Elder Averett.

"So why are you talking to me?" the man asked, still walking.

"We want to come to your house and teach you about the gospel of Jesus Christ," asserted Elder Roberts. He silently prayed that they would be able to get an appointment with this man.

"Already heard it," replied the man, but not too firmly. "When I was a kid."

"Yes, but we're going to tell you to repent," retorted Elder Roberts with a smile.

"Yeah, I heard that too." The man walked through a puddle as if to emphasize his rebelliousness.

"But it didn't do any good, did it?" added Elder Averett.

"Nah, I guess not." The man enjoyed this banter. People didn't usually talk with him much.

"So how about Sunday at three-thirty?" asked Elder Roberts. "We'll come to your house and share a message with you about Jesus Christ, okay?"

"Three-thirty?"

"Yeah."

"Can I bring some friends?"

Elder Averett and Elder Roberts exchanged glances. This could be the beginning of a group conversion or a group beating. Elder Averett shrugged. They were on the Lord's errand, so they'd let him take care of them.

"Sure, bring as many as you'd like," said Elder Roberts. "Three-thirty, Sunday."

✧ ✧ ✧

At church or in the discussions, someone had apparently read Third Nephi, seventeen to the Kressmanns, because on the sixth Friday and every other Friday after that when J.P. visited the Kressmanns, Uwe begged, "Please . . . please read . . . about Jesus healing the people."

The missionaries obliged, and J.P. did the honors. Remarkably, it did not dawn on J.P. why Uwe might have a peculiar affinity for this chapter until he read the familiar verses about Jesus asking Lehi's descendants to bring forth their lame and their sick.

For the first time in his life, as Jon Prentice read the words, he imagined Jesus Christ as a real person. He imagined some Lamanite or Nephite widow like Frau Kressmann, struggling to carry her crippled son forward to the Savior.

Elder Prentice's voice cracked as he read of the Lord's healing power and of the Lehites pouring out their gratitude through their tears at Jesus' feet. When he paused between verses to wipe his eyes, Elder Prentice saw that tears were rolling freely down Uwe's face. He hoped he could be there to see the Savior heal Uwe one day, to free him from his malfunctioning frame.

✦ ✦ ✦

Sunday after church, the hour of reckoning finally arrived. Elder Roberts enjoyed the warmth of members' homes, not to mention the food. But with many members, the missionaries had to struggle to keep the visit appropriately short. The bulk of the problem, however, lay with the missionaries who simply ignored the white handbook's one-hour rule and stayed as long as the members allowed.

Schwester Schmidt greeted the elders at the door, with two children peeking out from behind her. "Elders!" she exclaimed, as if they were family she hadn't seen in years. "Please do come in."

Schwester Schmidt showed the missionaries in to her living room, where she asked more questions about Elder Roberts and his background than any other member on his mission yet. He then learned that Schwester Schmidt was a widow who had a son on a mission herself. As she spoke about her missionary son, her eyes glistened with pride and emotion. "I just pray the members in England are taking good care of my Thomas," she sighed.

Chris enjoyed talking with Schwester Schmidt and her children, but he grew nervous as the minutes passed without any mention of dinner. It was now two-fifteen, and the elders had an appointment at three-thirty.

Finally, Schwester Schmidt stood up and said, "Well, I need to finish preparing the meal. Would you elders be so kind as to take the dog for a walk with Peter? Peter will show you where to take him. It shouldn't take you much more than half an hour, and I should have dinner ready by then."

Elder Roberts glanced at his watch, but realized they had no choice in the matter. He and Elder Averett spent the next half hour talking with ten-year-old Peter Schmidt and following around the Schmidt dachshund.

When they returned, it was another ten minutes before dinner was finally ready. The missionaries had only thirty-five minutes before their discussion was to begin, and it would take five or ten minutes to get there.

The meal was delicious, and the missionaries enjoyed the conversation with Schwester Schmidt and her children. The whole family seemed to care about the missionaries as individuals because one of their own was currently a missionary.

But Elder Roberts grew anxious as the time for the appointment neared and Schwester Schmidt kept insisting that they eat third and fourth helpings. The missionaries' opportunity finally came when Schwester Schmidt commented, "Elder Roberts, you keep looking at your watch. Do you have somewhere to go?"

"Actually, we do have an appointment at three-thirty," he answered.

"Ach!" exclaimed Schwester Schmidt, genuinely chagrined. "What a shame! You'll miss dessert, and the people probably won't even show up for the appointment. You could have stayed here for a couple more hours if it weren't for this."

Elder Averett smiled ever so slightly at Elder Roberts. Elder Roberts decided to try to solve the problem not just for today but for future appointments as well. He silently prayed that he could do this without offending Schwester Schmidt.

"Schwester Schmidt, in a way, we wish we could stay here all afternoon. There is a wonderful spirit in your home. But we do have an appointment to teach some people. And even if we didn't have an appointment, we would need to get going so that we could get back to work."

"What? You mean tracting? But you won't find anyone that way. Wouldn't you rather just relax for a while here?"

"Part of me would," replied Elder Roberts honestly. "Tracting isn't easy, and we may not find anyone. But we just might have found someone in that hour or two that we missed while staying here. That would be a shame. Spending time here is much easier and warmer, but we've been called by a prophet of God to preach the gospel to the people here."

"And also, there's this white handbook, a set of rules missionaries everywhere are supposed to follow," interjected Elder Averett. He welcomed the opportunity to indirectly explain to Schwester Schmidt why he'd been so antsy during the many hours he had spent in her home with Elder Johnston. "It says we're not really supposed to stay in members' homes longer than an hour."

For a moment there was silence and Schwester Schmidt looked stunned, if not offended. Then, to the elders' relief, Schwester Schmidt said slowly, "You are good missionaries. Why no missionary has ever told me this before, I don't know. I thought the best thing I could do to help the missionaries was to let them stay here as long as they wanted to stay. I never knew about this rule. And I didn't think anyone actually wanted to tract."

"It's all right, really," answered Chris. "We do very much appreciate your kindness. But next time you have missionaries who want to stay two or three hours, the best thing you can do is help them on their way."

"Yeah," added Elder Averett. "Ask them if they've read their white handbook lately."

When Elder Averett said this, a light seemed to go on in Schwester Schmidt's head as she recalled the hours Elder Johnston and Elder Averett had spent in her home and how uncomfortable Elder Averett had appeared. She assumed his awkwardness stemmed from his shyness, but she now understood it much better. "I'll do that," she promised.

Schwester Schmidt took a deep breath and surveyed her dinner table. "But now for the problem at hand. You elders had better get going if you're going to make it across town by three-thirty. But what about my dessert?"

"Why don't we stop back briefly for dessert after our discussion?" suggested Elder Roberts. Schwester Schmidt hadn't really known about the elders' time limit, and he didn't want to be rude.

"That's a splendid idea," replied Schwester Schmidt, relieved. "And I promise not to keep you more than fifteen minutes."

✦ ✦ ✦

The stringy-haired man answered the door when the missionaries knocked.

"So you came," he said, and walked back into his smoke-filled apartment without closing the door.

Elder Roberts and Elder Averett took this as an invitation to come in, so they followed. The apartment was dimly lit and filled with people. What it lacked in light, it made up for in noise and smoke.

"So, these are some of my friends," said the host, whose name was Karl. "I'd tell you their names, but you'd just forget. So where you guys from?"

Karl and his six beer-drinking friends had never heard of Utah, but they were excited when Elder Roberts said he was from Seattle.

"All right, man. We love Nirvana and Pearl Jam, you know? Too bad about Kurt Cobain, huh?" one of the drinkers said, as if the rocker had taken his life only recently.

"Hey, if you're from Seattle, how come you don't wear Grunge?" Karl asked, using the English fashion word.

Elder Roberts and Elder Averett spent the next fifteen minutes trying to fight off questions about why they wore suits and why they insisted on using formal rather than the familiar form of German.

The group of four men and three women finally let Elder Averett say a prayer. Elder Roberts ran with the discussion as soon as his companion said amen, sensing they would not have many uninterrupted opportunities to teach these people. With dim light, smoke, and bad German rock music playing in the background, the missionaries couldn't have found a less conducive environment for the Spirit.

Fighting off constant heckling, Elder Roberts and Elder Averett struggled through a couple of concepts in forty-five minutes. They were making no headway.

"Look," said one of Karl's somewhat drunk buddies. "I get along just fine without having to have religion as a crutch. The idea that there's, like, some cosmic father figure hovering over the universe—I just can't imagine it. No, you can keep your American religion. But I'll take your Seattle music."

In the darkness Karl's friends laughed and clanked their beer bottles together in a toast of agreement.

"So what happens when you die?" asked Elder Roberts. "Is that it—everything's over?" The noise level subsided slightly. "I mean, think about it. Can you imagine an eternity of nothing? You think whatever it is that's inside your body now, the part of you that thinks and feels . . . you think that just turns off forever when you die?"

Elder Roberts thought he actually heard one of Karl's friends say something like, "Yeah, what about that, Peter?"

Elder Roberts saw his sliver of opportunity. He poured out his testimony as directly and boldly as possible. "It doesn't work that way. Our spirits never die. We live on. I know this. We will live forever, and how happy we'll be depends on how we live here.

"We can try to ignore God now, but we won't be able to when we die. One day we will each come into his presence, if only for a brief time, and we will have to answer for what we have done with our lives. God and his Son, Jesus Christ, have sent us to tell you about his commandments, commandments that will make you happy now and for eternity."

The sun had gone down outside, and the room was almost completely dark. The reaction to Chris's testimony was almost hostile.

"Right. American messengers of God, come to tell us how to live," said Karl in a tone noticeably antagonistic. "Why don't you just take your religion and get out."

Having done all they could, Elder Roberts and Elder Averett thought getting out sounded like a good idea. They asked if they could say a prayer before they left. Elder Roberts kept it short to avoid trying anyone's patience further.

On their way out, Elder Averett asked if anyone wanted them to come back. Someone belched loudly, but someone else shouted, "Why not?"

Elder Roberts could think of a dozen good reasons why not, but Elder Averett said they'd come back next week at the same time.

"Sorry about that," explained Elder Averett as he and Elder Roberts rode back to Schwester Schmidt's. "Maybe they won't be there. It's just that President Cook is always talking about us being responsible for people's sins if we don't teach them properly. These guys seem to have lots of sins, and I want to make sure I don't have any of them on my shoulders."

Elder Roberts laughed and admired his companion's dedication.

✧ ✧ ✧

On the seventh Friday that Elder Prentice and Elder Olson visited the Kressmanns, Frau Kressmann invited the missionaries to sit down before bathing Uwe, a task they had volunteered to do from the third week on.

"I have some news," declared Frau Kressmann. "Uwe and I are going to be baptized in two weeks, on March eleventh."

"Fantastic!" exclaimed Elder Prentice. In his ignorance, J.P. had realized only after three weeks of visiting the Kressmann's that Uwe's disabilities were only physical, making him eligible for baptism.

"That's wonderful," added Elder Olson.

"Would . . . would you . . . please . . . baptize me, . . . please . . . Elder Prentice?" asked Uwe.

J.P. joked quickly to avoid getting emotional. "You think I strong enough?"

"No," retorted Uwe. "But . . . you drop me . . . in the tub . . . every week . . . so I'm . . . used to it." Uwe's head hung slightly to the side as always, but his eyes glistened with joy.

16
Game Over

As he changed into his whites, Jon Prentice was nervous. He called his baptismal clothes his whites as if they were his game uniform in a sport he played frequently, but Jon Prentice had never actually used his baptismal clothes before. He and Elder Lafferty brought two investigators to baptism, but a member had baptized one and Elder Lafferty the other. This would be J.P.'s first time in the waters of baptism as a priesthood holder.

All morning he had repeated the baptismal prayer to himself, and when Elder Olson was out of the room he even practiced it with the motions. "Of the Father, and of the Son, and of the Holy Ghost," he repeated in German, knowing every word must be correct.

To complicate matters for his first baptism, Elder Prentice not only had to get the words right in German, he had to do it with someone whose legs didn't work. Elder Olson and he had asked the district leader how to perform the baptism, and the question had gone all the way up to President Cook.

His instructions were that the baptizing elder's arm had to remain at the square during the prayer, but that another Melchizedek Priesthood holder could assist in holding Uwe. After the prayer, the baptizing elder could simply hold Uwe in his arms, bend his knees, and submerge Uwe completely, even if it meant submerging himself as well.

But as he sat in the makeshift locker room in his ill-fitting white pants and shirt, J.P. was troubled by more than just the logistical concerns. Perhaps it was Uwe's innocence, or the emphasis Uwe had placed on his baptism. He'd spoken of almost nothing else during their last three visits.

Maybe it was just that J.P. would be performing the baptism. Whatever the reason, J.P. was feeling overwhelmed by the significance of what he was about to do, awed at the prospect of wading into water and performing an ordinance that would wash someone's sins from his soul.

It was not a game, not anything like a game. Deep in his own soul, J.P. had come to understand over the past couple of weeks that what he was about to do mattered. Like perhaps nothing he had ever done before, this mattered. It defied all the trite, almost irreverent phrases missionaries sometimes used to describe the sacred ordinance.

Along with a growing sense of the significance of this rite came a growing sense of shame. Uwe had asked J.P. to baptize him, and J.P.

could not disappoint him. But if there had been an easy way out, J.P. would have taken it, just like he got out of blessing the sacrament on Sunday mornings after he'd kissed too much Saturday night.

Elder Prentice figured he was worthy in a technical sense: he had been careful not to wander into any real trouble on his mission. But as he sat on the toilet with the lid down, waiting for his companion and the ward mission leader to get Uwe into his baptismal clothes, feelings of guilt stirring within him over the last few weeks made their way to the emotional surface.

J.P. was becoming increasingly convinced that he had deeply disappointed the Lord. He could not erase words Uwe had spoken in his guileless, halting German during their visit last week. "I . . . I wish . . . . I wish I could be a missionary . . . to tell people . . . about Heavenly Father . . . and Jesus . . . and how happy . . . the gospel . . . has made me, . . . that's what I wish."

Of course, Uwe would never be able to be a missionary on this earth. No, J.P. was the one who had the opportunity to be a missionary here, and he had been one in name only for over thirteen months, thinking he could perhaps game God's system.

Now, as J.P. stood on the verge of performing the most sacred priesthood ordinance of his life, he felt empty. He buried his face in his hands and pleaded to the Lord that at least he wouldn't botch the prayer, that at least he wouldn't detract from the moment for Uwe.

Get down on your knees. The thought came to J.P. distinctly, almost urgently, though not audibly, nor even in words at all. Elder Prentice hesitated only a moment before kneeling on the hard tile surface of the bathroom floor. He knelt like he'd knelt in the MTC, resting his weight almost completely on his knees. He bowed his head and opened his heart, praying without using words himself. What poured out was sorrow, shame, guilt. Like nothing J.P. had felt before, his heart hurt.

After a few moments of allowing his anguish to flow freely, dressed in white, kneeling in a bathroom stall in Bremerhaven, Germany, Elder Prentice told Heavenly Father he was sorry, not for any single act, but for who he was, who he had let himself become. Almost as an afterthought, J.P. asked the Lord to forgive him. And he asked again that the baptism would go well—for Uwe's sake.

"Yo, comp, you comin'?" called Elder Olson in English from the other side of the stall door.

"*Ja, ich komme,*" replied Elder Prentice, rising to his feet and grabbing some tissue for his nose.

Elder Olson laughed at his companion, whose face he couldn't see. "That's right, you'd better start speaking German. You'd better learn German quick."

J.P. was unable to concentrate during most of the baptismal service. Finally, after a branch member baptized Schwester Kressman, Elder Olson pushed Uwe's chair to the stairs leading to the baptismal font.

Together Elder Prentice and Elder Olson lifted him from his chair, much more proficiently than the first time they'd lifted him to be bathed. As they edged their way carefully down the steps, Uwe clung to the missionaries with an arm draped around each of their necks.

When they reached the bottom of the stairs and positioned themselves in the center of the font, Elder Olson removed Uwe's arm from around his neck and helped him place his right hand on Elder Prentice's extended left arm.

"I . . . I am ready now," declared Uwe as he looked up at Elder Prentice trustingly. "You . . . you can do it, Elder Prentice." J.P. took heart.

As Elder Olson supported Uwe's weight, Elder Prentice raised his right hand to the square. "Uwe Kressmann, having been commissioned of Jesus Christ," recited Elder Prentice slowly and with a heavy accent. "I baptize you in the name of the Father, . . . and of the Son, and . . . of the Holy Ghost. Amen."

J.P. dropped his arm and slipped it under Uwe's back, while positioning his left arm under Uwe's knees. J.P. nodded to Elder Olson, who allowed Elder Prentice to carry the full load alone. Holding Uwe to his chest like a parent holds a sleeping child, Elder Prentice bent his knees as far as he could. When the water rushed in over his own head, he knew he had completely immersed his friend. With a mighty heave he straightened his legs, raising himself and Uwe from the water.

Uwe sputtered until Elder Olson wiped his eyes. "I am clean . . . now . . . , right?" he asked J.P. when he ventured to open his eyes again.

"Yes," answered Elder Prentice with conviction, pulling Uwe to him tightly. "You are clean. You are clean."

When he prayed that night, Elder Prentice ventured another request of the Lord. "I need to get out of this city, and I need to learn German," he prayed silently. "I'm ready to be a missionary. I'm sorry. I'm sorry it's taken me so long." And then, for the first time in eight months, Elder Prentice set his alarm.

✧ ✧ ✧

This time, no transfer came in response to Elder Prentice's prayers. Elder Prentice decided he must press forward anyway, as difficult as it would be.

He began by getting up at six a.m., a fact presumably lost on Elder Olson, since he was dead to the world until at least seven. He also started speaking German whenever he was outside of the apartment. This change was not lost on Elder Olson, since J.P. had rarely spoken German to his companion.

"Yo, comp," he said between doors one day after Uwe's baptism. "I didn't really mean anything when I said you oughta pick up German one of these first months. Hope you're not doing this 'cause of me."

"Worry you not," answered Elder Prentice in German. "I not it for you do. I no learn German, then parents, them me think no go really on mission maybe."

"Your parents speak German?"

"No, but uncle of I, he speak German. He tell parents."

"All right, just checking to make sure I hadn't offended you or anything. But by the way, as long as you're gonna speak German, would you mind cleaning it up some? It's murder on my ears."

"Yes, oh, yes, you much help me have been, Mr. Senior-Companion-no-need-language-study-today-morning have," countered Elder Prentice in a stream of animated but terribly ungrammatical German.

"All right, all right, you wanna learn German? I'll teach you German."

Given Elder Olson's own limited German skills, his offer was not particularly valuable, but Elder Prentice appreciated it nonetheless. Until he got a companion who spoke better German than this one, he would learn everything Elder Olson had to offer.

❖ ❖ ❖

April transfers sent Elder Hawthorne from Luebeck to Rendsburg to join Elder Roberts. The two missionaries had established a good relationship, if not a friendship, in the MTC. As was the case with all of Elder Greisel's companions when they were transferred, Elder Hawthorne was thrilled with the change.

Persistent tracting, GQ-ing, and even a member referral had steadily increased the Rendsburg teaching pool. The people in Rendsburg were much slower to open their doors to the missionaries than were the people in Goettingen. However, once they did they were much more likely to open their hearts.

No investigator demonstrated this phenomenon better than Frau Hildebrand. A cantankerous, chain-smoking, foul-mouthed thirty-year old, Frau Hildebrand was one of only two of Karl's friends to show up the second week when the missionaries returned. She challenged and taunted the elders at nearly every opportunity in the first discussion.

Elder Roberts didn't mind earnest and even difficult questions—in fact, he welcomed them. But Frau Hildebrand was toying with the elders, and they knew it. The experience was not pleasant. The language the missionaries could understand was offensive, and they assumed the language they couldn't understand was even worse.

Chris was again tempted not to ask Frau Hildebrand and her friends for a return appointment. She clearly was not interested in sincerely investigating the gospel, and an hour spent with her was probably spiritually damaging to the missionaries. But Elder Roberts dutifully followed his companion's example and asked the motorcycle queen whether they could visit her another time.

"Sure," replied the burly smoking machine between puffs. "Why not?"

None of Frau Hildebrand's friends were interested in a third discussion, so the missionaries went to her apartment together with a sister from the ward. They tried to prepare their "joint teach," Schwester Pinka, as best they could. Schwester Pinka testified meekly, and the missionaries testified boldly. But the Spirit seemed unwilling or unable to carry the message through the cloud of smoke to Frau Hildebrand's heart, regardless of how it was delivered.

Elder Roberts did see some success when he returned a few of Frau Hildebrand's barbs with good-natured ribbing of his own. Frau Hildebrand welcomed Chris's teasing, like a gladiator happy to have finally found a foe courageous enough to fight.

When they came to the end of the discussion, Frau Hildebrand surprised the elders. "So, I suppose you religious zealot-types wanna come again. How 'bout next Wednesday?"

The fourth visit began much the same as the first three had. Frau Hildebrand opened the door when the elders and Schwester Pinka arrived, five minutes behind schedule. "So, is this part of your religion or what? Are you always five minutes late?" This was her greeting.

"No, for typical members it's more like fifteen," dead panned Elder Roberts. "We're just more righteous as missionaries, so we're only five minutes late." Frau Hildebrand would later learn how much truth there was to Chris's comments.

Elder Roberts decided to waste no time turning the tables on Frau Hildebrand. "So what's with the constant smoking? Is it just to give your apartment and clothes that scent of tobacco? Maybe you could just use some perfume, like Essence of Nicotine or something."

The missionaries had asked Frau Hildebrand not to smoke during each of her their visits, but to no avail.

"No, I happen to like the flavor. And I suppose you're going to tell me smoking's a sin?"

"Yes," replied Elder Hawthorne, and they left it at that.

The discussion was turbulent as usual. Frau Hildebrand would simply not allow herself to be shepherded through any discussion prepared in advance. In fact, as soon as she caught on to the fact that the missionaries had certain points they were supposed to address, she made it her job to sidetrack them.

When Elder Hawthorne asked Frau Hildebrand to read Ether four, eighteen and nineteen, midway through the discussion, her initial reaction was typical. She took the Book of Mormon and flipped the page. She began reading, mostly to herself, much earlier in Ether four. Neither Elder Roberts nor Elder Hawthorne could remember anything significant from the rest of Ether four, and they were beginning to get annoyed with Frau Hildebrand's complete unwillingness to cooperate.

Finally, she began reading aloud, practically mumbling at first. "And in that day that they shall exercise faith in me, saith the Lord, even as the brother of Jared did, that they may become sanctified in me, then will I manifest unto them the things which the brother of Jared saw, even to the unfolding unto them all my revelations, saith Jesus Christ, the Son of God, the Father of the heavens and of the earth, and all things that in them are."

Frau Hildebrand paused for a long drag from her cigarette and glanced quickly at the elders to see if she was annoying them. She was, so she continued. "And he that will contend against the word of the Lord, let him be accursed; and he that shall deny these things, let him be accursed; . . ."

She paused for a moment, but her eyes did not leave the page. Elder Roberts thought he heard a slight tremble in her otherwise assured and caustic tone as she continued: " . . . for unto them will I show no greater things, saith Jesus Christ; for I am he who speaketh."

Again Frau Hildebrand paused. She rubbed out her half-used cigarette in the ashtray. "And at my command the heavens are opened and are shut; and at my word the earth shall shake; and at my command the inhabitants thereof shall pass away, even so as by fire."

Frau Hildebrand's voice was now quivering noticeably. The two elders sat on the edge of their chairs and heard the words of Ether four as they had never heard them before.

Frau Hildebrand read on. "And he that believeth not my words believeth not my disciples; and if it so be that I do not speak, judge ye; for ye shall know that it is I that speaketh, at the last day."

As Frau Hildebrand read this last phrase, both missionaries felt a rush of the Spirit as powerful as few other times in their missions. The Spirit also let Elder Roberts know that in that instant, the Spirit had spoken to Frau Hildebrand's soul and she had heard.

"But he that believeth these things which I have spoken, him will I visit with the manifestations of my Spirit, and he shall know and bear record. For because of my Spirit he shall know that these things are true; for it persuadeth men to do good."

Frau Hildebrand's hands were now shaking as well as her voice, but she pressed on. She read each word deliberately, as if reading a scroll handed her by an angel. "He that will not believe my words will not believe me—that I am; and he that will not believe me will not believe the Father who sent me. For behold, I am the Father, I am the light, and the life, and the truth of the world. . . . Behold, when ye shall rend that veil of unbelief which doth cause you to remain in your awful state of wickedness, and hardness of heart, and blindness of mind . . ."

Frau Hildebrand looked pained as she read of the veil of unbelief. A tear rolled down her cheek. "Then shall the great and marvelous things which have been hid up from the foundation of the world from you—yea, when ye shall call upon the Father in my name, with a broken heart and a contrite spirit, then shall ye know that the Father hath remembered the covenant which he made unto your fathers, O house of Israel."

Frau Hildebrand was now openly crying. She wiped her nose on her shirt sleeve before reading the final verses of the chapter. "Therefore, when ye shall receive this record ye may know that the work of the Father has commenced upon all the face of the land. Therefore, repent all ye ends of the earth, and come unto me, and believe in my gospel, and be baptized in my name; for he that believeth and is baptized shall be saved; but he that believeth not shall be damned; and signs shall follow them that believe in my name. And blessed is he that is found faithful unto my name at the last day, for he shall be lifted up to dwell in the kingdom prepared for him from the foundation of the world. And behold it is I that hath spoken it. Amen."

Frau Hildebrand set down the book slowly but did not stop looking at it. Finally, she drew a deep breath and looked up at the missionaries. "This is why you've come, isn't it?" she asked as she tried to choke back the tears.

"Yes," replied Elder Hawthorne through his own tears.

"You're here to baptize me?" she said, only partly as a question.

"Yes," answered Elder Roberts. "We want you to come unto Christ, to repent, and to be baptized. It won't be easy: you will have to change. But you will never regret it. You will experience joy in this life you have never known, and you'll receive joy in eternity you have never imagined possible."

The discussions did not call for a prayer at this point, but the Savior's words about praying to the Father with a broken heart and a contrite spirit still echoed in Chris's mind.

"Schwester Hildebrand," he said as he dropped to his knees, "would you please join us in prayer and tell the Father what is in your heart?"

Elder Hawthorne immediately knelt down as well. Frau Hildebrand, who had previously refused to do almost anything the missionaries asked, got on her knees and prayed aloud for the first time in her life.

"Dear God, . . . I'm sorry. I'm so sorry." For the next minute or more, Frau Hildebrand simply cried. "Please help me change. Please. Thank you for letting me feel these strange feelings, for showing me the way. Thank you for sending these two American messengers. I'm sorry I give them such a hard time. I don't mean anything by it. Thank you for sending me this book. I'm sorry I haven't been reading it. I will. I promise." Frau Hildebrand looked up at the missionaries. "How do I end?"

"In the name of Jesus Christ. Amen," whispered Elder Hawthorne.

Frau Hildebrand repeated the phrase and meant it.

As they climbed back into their seats, Elder Hawthorne asked, "So how do you feel?"

"Drained. I felt real warm, like, and then real dark for a few seconds, and then real warm again, you know? I've never felt so high or so low."

"We'll have you read Alma thirty-six before our next visit," replied Elder Roberts. "A prophet in the Book of Mormon once experienced similar feelings."

"So did you say you baptize by dunking?" asked Frau Hildebrand.

"We generally call it immersion," answered Elder Hawthorne.

"I want you to do it," she said to Elder Hawthorne. Nodding toward Elder Roberts she added, "I don't think he's strong enough to get me back up. I'm afraid I'd drown."

Elder Roberts laughed and acted offended, but feared she was right.

Elder Roberts and Elder Hawthorne left with two bags of cigarettes and alcohol that night. They had not yet explained the Word of Wisdom in detail, but promised to do so during a future visit. For now, they explained, it was enough for her to know that God didn't want her to use these things anymore and that she might as well stop tonight while she felt the Spirit.

The missionaries practically floated home as they looked for a place to dispose of their contraband.

17
Digging In

Getting out and staying on the work was the most difficult challenge for Elder Prentice. For the most part, though, Elder Prentice resisted temptation and pushed himself to press on with the work. Unfortunately, Elder Olson had not undergone a similar change of heart.

"Hey, where's your U-2 CD?" asked Elder Olson one March afternoon after a typical lunch of rice, gravy, and bread with Nutella.

"I've, uh, well . . ." hesitated Elder Prentice, not wanting to appear self-righteous.

"What?" demanded Elder Olson.

"I'm over them. They don't do anything for me any more."

"Over them?" asked Elder Olson incredulously.

"Yeah," dismissed J.P., who quickly changed the subject. "Say, what do you think's the best way to get Herr Werner to come to church?"

"I'm talking CD's here, not investigators," insisted Elder Olson. He sounded earnest as he continued. "Look, don't think I haven't noticed you slipping out of bed early in the morning to study. I seen you speaking German all the time, always tryin' to get us to go out on the work and stuff. 'Fess up. What's the deal?"

"What?"

"You heard me," repeated Elder Olson. "You turnin' into some kind of straightlaced zone leader wannabe?"

"I'd say it's a little late for that," joked J.P., who now had only ten months of his mission left. "I just, um, yeah, I wanna do it right, that's all."

"I knew it," declared Elder Olson as he slapped the table, like a detective who had cracked a case. "I seen it in your eyes when you was holding Uwe there in the font. I knew it."

"So are you in?" J.P. decided to go on the offensive.

"What?" asked Elder Olson.

"Are you in? Whadya say we turn things around in this city? I want to teach."

Remembering part of *Alice's Restaurant*, a quirky hippy ballad from the 1960's to which Elder Olson had introduced him, Elder Prentice decided farce was the best chance he had to defend his new zeal for the work without seeming too pious. "I want to teach people, all kinds of people."

J.P. did his best Arlo Guthrie imitation. "At first it may just be one German person, comin' into the Church, checkin' it out, and decidin' to stay. The members, well, they won't think anything of it. Then pretty soon we'll have two German people, I'm talking about two German people, comin' into the Church, askin' all kinds of questions, checkin' it out, singin' hymns, and gettin' baptized."

Elder Prentice was on a roll now. "And then pretty soon we'll have all kinds of German people, fat people, old people, young people, good people, sinners, Muslims, Lutherans, Seventh-Day Adventists, I'm talkin' 'bout all kinds of people, comin' into the Church and demandin'—to be baptized. We'll be teaching all kinds of people! And then the members, well, they'll say, 'We got ourselves a movement!'"

Inexplicably, Elder Prentice's bizarre antics proved contagious, and soon the two Americans were jumping up and down in their apartment mumbling about teaching all kinds of people. Although Elder Olson was older than J.P., J.P. was hip and Elder Olson knew it. When his junior companion got on a roll, Elder Olson usually went along for the ride, wherever it took him.

✧ ✧ ✧

A remarkable thing happened to the work in Bremerhaven as the April flowers began to bloom. Elder Prentice, followed by Elder Olson, worked harder than any elders had worked in that city for at least a year. They left the apartment every morning at nine o'clock, took no more than one hour for lunch, and returned again to the apartment no earlier than nine every evening.

On the work they pushed hard rather than coasting, climbing stairs two at a time until they were out of breath. Instead of checking on lukewarm contacts scattered around the city for much of the day, the missionaries plowed new ground. They tracted, they GQ-ed, they even spoke with people on the street in between houses while they were tracting. For three weeks they radically changed the way the work was done in Bremerhaven.

But the results were the same. They still had only three investigators, one of whom was probably not mentally competent to be baptized. They'd worked themselves silly and had nothing to show for it.

"This stinks," said Elder Olson in English during a break from some rigorous Saturday morning street contacting. "It's like giving up ice cream, potato chips, chocolate, and soda pop and eating nothing but grapefruit and water for three weeks, without losing any weight. If working hard doesn't make a difference, we might as well enjoy the ride, don't you think?"

"Yeah, I thought thing around faster coming would also," sighed Elder Prentice in German.

Elder Olson looked hopeful. Perhaps his companion would slacken the pace a bit.

"But I in the mirror better look can, Elder," Elder Prentice said, as he slapped his senior companion's leg. "Let's go."

Elder Olson watched in amazement as his junior companion jumped back into the fray, stopping almost every person he could, gesturing, pleading, pressing, refusing to give up until people walked away. It was the new Elder Prentice, and he showed no signs of relapsing into his discarded pattern.

18
Fishing for Men and Pizza

The baptism of Sister Hildebrand in May marked a turning point for the Rendsburg branch and the end of several fairly unproductive and frustrating months for Elder Hawthorne. As with all Rendsburg baptisms, the Hildebrand baptism was held about twenty kilometers away in the Neumuenster building, which had a font.

Virtually all thirty-four active members of the branch attended. Unlike most convert baptisms back home, which tended to feature only the assigned member of the bishopric, the ward mission leader, and a smattering of hard-core members, baptisms in Germany were celebrations of renewal. They provided new hope that the branch would not disappear when the widows died and the kids grew up and moved away.

Initially, Elder Roberts and Elder Hawthorne worried about how the members would react to Sister Hildebrand and how she would react to them. But the summary of her first homemaking meeting put the elders at ease. "They do bizarre things with Popsicle sticks, but the people are nice," Sister Hildebrand concluded.

The baptism—the first bona fide convert baptism in Rendsburg in over two years—energized the branch. The young branch president gave a stirring talk on Sunday about the importance of doing missionary work. Sister Schmidt raved about the missionaries in her testimony on fast Sunday. By the end of the month, the elders had received three solid member referrals. Slowly, but surely, the work in Rendsburg was growing.

✦ ✦ ✦

When the call finally came in early June—months after Elder McKinstry had convinced Elder Roberts that it might come—Elder Roberts was almost surprised. The work with Elder Hawthorne was going so well that it occupied nearly all of Elder Roberts' thoughts. Yet Elder Roberts was programmed so deeply to excel, to figure out what the next step on the ladder was and then pull himself up to it, that no pre-transfer Tuesday night passed without him wondering whether he might receive a call from the president.

The best news for Elder Roberts was that he was going to become a district leader without having to leave Rendsburg and Elder Hawthorne. The district leader in Neumuenster had gone home, and rather than transfer Elder Roberts to Neumuenster, President Cook had decided to make Rendsburg the district leader's city.

For his part, Elder Hawthorne was thoroughly pleased to stay with a companion and in a city he liked. But he was distraught about the one added duty thrust upon him by his companion's new assignment: he would regularly have to travel by train to the other three cities in the district to split with the junior companions while the senior companions came to Rendsburg to split with Elder Roberts. Elder Hawthorne became almost physically ill each day he was forced to travel by train for splits.

✧ ✧ ✧

Elder Prentice began to reform his ways at least a month before the May transfer, but when he was finally transferred out of the city, he felt as if he had a new lease on life. He was transferred to Minden to work with Elder Hunter—a Salt Lake native whose missionary skills and talents bordered on intimidating.

Working with Elder Hunter reminded Elder Prentice of a game of pick-up basketball he stumbled into at BYU before his mission. Three or four players who sat on the bench for the BYU varsity team were playing, and J.P. figured that as a starter from a decent high school team, he would at least be able to hold his own in the game. To his surprise, the varsity bench warmers scored at will against J.P. when they had the ball and completely suffocated J.P.'s offense with their quickness when they didn't have the ball. He'd been fooling himself when he thought he could run with them.

As he turned things around in the last month or so, Elder Prentice knew he had months of lost ground to make up. But because he'd never had a stellar senior companion, he had no idea just how far he had to go, just how much better he could be, until he met Elder Hunter.

Elder Hunter spoke the language so effortlessly that members and investigators alike routinely assumed he was a native German. Scriptures and discussions rolled off his tongue with ease and emphasis, revealing no hint of rote memorization.

In the apartments, on the doors, in investigators' homes, and at church, the slender, six-two elder presented the same face. He handled himself with confidence, not arrogance, speaking almost quietly, yet with an edge of urgency. There was no trace of affectation or insincerity in his voice; if he asked someone how they were doing, he actually wanted to know.

Not coincidentally, Elder Hunter was able to establish relationships with people and earn their trust with remarkable quickness. And members acted differently toward Elder Hunter than to any missionary Elder Prentice had observed at home or on his mission: they treated him not as a priest—two years removed—but as a servant of the Lord.

Nowhere was Elder Prentice's new senior companion more impressive than in teaching situations. The discussions generally called for missionaries to testify of the truthfulness of the principle they had taught after explaining it, but Elder Hunter didn't wait. He subtly wove his testimony into almost every sentence, even when speaking words that sounded merely explanatory when used by most missionaries.

Meekness and boldness seemed opposites, but Elder Hunter was somehow meek and bold simultaneously as he taught the gospel of Jesus Christ. The result was so powerful that even some of the most antagonistic investigators he taught acknowledged that they felt something unusual as he spoke.

What amazed and impressed Elder Prentice most was that despite his tremendous spiritual commitment and power, Elder Hunter didn't seem to take himself too seriously. When Elder Prentice asked what the key was to successful missionary work, Elder Hunter leaned forward, resting his arms on his knees, and replied earnestly, "Good dental hygiene." Elder Prentice wasn't sure until several seconds later that his senior companion was joking.

Before their second day together came to a close, Elder Prentice found himself describing his evolution as a missionary, mostly as an apologetic explanation of why his German sounded like he'd been in the field for only two or three months. Elder Hunter didn't flinch as Elder Prentice described the months he'd wasted in Bremerhaven. He only nodded his acknowledgment and support.

When Elder Prentice was finished with his story, Elder Hunter asked simply, "What can I do to help?"

"Train me," requested Elder Prentice of his senior companion, who had been in the field three months less than Elder Prentice. It was perhaps the first time in Jon Prentice's life that he had solicited any kind of instructional help from anyone. "Teach me German. Teach me how to teach. Teach me the scriptures. Teach me everything you know. Pretend I'm an inexperienced golden, and you won't be too far off."

"Well," answered Elder Hunter softly, "I'm happy to do what I can. We'll start with flossing." He smiled and then laughed lightly at his own joke. "No, really, how about fasting tomorrow for starters? We can't do much without the Lord's help, and I've always found fasting to be a good way to show the Lord I'm serious about something."

Elder Prentice had never fasted when it wasn't fast Sunday, but he was ready to follow his new companion anywhere. As he knelt in companionship prayer with Elder Hunter that evening, Elder Prentice's heart was filled with a wonderful new sensation—hope.

❖ ❖ ❖

July's even bluer skies and balmier weather would have been a welcome change for Elder Hawthorne, had they not also accompanied the biggest change yet of his mission. Elder Hawthorne became a senior companion because Elder Roberts was transferred to Bielefeld to serve as zone leader.

The only time the idea of being senior companion had even remotely appealed to Elder Hawthorne was when he worked with Elder Greisel. But with great senior companions, or even half decent ones, laboring diligently in the role of junior companion was easily preferable to the inevitable pressures of leadership and responsibility. Had Elder Hawthorne lived at the time of King Mosiah and Alma, he would have voted to keep the kingship rather than face the prospect of voting for judges and receiving greater individual responsibility.

Even though each of his senior companions had given Elder Hawthorne substantial responsibility in their companionships, the senior companions had still been ultimately accountable for the final decisions. The district leader always looked first to the senior companion in the weekly interview when things weren't going as well as they should. And Elder Smith and Elder Roberts had always been there to move the work along if Elder Hawthorne got discouraged. With them, there was a feeling of inevitable success—that things would somehow work out.

Now, Elder Hawthorne was charged with responsibility for the work in Rendsburg and his only help was a missionary who'd been in Germany only three months. Elder Sampson seemed to have a good heart, but he actually knew less about missionary work than Elder Hawthorne did.

Jolted out of his comfort zone once again, Elder Hawthorne longed for the security of his own home. Eight months to go, he caught himself thinking.

✦ ✦ ✦

Finding and meeting a new companion was always an interesting event in the Germany Hamburg Mission. There was no friendly gathering of missionaries and pickup-driving members at a stake center to transport the missionaries' growing cache of worldly possessions. Instead, the missionary being transferred simply sent the new companion a postcard indicating what time he would arrive at the train station on transfer day. The new companions would meet at the designated time.

Elder Roberts decided to test the capacity of his new companion for bizarre humor. After an extensive four-minute search, Elder Roberts found the perfect postcard on which to send notice of his arrival time. The caption-less photograph featured a rather frazzled looking terrier standing on its hind legs in front of a red velvet blanket. The card made no sense whatsoever, making it quite a find.

On the back, Elder Roberts wrote a quick note to Elder Keil, whom he had never before met:

> Looking forward to seeing you and the kids again—it's been years. Hope everyone is doing well. I'll be coming in at three twenty-three this Thursday. Until then, I remain—*Elder Roberts.*

When Elder Roberts finally stumbled off the train, no companion was in sight. As with most of his new companions, Elder Roberts had no idea what Elder Keil looked like, but few twenty-year-olds had short hair and wore dark suits with name tags.

Elder Roberts scanned the crowd again for a name tag and came up empty. He realized that it wouldn't take much for companions to miss each other in a train station this size. Dozens of passengers got off a train from several different cars, quickly merging into a bustling crowd. In fact, thought Elder Roberts, it's a miracle that companions didn't miss each other more often.

He scanned the constantly moving crowd again, but still saw no one likely to be his companion. As he slowly came to the conclusion that he had somehow missed his companion, Elder Roberts had the same sinking, desperate feeling he'd had on a Scout hike when he finally came to the conclusion that he was lost.

Just as his anxiety was beginning to mushroom into panic, a young German man with two small children approached him rapidly. "Children, it's Uncle Kris!" exclaimed the man in German.

The children hesitated, but the man encouraged them. "Go on, don't be shy, give him a hug."

The man himself then gave Elder Roberts a giant embrace. "Ach, how good to see you. You do look well," continued this stranger, now pumping Elder Roberts' hand.

"And, uh, you would be?" asked Elder Roberts as tactfully as possible.

"Ralf Keil, of course," replied Elder Roberts' new companion, pulling out his name tag and slipping it onto his jacket. "Welcome to Bielefeld!" Elder Roberts knew then this would be a great companionship.

That evening, after he and Elder Keil returned the borrowed children to a church member's home, Elder Roberts pumped his new companion for information about the ward, as he did in every city.

Elder Keil gladly obliged, giving colorful background information about each of the key players in the ward. After going through most of the ward, the new companion played his ace. "Have you heard about the Family Schumann, Elduh?" Elder Keil never fully pronounced his R's in English.

Elder Roberts answered that he had not.

"They are . . ." Elder Keil paused, searching for the most appropriate English adjectives. (Elder Keil preferred to practice his English in the apartment.) "They are in danger of being translated."

Elder Roberts laughed, impressed at Elder Keil's adept use of American missionary colloquialisms. "What's so special about them?" He asked as he greedily spread some Nutella on a piece of sturdy German bread.

"You'll see when we go to their apartment for our weekly discussion this Friday," replied Ralf Keil as he spread liverwurst on his bread, a German snack Elder Roberts still couldn't stomach.

After a few seconds, Elder Roberts realized what Elder Keil had said. "Weekly? What? Do they just get together with the missionaries every week?" asked Elder Roberts.

"Nope," responded Elder Keil as he slapped a tomato slice on his bread and took a huge bite. "With investigators," he continued with his mouth full. "Every Friday."

"I assume we bring the investigators," said Elder Roberts, who had received only five or six genuine referrals his entire mission.

"Nope," said Elder Keil, still chewing. "They do."

"These people really are in danger of being translated," admitted Elder Roberts.

Sharing the gospel in Germany was even more difficult than in the States, and Elder Roberts had never heard of such member missionaries even in the U.S. "Either that or they're nuts," he added, mostly to himself.

"They're not nuts, Elduh," persisted Elder Keil as he finished his sandwich. "You'll see. They're just wighteous."

Elder Roberts soon learned that the Schumanns were anything but crazy. The next Friday afternoon, the rain had not let up, and no one would let the missionaries in. They were soaked when they arrived at the Schumanns' apartment.

"Come in, Elders, please come in," said Brother Schumann warmly as he greeted the missionaries. "It's a pleasure to meet you, Elder," he said to Elder Roberts. "I'm Rudy Schumann."

"It's a pleasure to meet you," responded Elder Roberts. "Elder Keil tells me wonderful things about you and your wife."

Brother Schumann was quick to downplay the compliment. "You mustn't believe Elder Keil—we feed him occasionally, so he's biased."

The Schumanns' apartment was small but warm, particularly after the afternoon soaking. The elders peeled off their coats at the Schumanns' invitation and made their way into the living room.

Sister Schumann greeted the missionaries as they entered the room. "Elder Roberts, pleased to meet you. Let me introduce you to our friend, Brother Puttermark," said Sister Schumann as she gestured warmly toward an elderly gentleman hunched on the couch.

"Brother Puttermark, these are the missionaries—Elder Keil and Elder Roberts."

Sister Schumann raised her voice for the benefit of the older brother. Then she turned again to the missionaries and explained in a more hushed tone, "He lives in a rest home about twenty kilometers from here. Rudy discovered him when he was going through the ward records last month. Brother Puttermark joined the Church about ten years ago, but stopped coming shortly after his baptism when he was placed in the home."

"It's true, it's true," nodded Brother Puttermark from the couch. "Ten years, no church. Forgotten, I was. Until them." Brother Puttermark's countenance brightened with these last two words. "These people, they're good people, good people."

His gravelly voice creaked with gratitude as he spoke. His face bore the white stubble of one that won't shave well because of the wrinkles. His eyes were tired but peaceful.

"We pick him up for the weekend so he can attend church, and then we take him back Sunday afternoon," added Brother Schumann matter-of-factly. It occurred to Elder Roberts that the Schumanns didn't need to pick up Brother Puttermark on Friday night in order to attend church on Sunday.

"Would it be all right if Brother Puttermark joined our discussion tonight, Elder Roberts?" asked Sister Schumann.

"Of course," replied Elder Roberts. "We would like that."

"God be thanked, God be thanked." Brother Puttermark, Elder Roberts soon learned, was a rare German Baptist before joining the Church.

"Elders, I've prepared some cold cuts for you to eat before our discussion with Frau Lohsa," said Sister Schumann as she guided the missionaries into the kitchen and dining room area.

As the missionaries quickly stacked meats on bread and consumed the open-face sandwiches, the Schumanns asked Elder Roberts a few questions about himself and his family. The conversation then turned to the evening's discussion.

"I hope this woman accepts the gospel," sighed Sister Schumann. "We've been doing this every week for quite some time, and we haven't seen success in over a year."

Elder Roberts was a bit surprised at the remark, yet relieved to see that the Schumanns were human.

"The Lord will guide us to his sheep," Brother Schumann assured his wife and the elders. "Brother Roberts, do you know how my wife found the woman you'll be teaching tonight? She asked the Lord who we should invite over next. The prompting she received was to invite the cashier from the grocery store. Imagine that—the cashier from the grocery store! We have gone through this woman's line for five or six years, but we didn't even know her name."

"I'm afraid I would have hesitated," confessed Brother Schumann. "But not my Sandra; she is not one to doubt the promptings of the Spirit."

In Germany, thought Elder Roberts, acting on such a prompting must have required even more faith. Elder Roberts recalled the scowl he'd received during his first day of tracting when he had naively asked a woman how she was doing.

"In Germany that's viewed as a rather personal question," explained Elder Thomas later. "It's not the kind of thing you ask strangers."

"So, how did you invite her over?" asked Elder Roberts, still trying to imagine himself doing this kind of inspiration-intensive missionary work as a member one day.

"I was scared," replied Sister Schumann honestly. "The next day as we stood in line at the store, I knew I had to invite her over, but I didn't know how. I prayed, 'Please Heavenly Father, give me the courage to share the gospel with this woman, and help me know what to say.' When it came our turn to pay for our groceries, we began chatting. Then I said, 'I know this may seem unusual, but my husband and I would like to invite you over tomorrow night.' She said yes, and she seemed genuinely pleased that we'd invited her. I was so relieved."

"So does she know we're going to be here?" asked Elder Roberts, a little worried that this might look like an ambush.

"Yes," said Brother Schumann. "We had her over last night alone first. I hope you don't mind, but we thought it might be best to get to know her a little more first and then invite her back when you were here. So we did, and she's coming back tonight."

"We don't mind, Brother Schumann," said Elder Keil. "You're amazing. I've never had so many referrals from a member. And this food is excellent. So you can do it however you want."

"Did I tell you, Elder?" asked Brother Schumann of Elder Roberts. "This man's loyalties can be bought with food."

"Not just any food, though," added Elder Keil, trying to speak as if his mouth weren't full. "It has to be very good food, and this is."

"I'm not sure if I should be flattered or offended, Elder Keil," responded Sister Schumann in mock indignation.

Soon Frau Lohsa arrived. She was a rather nervous but pleasant-looking woman in her fifties, cautious in her small talk but obviously taken with the Schumanns. After introductions, everyone took their appointed seat.

Elder Roberts realized that the he and Elder Keil hadn't talked with the Schumanns about what role their hosts would play in the discussion, but his thought was interrupted by Brother Schumann's firm voice.

"Frau Lohsa, as you know, we have invited you here tonight to hear a message from our two young friends, Elder Keil and Elder Roberts." Brother Schumann paused and nodded toward the missionaries. "These two men—these missionaries—are actual messengers of the Lord Jesus Christ."

A surge of energy rushed through Elder Roberts' soul as he heard these words. Brother Schumann continued, "The words they tell you are the words the Lord wants you to hear tonight. I personally know that what they will tell you is true. I am sure of this. I am sure because I have felt it through the power of God." Brother Schumann looked directly into Frau Lohsa's eyes and spoke without hesitation.

"But please, do not take my word for it. Listen with your heart. You will feel a warmth, a peace, perhaps a calm. These feelings come from the power of the Holy Ghost and are God's way of confirming the truthfulness of the missionaries' words. When you go home tonight, pray and ask your Heavenly Father if what they have said is true."

"Pray," chimed in Brother Puttermark from the couch. "That's right; pray."

"If you pray with faith that God lives and will answer your prayer," continued Brother Schumann, "these feelings will again come into your heart." Brother Schumann then turned to Elder Roberts, the senior companion, and said simply, "Elder Roberts."

The overwhelming conviction of Brother Schumann's introduction rang in Elder Roberts' ears as he began the discussion. He was humbled and honored by Brother Schumann's powerful reminder of the role he and Elder Keil played as missionaries.

The discussion was among the most spiritually potent in which Elder Roberts had participated. The words seemed to flow naturally, even effortlessly from his lips. He felt almost as if he were watching someone else teach when he spoke.

Elder Keil quickly established rapport with Sister Lohsa. He bore strong testimony while demonstrating that this spiritual knowledge made him joyful rather than prudishly pious.

But the backbone of the discussion was clearly the frequent testimony of Brother and Sister Schumann. Elder Roberts was amazed at how boldly they spoke to this person whose name they had not known three days before. He was also impressed that as forceful as their testimonies had been, they were always couched in such love that they were not overpowering.

Next week, Elder Roberts thought at the conclusion of the discussion, I'll make sure to ask the Schumanns what they want us to do.

✧ ✧ ✧

May, June and July were brutal but exhilarating months for Elder Jon Prentice. In fact, years later he would still remember that summer as one of the best seasons of his life.

Mimicking his senior companion's every move, he began the day with forty belly busters and forty pushups to the accompaniment of Beethoven's Seventh Symphony.

"Classical calisthenics," Elder Hunter had explained as he turned on the music. "I see you're a Beethoven fan yourself."

"Not exactly," J.P. had said sheepishly. "I'm afraid you can't always judge a CD by its jacket."

Elder Hunter had just smiled and shaken his head slightly. "Let's hear the first discussion," he asked firmly as soon as Elder Prentice stepped out of the shower on the first day of Elder Prentice's new training regimen. J.P. obliged, paraphrasing the discussion as had his companions in Bremerhaven.

After the first concept, Elder Hunter interrupted with a question. "Can you do it word for word?"

"Well, probably," replied J.P. as he began shaving. "But you don't, do you? I prefer the customized approach."

"Actually, I pretty much give it word for word, at least as the basic framework for my discussion. I do add some things as the Spirit directs. But I've made the discussions' words my own, so hopefully it doesn't sound memorized.

"I've just found that mastering the discussions as written is a great way to learn the language. Once you get down the grammar and word patterns in the discussions, it's easier to speak properly when you're improvising. And believe me, it matters to these Germans."

Not until Elder Hunter began correcting him did Elder Prentice realize just how much he had been abusing the German language. While getting dressed, making meals, or cleaning in the apartment, Elder Prentice spewed out discussions in German. Out of the apartment, Elder Hunter and Elder Prentice spoke nothing but German.

Elder Hunter was polite but merciless in his ongoing critique, which Elder Prentice had invited. For the first few days, he could rarely utter a sentence without some correction from his senior companion. But by the end of the second week, he was beginning to master the discussions word for word. By the end of his fourth week with Elder Hunter, proper grammar was creeping into most of his speech.

From the first discussion he taught with Elder Hunter, Elder Prentice was taken with his companion's teaching style, which really was an extension of his finding style. What struck him most of all about Elder Hunter's approach on the doors and in discussions was his honesty and boldness.

There was no embarrassment or effort on Elder Hunter's part to postpone disclosing the true purpose of the missionaries' message. To the contrary, beginning in conversations with potential investigators at the doors and in the streets, Elder Hunter spoke candidly.

"We're messengers of the Lord Jesus Christ," Elder Hunter often said in a tone that was somehow both convincing and meek. "We have a message that will change your life. May we come in?"

This was a radical departure from the proselyting philosophy of Elder Lafferty, who—Elder Prentice now realized—had unfortunately been the major influence to date on his own tracting and teaching style.

The Texan's lowest-common-denominator approach involved saying as little as possible at the doors that was in any way controversial or objectionable. "Build on the beliefs we share, and don't throw your pearls before swine," Elder Lafferty had explained. "Why scare 'em away before ya even get in the door?"

Buoyed by this rationale, Elder Lafferty's favorite approach was to suggest that he and his companions were American students on a sabbatical of sorts, and they were exchanging opinions with people in the neighborhood, wondering how people felt about the importance of family.

Running a close second among Elder Lafferty's tracting techniques was not a canned dialogue, but a game. The first companion would throw out a word—the more unexpected and seemingly unrelated to religion, the better—just before the other companion began his door approach.

The second companion's challenge was to work the word into his dialogue. The result was rarely an inspired door approach and often missionaries who had difficulty maintaining their composure.

Elder Hunter appeared almost saddened when Elder Prentice told him of Elder Lafferty's approaches. "It's tough when you speak to so many people in a day. But instead of viewing each door as just one of dozens of doors I'll knock on that day, I try to think of the door approach, of the conversation we're about to have, as one of maybe two or three real encounters this person will have in their entire life with representatives of the Lord," explained Elder Hunter.

"I sort of imagine this person's guardian angel up there, rooting for us, praying for us, waiting nervously as this guy gets his first real shot at hearing the gospel. Our job is to find some way in those few seconds we speak with the people to let them feel the electricity of the Spirit, to let them know we're talking about something that's more meaningful than anything they've ever heard.

"I don't want anyone to miss out on their chance to hear the gospel in this life because I was trying to entertain my companion." Elder Hunter stopped, as if he'd said too much. It was the most critical comment Elder Prentice ever heard his companion make.

Ironically, some of the words Elder Hunter used in his door approaches were quite similar to words used by Elder Greisel. But that's where any resemblance in the two missionaries' styles ended. Elder Greisel had frequently warned investigators that he would be called on at Judgment Day to testify that he had delivered the gospel message to them, but they had rejected it. J.P. suspected that if this actually happened, Elder

Greisel might throw in an "I told you so" for good measure. Elder Hunter, on the other hand, would cry.

❖ ❖ ❖

During the last week in July—his fourth week together with Elder Sampson—Elder Hawthorne experienced a first. He and Elder Sampson found a complete family while tracting, and the whole family was interested in the gospel. Herr Ulrich was a portly, distinguished looking man in his late thirties or early forties. Frau Ulrich sang in her church choir together with her fifteen-year-old daughter, Simona, who also participated weekly in a Bible study group.

The youngest family member, three-year-old Martin, had enjoyed rolling up Elder Sampson's tie and then letting it go. By the end of the discussion, he was asleep in his mother's arms. The Ulrichs were a happily wedded couple with two lovely children, and they were religious. This was a rare combination in northern Germany.

Many already religious people were somewhat bored with the first few concepts of the first discussion, since the subjects were already familiar to them. But with the Ulrichs, Elder Hawthorne thought the discussion of Heavenly Father and Jesus Christ felt crisp and fresh.

Herr Ulrich's ears seemed to perk up as the missionaries discussed prophets generally. As Elder Sampson told a condensed version of the Joseph Smith story, both Herr and Frau Ulrich were on the edge of their seats. "What would it mean for you if this story we have just told you is true?" Elder Hawthorne asked Frau Ulrich.

She looked down at her husband's hand, clasped in hers, as she paused before answering. "It would mean your church is led by Jesus Christ."

Elder Hawthorne was shocked, since the fuller explanation of the Restoration did not come for another two discussions. "Yes," he agreed. "That is what it means."

Both elders felt the Spirit strongly as the discussion concluded. Elder Hawthorne asked Herr Ulrich what sort of feelings he had in his heart.

"I feel unusually at peace," said Herr Ulrich. "I feel calm and at peace."

"These feelings are the feelings we mentioned at the beginning of our discussion," reminded Elder Hawthorne. "They come from the Holy Ghost and are God's way of confirming the truthfulness of our words. Remember this feeling," added Elder Hawthorne. "After we have been gone for a while, see if you notice a difference."

Making this kind of bold statement was exceptionally difficult for Elder Hawthorne. He had always let Elder Smith or Elder Roberts do it when he could. But in their absence, he did what he could.

Elder Sampson then reviewed the basic steps of prayer with the family and asked Herr Ulrich if he would mind saying the closing prayer.

From his hesitation it was evident that he had not prayed aloud before with his family.

"Why don't one of you offer the prayer," suggested Herr Ulrich. "You're more experienced in this than I am."

"No, Lord like if you pray," assured Elder Sampson with his fledgling German. "It's simple. Begin, 'Father in Heaven. Closing, 'In name of Jesus Christ," and between talk, okay?" With that Elder Sampson and Elder Hawthorne bowed their heads, not wanting to give Herr Ulrich another chance to back out. Simona smiled at her dad and bowed her head, as did her mother. Herr Ulrich had no choice but to pray.

"Um, dear God," he began slowly. "We thank thee . . . for the pleasant discussion we had tonight, for Jesus, and for what he has done for us. And we thank thee for sending these two young men to teach us. Please bless us that we can know thy will and obey it. In the name of Jesus Christ. Amen." Herr Ulrich looked up rather sheepishly, and Frau Ulrich and Simona positively beamed.

The elders would have loved to languish in the warmth of the Ulrich home for another hour, but they were careful not to overstay their welcome. Elder Hawthorne remembered President Cook's advice. "Have some small talk before the discussion—get to know the people a little. But never forget that you're messengers of the Lord. Don't diminish the glow from a great discussion by spending forty-five minutes talking about or sports other things after you're done. Leave them with the taste of your powerful testimonies still fresh in their hearts."

President Cook frequently mixed his metaphors, but the missionaries understood what he meant. So Elder Hawthorne and Elder Sampson had made another appointment and excused themselves over the family's objections.

In companionship prayer that night, the elders jointly offered their thanks to the Lord for helping them find such a wonderful family. "Please bless us with the faith we need," asked Elder Hawthorne, "so that we can teach the family with the Spirit . . ." Elder Hawthorne paused. He hesitated to get his hopes up or appear naive. But he knew that without faith he and Elder Sampson could not do their part. He completed the thought: "so that they might be converted and join the Church." A man like Brother Ulrich would make a great priesthood leader, and his family could become the strength of the ward.

✧ ✧ ✧

It was a sizzling Saturday in August, and Minden's pedestrian zone was abuzz with shoppers, mimes, musicians, political activists—and two American missionaries. Elder Prentice approached people with the same intensity that had filled him since late spring, but now he was actually able to speak German reasonably well, which proved remarkably useful.

Along with the language, Elder Prentice had learned most of Elder Hunter's best approaches. Moreover, in the last two weeks, he had been teaching his junior companion about perhaps the most useful but underutilized missionary tool of all—following the Spirit.

Like an expert fisherman, Elder Hunter cast his line not only frequently but in carefully selected spots. Soon J.P. was praying more frequently and intensely about whom to approach and what to say.

The first man Elder Prentice approached that afternoon dismissed him quickly. A year earlier he would have decided it was time for an hour-long ice cream break. Two months earlier he would have immediately stopped the next pedestrian who came into sight. But now that he was experimenting with the Spirit, he stopped and surveyed the square for a moment.

Three bearded students smoked on a park bench as they argued about something. An older gentleman escorting an immaculately groomed poodle walked briskly through the heart of the square. A tramp foraged through a garbage can. A middle-aged couple strolled past shop windows. Strangely, Elder Prentice felt perhaps he should speak with the tramp.

The thought was so contrary to his own personal inclinations that J.P. assumed it must have come from some external source. From Elder Hunter, he had learned to heed virtually every thought not inconsistent with gospel teachings. Reluctantly, Elder Prentice made his way over to the garbage can.

"Um, excuse me sir," interrupted the Californian.

The tramp continued pawing through the trash container without looking up. Finally, he paused momentarily, but not for J.P. "Ah, pizza!"

When the hobo pulled the half-eaten slice of pizza out of the garbage and to his mouth, Elder Prentice saw to his surprise that the man was only about twenty years old. The similarities between missionary and his contact ended there, however.

Elder Prentice's blond hair was short and fashionably styled. The scavenger sported a head of long, brown hair that sat in a jumble of loose, natural curls. It could not have been washed or combed for over a week.

While Elder Prentice stood out from the crowd in his white shirt, tie, and pressed slacks, his contact was distinguished from other pedestrians by a pair of rugged but worn wool trousers and a dirty long-sleeved denim shirt. Neither of these items of clothing were a good match for the August sun.

Elder Prentice decided that he had no more promising alternative, so he followed through with what he had first feared was simply his own imagination, not a legitimate prompting of the Spirit. He hoped to improve at recognizing the Spirit with time.

"Excuse me, sir, but do you believe there is a Supreme Being who gives his creations commandments?" The word "commandments" in this approach often drew objections from younger people with whom Elder Prentice spoke.

"But of course," answered the street person without hesitation.

"Oh," replied J.P. After a moment he pressed, "How do you think he conveys these commandments to us?"

"Through the Holy Scripture and through his Spirit, naturally," responded the man casually between bites.

Most people the missionary approached seemed surprised to be asked a question about religion, but this man answered J.P. as effortlessly as if he had just been asked directions to City Hall.

"I see," said Elder Prentice, who had to figure out where to go next with this approach, since no one had ever answered his second question so astutely. Finally, in what he later recognized was an effort to shake his shabby street contact, he asked, "Are you willing to keep all of God's commandments?"

"Yes, I am," replied the man as he wiped his mouth with the unused corner of a napkin he'd also found in the trash can. "That's why I'm here."

Mental case, thought Elder Prentice immediately. At least once a month he had a fascinating discussion with someone who asked remarkably insightful, childlike questions but who proved to be receiving medical treatment for their mentally unstable condition. Out of the corner of his eye, Elder Prentice saw that Elder Hunter had just completed a conversation, so he signaled for help.

Elder Hunter strolled over and approached Elder Prentice and the tramp as if he were meeting a visiting dignitary. "Hello, my name's Elder Hunter," he said as he offered the man his hand. "I'm Elder Prentice's companion."

The man's mouth was full with a bite of an apple he'd produced from his pocket, so he quickly choked down his morsel of food while wiping his hand with what was left of the napkin. "Leo, my name's Leo," offered the man as he shook hands with Elder Hunter. "Two by two, that's even scriptural," Leo commented as he sized up the two Americans with seeming approval. "Very nice."

"Yes, we're missionaries, called by the Lord Jesus Christ and sent into the world, two-by-two, just as his disciples were when He lived on earth," explained Elder Hunter, picking up on Leo's comment.

"So am I," responded Leo without any trace of pride. "Except for that two-by-two part. That would be nice."

As Elder Prentice tried to figure out how to shake this nut case, his companion seemed to be taking a different approach. "Here," said Elder Hunter, pointing to a vacant bench. "Do you mind if we sit down while you tell us what you mean?"

Leo was happy to have an audience. He explained enthusiastically how he had begun reading the Bible for no apparent reason when he was seventeen. The book fascinated him beyond anything he could have imagined. By age nineteen he had read the book four times. As the Savior's teachings lodged deeper in his heart, he came to understand the importance of sharing them.

"I just don't see how you can keep your mouth shut about it, if you believe Jesus when he said there is no way back to the Father except by him. Unless you don't much care about whether anyone else makes it back to the Father, I suppose."

Finally, Leo had felt impelled to go into the world without purse or script to preach the word. Having no money, he walked. Beginning in February, he wandered through Germany and eventually decided he could do the most good in the Balkans.

"I saw all the unrest, all the hate, all the killings on TV, and I thought those people could benefit the most from the peace Christ's word brings."

Leo was ultimately placed in a refugee camp by one of the ethnic factions in the former Yugoslavia. "I never could keep those groups of people straight or figure out how they got started hating each other," Leo explained. He preached "Christ's word," as he called it, to anyone within earshot. When the guards decided they could endure his sermons no longer, they put him in a truck headed for Austria and told him they'd shoot him if he ever returned.

"Of course, that's not what kept me from going back," insisted Leo as the missionaries listened with fascination. "I'm not afraid of dying. In fact, I was thinking about heading for Jerusalem, hoping I might be one of the two prophets who get killed in the streets. That would be phenomenal, don't you think?" Leo's eyes sparkled as relished the thought for a moment. "But the Spirit told me it was time for me to come back. I don't know why."

"I think I do," offered Elder Hunter. For the next hour and half, Elder Hunter and Elder Prentice taught Leo the principles contained in the first discussion. Many individuals who already had a religious foundation felt patronized by the concepts they already believed and defensive about the ones they did not. Not Leo.

When given the sneak preview of the Book of Mormon, Leo would not let go of the subject until Elder Prentice finally gave him a copy of the book. Like a deprived child given his first toy, Leo could focus on nothing else once he had the book in his hands.

Elder Hunter ultimately gave up on trying to teach him any more that night, so he gave Leo a brochure that contained the Church's address and meeting times. Leo nodded without looking up from the book.

"I wonder if we'll ever see Leo again," wondered Elder Hunter aloud as he and Elder Prentice rode their bikes home that night.

"I bet one day we see his picture in the Church News under new stake presidents," responded Elder Prentice, only half joking.

"He is a remarkable individual," agreed Elder Hunter. "He would have gone into the wilderness to hear John the Baptist."

The missionaries spent the rest of the ride home marveling at Leo's understanding of the Bible. Although they hoped Leo's story would one day have a remarkable ending, they did not anticipate being part of it.

19
Water Up the Nose

The second discussion had gone as well as the first with Sister Lohsa, who attended church at the invitation of the Schumanns, who also provided her a ride.

"This is almost like cheating," commented Elder Roberts to his companion after the second discussion.

"I know," agreed Elder Keil with a grin. "President Cook always thinks his zone leaders are doing great work down here. But all they have to do is show up at Schumanns."

❖ ❖ ❖

Before the second discussion, Elder Hawthorne and Elder Sampson visited the Ulrichs twice. Almost like a missionary training film produced by the Church, the family greeted the missionaries enthusiastically at the door and invited them in to say a word of prayer.

With each contact, the missionaries' hopes rose. Even the usually guarded Elder Hawthorne found himself imagining the Ulrichs in baptismal clothing.

For their second discussion with the Ulrich family, Elder Hawthorne and Elder Sampson brought along a fellowshipping member, Brother Moelke. Brother Moelke was about fifty, but it was the first time he had ever gone out with the missionaries. He was rather bashful and nervous about the whole notion of teaching strangers about religion, but the Ulrichs soon made him feel welcome in their home.

After a few minutes of sharing pleasantries and nibbling sweets, Brother Ulrich cleared his throat and said, "Well, we're happy to have you in our home tonight. I think we should begin with a word of prayer. Would you offer it, Simona?"

Elder Roberts and Elder Keil exchanged muted looks of amazement; Brother Moelke assumed such behavior was normal for investigators.

The presentation of the plan of salvation went even better than the first discussion. As it came to an end, the elders found their faith mushrooming. Brother Moelke had been great as he humbly added testimony when appropriate. He even seemed to enjoy explaining the resurrection, the concept that had worried him so much when the elders asked him earlier in the week if he would teach it.

After they left the Ulrichs' apartment, the missionaries and Brother Moelke shared their excitement as they walked toward his apartment. Brother Moelke talked with much more animation than usual, and he seemed to feel that special bond that comes from working together in a cause of eternal importance.

The three anticipated next week's discussion with special hope. It had been years since such a family had joined the Church in Bielefeld, and they all knew how important this next visit would be—if one could call something of such magnitude a visit.

✧ ✧ ✧

Elder Prentice wasn't sure whether he was more pleased or embarrassed when Leo showed up at church the next Sunday. His clothes were no cleaner and his hair no less unkempt than when the missionaries had taught him earlier the week in the pedestrian zone. When he first saw Leo walk through the door, J.P.'s first reaction was to scan the members' faces.

Elder Hunter immediately joined Leo, threw an arm around his shoulders, and pulled Leo toward the president of the elders quorum. While Elder Prentice schemed about how to get Leo into the bathroom for a good wash before he did any more damage, Elder Hunter began introducing Leo to ward members as "a remarkable follower of Christ."

Some of the members undoubtedly shared Elder Prentice's apprehension about the unusual investigator, but if they did, they didn't show it.

After church, the two missionaries taught Leo the second and third discussions. Leo had read through the book of Mosiah and was full of questions about the Book of Mormon and Joseph Smith. When told the young prophet had been martyred, Leo seemed in awe. "That's perfect, just perfect. It makes it all the better," exclaimed Leo slowly.

While the discussions went as well as any Elder Prentice had ever taught, he was still surprised when his senior companion challenged Leo to baptism. The missionaries didn't even know the man's last name.

For forty-five minutes Leo asked questions about the significance of baptism, the structure of the Church, and the obligations of its members. "What about ties?" pressed Leo. "Are they a requirement?"

Even Elder Hunter seemed unsure of how to answer this question. "I suppose, well, no, ties are not a requirement," Elder Hunter finally concluded. "But we like to wear our best clothes when we attend church to show respect for the Lord."

"You mean the Lord likes ties?" snorted Leo. "What about humility? What about sack-cloth and ashes?"

"Oh, we do that every third Sunday," joked Elder Prentice, hoping to divert Leo's attention. Leo laughed.

Elder Hunter took the initiative. "Being baptized a member of The Church of Jesus Christ of Latter-day Saints will change your life forever. It will bring you an even greater level of happiness than you've experienced so far in life. And it will mean embracing a . . . a different lifestyle, a different culture. Things like sustaining and obeying church leaders might not be easy for you, but it will be part of the commitment you make when you enter the waters of baptism."

"Jesus Christ is my church leader," answered Leo. "I follow no master but him."

"Unless he asked you to follow an earthly master, right?" interjected Elder Prentice.

"I suppose," conceded Leo begrudgingly. "But I'd be like Paul, telling Peter how it was, no matter how long he'd been an apostle."

The missionaries made some progress but were unable to commit Leo to baptism. Finally, Elder Hunter decided to try to arrange to meet Leo again somewhere to teach him the remaining discussions.

"There's something you should know," announced Leo. "I feel the time has come for me to finish my journey and return to Neumuenster. I'll be leaving tomorrow. Do you have faith brothers there?"

Elder Hunter told Leo that Neumuenster had a chapel, a ward, and missionaries. He gave Leo the number of the mission office and encouraged him to call for the address of the chapel when he arrived.

After committing Leo to completing the Book of Mormon and visiting the Church in Neumuenster, Elder Hunter gave Leo a big hug. To his surprise, Elder Prentice found himself hugging Leo as well. It was the last time he ever saw Leo.

✦ ✦ ✦

With many investigators, issuing the baptismal challenge on the second or third discussion felt like a stretch. But with the Schumanns leading the charge, Elder Roberts felt as if he could have challenged Sister Lohsa to baptism on the second discussion, or maybe even the first. Because of the Schumanns' boldness and candor, Sister Lohsa was not in the least surprised when Elder Roberts asked her early in the third discussion if she would follow the Savior and be baptized.

"Ah, baptism, yes, baptism," chimed in Brother Puttermark, who beamed at the mention of the word. Elder Roberts had become accustomed to Brother Puttermark's affirmations and was almost wishing he had a Brother Puttermark with him and Elder Keil for all their discussions.

"How do you, well, how do you baptize people in your church?" asked Sister Lohsa, seeming perplexed.

Elder Roberts hesitated, unsure of what Sister Lohsa was getting at. Elder Keil jumped in with the answer. "We baptize by immersion, just as Jesus Christ did."

"Immersion," answered Sister Lohsa with some apprehension. "Oh."

Elder Roberts assumed Sister Lohsa doubted the propriety of baptizing through immersion, so he quickly opened to some New Testament scriptures that suggested Christ himself was baptized by immersion.

"See, here it says that Christ came forth out of the water . . ." began Elder Roberts.

Sister Schumann cut him off politely. "One moment, elders," she said, slowing the missionaries down with one hand and touching Sister Lohsa's knee with the other. "I don't think Sister Lohsa is questioning whether Christ was baptized by immersion. I think her concern is more practical. Am I right?"

"Well, yes," confessed Sister Lohsa sheepishly. "I just hate getting water up my nose."

The missionaries breathed a collective sigh of relief. Brother Puttermark smiled and nodded, "Ah, up the nose, yes, up the nose."

"Don't you worry about a thing," assured Sister Schumann. "Here, Elder Keil, let's show her how it works." Elder Keil and Sister Schumann then demonstrated how Sister Lohsa would be baptized, with a heavy emphasis on how she would be able to hold her nose.

The demonstration seemed to alleviate Sister Lohsa's fears. "So, will you follow the Savior and be baptized?" asked Elder Roberts again.

"As long as I can hold my nose, yes," replied Sister Lohsa. Once she'd said it, she seemed to feel better. "Yes," she said again, looking now directly at Sister and Brother Schumann, "yes I will be baptized."

After Sister Lohsa left that evening, the missionaries, the Schumanns, and Brother Puttermark celebrated the good news. The missionaries thanked the Schumanns profusely and gave them all the credit. The Schumanns thanked the missionaries and gave the Lord all the credit. Brother Puttermark agreed with everyone and kept mumbling about baptism and holding the nose.

Sister Schumann cut the celebration short by reminding everyone that Sister Lohsa still had a long way to go. "Remember, we haven't taught her about the commandments yet. I have the feeling that she will be able to accept the Word of Wisdom without much trouble, but I'm worried about tithing. I think that may be our big challenge. We should start praying now for help in teaching her about tithing."

"Ah, prayer," exclaimed Brother Puttermark as he immediately but slowly got down on his knees by the coffee table. Elder Roberts wasn't sure whether Sister Schumann had meant the group should say a prayer together at that very moment, but Elder Keil and Sister Schumann quickly joined Brother Puttermark at the coffee table. As Elder Roberts and Brother Schumann knelt, Brother Schumann asked his wife if she would offer the prayer.

"Dear Heavenly Father, we are so very thankful that thou hast led us to the wonderful Sister Lohsa. Please bless and protect her from the influences of the adversary as she prepares to enter the waters of baptism. Please bless her with faith and an obedient heart so that she can accept all thy commandments. Bless us to know how to help her. And please bless these two wonderful missionaries, Elder Keil and Elder Roberts. We thank thee that they chose to serve thee on missions and that they prepared for their missions well. Please bless their mothers and fathers for having taught them so well. In the name of Jesus Christ. Amen."

❖ ❖ ❖

When the evening appointed for the third discussion with the Ulrichs arrived, Elder Hawthorne felt more apprehension than he had since riding the train to Rendsburg on his last transfer. This would be the first time he taught a third discussion—at least one with some real promise—as a senior companion. He did not want to be in charge. He wished desperately that he were accompanied by Elder Roberts or Elder Smith rather than Elder Sampson, who had a good heart but no more confidence than Elder Hawthorne.

When Elder Hawthorne and Elder Sampson arrived, Brother Moelke awaited them on the street. They greeted each other warmly in the hushed voices of men discussing something important. In Elder Sampson's pack was a single copy of the Book of Mormon.

The Ulrich family again greeted the missionaries and Brother Moelke warmly. Brother Ulrich had purchased his wife a very nice edition of the Bible for her birthday, and he blushed as she spoke about how happy it had made her.

After politely devouring a couple of Sister Ulrich's marvelous German pastries, the missionaries shifted the conversation to the reading assignment. As usual, the Ulrichs had read the assigned chapters in the Bible as well as the brochures the elders had given them. Their questions showed that they had digested the materials as thoroughly as the missionaries consumed Sister Ulrich's treats.

Finally Brother Ulrich began the discussion by welcoming everyone again and then offering the prayer himself. "Dear Father in Heaven," he began. "We thank thee that we are able to gather this night to discuss thee and thy Son. We thank thee for sending thy Son into the world to atone for our sins that we might have the opportunity to return to thee. We also thank thee for these missionaries, thy messengers, whom thou has sent to us. Please bless them in their work, and bless us that we might have an enlightening discussion this evening. Please let thy Spirit be with us again as it has been in the past, we pray in the name of Jesus Christ. Amen." Those in the room assented to the words of the prayer with their own reverent "amens."

As the missionaries and Brother Moelke taught the Ulrichs of the Restoration, the Spirit was as strong as it had been in the first two discussions. After Elder Hawthorne told the story of the First Vision, he asked Simona what it meant if the story he had just told was true.

Simona hesitated and turned to her father. "It means we're in the wrong church," declared Brother Ulrich without animosity. Elder Hawthorne was amazed at how many people could hear the story of the First Vision without grasping this point.

"Yes, it means that The Church of Jesus Christ of Latter-day Saints is the only church established and led by the Lord," affirmed Elder Hawthorne. "We invite you to pray and find out for yourselves that the story we just told is true."

Elder Hawthorne thought about rolling right into the baptismal challenge, but decided not to. Somehow he didn't want to rush things with this family. He felt as if he and Elder Sampson were building a house of cards, and he didn't want to risk knocking it over just yet.

When Elder Sampson explained the Book of Mormon, he handed a copy of it to Sister Ulrich. She handled it carefully, even reverentially, and then passed it to her husband. "I feel a good spirit when I hold this book," said the head of the Ulrich home.

Elder Hawthorne, Elder Sampson, and Brother Moelke were euphoric when they left the discussion. They had introduced the principles at the core of the Restoration, and the family had not balked. "That, um, that went pretty well, didn't it?" asked Brother Moelke.

"Yes," answered Elder Hawthorne with a smile. "Very well."

* * *

The missionaries and the Schumanns had fasted in preparation for the commandments discussion, but the missionaries were still nervous when the appointed evening arrived. The first three commandments went smoothly. Even the Word of Wisdom seemed simple, given the anticipated problems with tithing.

Brother Schumann testified about how he quit drinking the day the missionaries had taught him about the Word of Wisdom, even though he'd been drinking ten bottles of beer a day. Sister Lohsa confessed that giving up coffee would be simple by comparison, and she promised to do so.

Elder Keil drew the assignment to explain tithing. "Ach, that's what I feared!" exclaimed Sister Lohsa. "Ten percent! That's impossible. That's simply impossible." Sister Lohsa's objection was neither obstinate nor mean. It was merely an exasperated statement of fact. She could not imagine, she explained, how she could get by on her fixed income with ten percent less than she was currently earning.

The missionaries barely uttered a word for the next thirty minutes. Brother and Sister Schumann alternately told of miracle upon miracle from their own lives involving the law of tithing. Finally, Brother Schumann moved in for the commitment.

"Dear Sister Lohsa, do you believe there is a God?"

"But of course, Brother Schumann," answered the grocery store checker who by now had become fast friends with the Schumanns. "You know I do."

"Do you believe he created this world?"

"But surely," affirmed Sister Lohsa, looking almost offended.

"Ah, the beautiful world, the beautiful world," chimed in Brother Puttermark, whom Elder Roberts had almost forgotten.

"Do you believe he is all-powerful?" continued Brother Schumann.

"Yes, he most certainly is." Sister Lohsa said this with conviction.

"Good," approved Brother Schumann. "Because there is a God, who is our Heavenly Father, and he created this world through his Son, and he is all-powerful. Now, do you believe the Book of Mormon is the word of God, or did Joseph Smith make it up?

"No, Joseph Smith would not have done that," replied Sister Lohsa almost indignantly. "He received the plates from an angel."

"An angel, the angel on the temple," echoed Brother Puttermark.

"How do you know this?" pressed Brother Schumann. "Because we told you?"

"Well, yes, I suppose . . . " offered a confused Sister Lohsa.

"Is that all?" demanded Brother Schumann.

"Yes, well, I mean, no, no it's not," declared Sister Lohsa, regaining her footing. "I know it's true because I asked Heavenly Father, and I got a warm feeling in my heart. That's how I know it's true."

"I see," nodded Brother Schumann, finally allowing himself a smile. "Now, Sister Lohsa, do you believe God revealed the law of tithing to Joseph Smith?"

"Well, yes, if it's in that book," explained Sister Lohsa, pointing to her triple combination, "then I guess I do."

"Yes, the good book, the good book," added Brother Puttermark, clutching his Bible.

"Do you believe God keeps his promises?"

"Certainly."

"Then Sister Lohsa, do you believe God will ever let you go hungry if you keep his commandment to pay tithing?"

Sister Lohsa looked almost sheepish at this point. "No, I don't."

"So will you keep the law of tithing?" Elder Roberts squeezed his hands together tightly as he waited for Sister Lohsa's response.

"Yes," committed Sister Lohsa, looking up at Sister Schumann and her husband. "Yes, I will. I don't know how I will get by, but I will."

"The Lord will take care of you, my dear Sister Lohsa," instructed Brother Schumann. "And if you ever lack for anything you need, you come to us and we'll take care of you. The Lord keeps his promises, Sister Lohsa, and so do we. So do we."

"That you do," nodded Brother Puttermark, his eyes glistening. "That you do."

❖ ❖ ❖

The Ulrich family called to cancel the next appointment because relatives from out of town came to visit. In the time leading up to the rescheduled appointment, Elder Hawthorne and Elder Sampson debated whether to challenge the family to baptism at the next discussion. To the missionaries' dismay, the argument proved to be moot.

"Come on in, brothers," said Brother Ulrich as he greeted the missionaries and Brother Moelke with a smile. The father of the dream investigator family somehow seemed more distant than usual, despite his outward cheeriness. "Please, sit down. We have something to tell you."

The entire family squeezed together next to Brother Ulrich on the couch. Sister Ulrich grabbed her husband's hand and squeezed it tightly. With her other hand, she clutched a paperback book.

"We've been doing a lot of thinking these last few weeks, and we want to thank you for all you've done to raise our religious consciousness," began Brother Ulrich. "Until you came, we were religious, or at least I was religious, out of habit, I suppose. You have gotten us thinking, questioning, and for that we thank you."

Elder Hawthorne's heart sank. Sister Ulrich moved even closer to Brother Ulrich.

"We've done a lot of soul-searching and praying these last two weeks in particular, and we've been speaking with our minister . . . . We've been reading a book he's given us, and it's helped us find Jesus Christ, to comprehend his grace, to . . . to understand just how simple his word is. We have accepted him as our Savior." Brother Ulrich clutched his wife's arm with his other hand. As he finished his well-rehearsed statement, he squeezed Sister Ulrich's arm.

"We are so truly grateful to you for visiting us and taking an interest in us," explained Sister Ulrich almost apologetically. "We want you to have this." Sister Ulrich held out the family's new guide to spirituality, a book by a theologian's name the missionaries did not recognize. "This will show you just how simple it really is."

Elder Hawthorne was too stunned to respond diplomatically. "Have you . . . did you . . . I mean, have you read any of the Book of Mormon?"

"Well, no," answered Brother Ulrich, struggling to maintain his cheery and confident veneer. "Please, don't be offended, but once we read this book," he continued, taking the book from his wife's hand and grasping it tightly, just as he had clutched the Book of Mormon the first night the missionaries gave it to him, "once we read this book, we saw we no longer needed to read your Book of Mormon."

The rest of the brief discussion was a blur for Elder Hawthorne. The missionaries were gone by eight-fifteen, but Elder Hawthorne had no heart for working any more that night. Brother Moelke did his best to comfort the distraught elders, but to no avail.

"What we done could have?" asked Elder Sampson in German as the companions ambled toward their apartment.

"I don't know," muttered Elder Hawthorne uncharacteristically in English. "I don't know. They were so good, so good. I don't know."

As the numbness from the shock began to wear off later that night, Elder Hawthorne managed to come up with several explanations of what might have gone wrong. His conduct or decisions were at the core of every explanation.

"We shouldn't have waited so long to challenge them. We should have challenged and committed them when the Spirit was there on the second or third discussion. Why did I wait so long?"

Elder Sampson did his best to console his senior companion, but Elder Hawthorne was now more sure than ever of his inability to lead a companionship. Without an Elder Smith or Elder Roberts at his side—or better yet, in front of him—he did not see how he could lead anyone into the waters of baptism.

20
Where Are the Porters?

"So, how's it going, Elder?" asked President Cook in Elder Prentice's monthly interview in the last week of August.

For most of his mission Elder Prentice had dreaded the monthly interview. President Cook never confronted J.P., but Elder Prentice always feared sure his mission president could see through the façade. Of course, J.P. never actually lied to President Cook. He just answered each question vaguely and did everything he could to avoid looking President Cook in the eye.

"It's going very well," he answered, finally able to look President Cook in the eyes.

"I know," smiled President Cook. "I know." President Cook slapped Elder Prentice on the knee and added, "Welcome to the Germany Hamburg Mission."

Now Elder Prentice glanced away for a moment and swallowed hard. "Sorry it took me so long to show up."

"What counts is that you're here now," assured President Cook. "You've been getting tutored by the best, you know."

"Yes, I know," answered Elder Prentice. "Thanks." Together with Elder Hunter he had participated in a baptism each month he had been in Minden.

"Soon we'll see what you can do on your own." President Cook nodded at Elder Prentice slightly, and then embraced him for the monthly hug. "The Lord loves you, Elder. Give it all you've got for him as you come down the stretch, okay?"

"Yeah," said J.P., his answer muffled by President Cook's polyester-wool suit. "I will. I will."

The next week, Elder Hunter was called to be a zone leader in Hamburg. Eighteen months after entering the MTC, Elder Prentice became a senior companion. The day they parted, Elder Hunter gave Elder Prentice Beethoven's Seventh, which Elder Prentice had actually come to love.

"You've earned it, Elder," commented Elder Hunter. It was one of the greatest compliments Jon Prentice had ever received.

❖ ❖ ❖

When the phone rang in Elder Hawthorne's apartment at ten p.m., Elder Hawthorne was troubled. On his mission, as at home, Elder Hawthorne had not been a heavy telephone user. He generally got by without calling people much, and they didn't often need to call Elder Hawthorne, especially at ten o'clock.

When he heard the president's voice on the other end of the line, Elder Hawthorne was even more concerned. He could not conceal his alarm. "What's wrong, President?" he asked without returning the president's greeting.

"Nothing's wrong, Elder," chuckled President Cook. "I just called to let you know I'd like you to serve as district leader."

"But . . . but President . . . " began Elder Hawthorne.

"Don't worry, I'm going to keep you right there in Rendsburg," assured President Cook, not addressing the concern Elder Hawthorne was going to raise. "You'll do great, Elder. The Lord loves you, and so do I. If you need anything, just call me. Good night."

✦ ✦ ✦

The chapel was full for the baptismal service of Sister Lohsa and three other investigators who were joining the Bielefeld Ward of The Church of Jesus Christ of Latter-day Saints. The other set of elders in Bielefeld had taught two of the other investigators, and Elder Roberts and Elder Keil had taught the third. Each of the four converts were solid, and the ward was brimming with enthusiasm. The previous Sunday the Bishop had announced plans for a new building because the ward had grown so much.

Elder Roberts sat next to Sister Lohsa, who was flanked by the Schumanns on the other side. For the opening hymn, the congregation sang "Nearer, My God, to Thee," a hymn Elder Roberts had never really fully appreciated. But singing together with Sister Lohsa, the Schumanns, Elder Keil, and a true congregation, Elder Roberts was flooded with emotion as he pondered the hymn's simple message.

Brother Schumann radiated joy and solemnity as he stood, dressed in white, with his arm to the square in the baptismal font. Sister Lohsa squeezed her nose and shut her eyes throughout the entire baptismal prayer, just to make sure she was not caught unprepared.

After Sister Lohsa came out of the water, she effusively embraced an embarrassed Brother Schumann briefly before hurrying up the stairs of the baptismal font into the open arms of Sister Schumann. Sister Schumann was drenched by the time the new member of the church finished hugging the person to whom she felt an overwhelming debt of gratitude.

"Oh, thank you, thank you, thank you for having the courage to share this with me," exclaimed Sister Lohsa amidst her tears of joy. "And you two," she said, turning to Elder Keil and Elder Roberts and squeezed each missionary's hands. "I will always remember you as my personal angels. When you taught me, you spoke with the tongue of angels. Thank you."

✧ ✧ ✧

"*Guten Tag, ich heisse* Elder Prentice," said Elder Prentice as his new companion—a golden—stepped off the train.

"Fine," answered Elder Oglesby, a rather rotund nineteen-year-old who looked more like a junior version of a fifty-year-old businessman than a fresh new missionary. He wore cufflinks, brightly polished Bostonian wingtips, and a shirt that somehow had a starched collar. His silk tie and suspenders matched a handkerchief that protruded fashionably from his wool suit's breast pocket. The new missionary reminded Elder Prentice of a four-year-old who had been dressed in a darling little suit by his mother.

"My name is Ryan Oglesby," continued Elder Prentice's golden as he set down one enormous suitcase and a bulging garment bag—a luggage item Elder Prentice had not seen before among missionaries.

"I don't speak German, I'm very tired because of this time zone thing, and I can't stand this humidity." Elder Oglesby was perspiring noticeably, and he paused to wipe his brow with the matching handkerchief. "Please take me to our apartment, and tell me it has air conditioning." Ryan began to walk in the direction of what he assumed was the exit to the train station, carrying only his garment bag.

It took Elder Prentice a few seconds to come to grips with what Elder Oglesby had said. He quickly joined his new companion without bringing along the bloated suitcase.

"We speak German, you'll get to sleep tonight, we have no air conditioning, and you forgot your suitcase," Elder Prentice said in German with as much restraint as possible.

"Oh, could you please get my bag?" Elder Oglesby almost demanded without breaking stride, and without acknowledging that his trainer had said anything at all.

Elder Prentice stopped. "*Nein*," he mouthed slowly and clearly.

Elder Oglesby finally halted. He stared at Elder Prentice as if Elder Prentice were an insolent child. As the senior companion was quickly learning, the golden was not accustomed to having any of his requests denied. "Junior Oglesby," as Elder Prentice came to think of him, snorted a sigh and turned back to retrieve his suitcase. "I see. It's going to be that kind of companionship, is it."

"Here, let me take this bag," offered Elder Prentice in German as he grabbed the garment bag from Junior. He hadn't wanted to be combative or discourteous, but he certainly wasn't going to be taken advantage of by some spoiled adolescent.

"Well, it's good to see you're good for something," sneered Junior as he lifted his suitcase. "Don't they have porters? Where are the porters?"

Elder Prentice shook his head and laughed to himself at this increasingly surreal scene.

"No, they don't have porters," he said in German, refusing to accede to his companion's desire to speak in English. "I'll get you a cart."

The two missionaries managed to get Junior's belongings to the front of the train station without any further exchanges. Elder Oglesby's face brightened when he saw a line of taxis.

"Oh taxi!" he called out immediately, without first asking Elder Prentice, and without making any attempt to pronounce the word in German.

Elder Prentice again shook his head and laughed. "No, we don't take taxis. We take the streetcar. Come on, this way," he directed as he walked toward the streetcar.

"You may get to the apartment however you like," huffed Elder Oglesby as he struggled to drag his suitcase over to the taxi. "But as for me and my suitcase, we will take the taxi. Don't worry, I have the money to pay for it."

Money was the main reason Elder Prentice had vetoed the cab. Yet even with that obstacle removed, taking a cab as missionaries seemed wrong as a matter of principle. He didn't want his golden—especially this golden—to be pampered. And he definitely didn't want this boy thinking he would get his way, as he apparently had at home.

"Come on," instructed Elder Prentice more sternly and slowly so that Elder Oglesby might actually be able to understand. "We . . . are . . . taking . . . the . . . streetcar." Elder Prentice pointed to the streetcar stop so that there was no question about his intent.

Junior dismissed Elder Prentice with a wave of the hand and dropped his suitcase next to a taxi driver.

"Here's my bag," the Utahn said in English. Then he pulled a piece of paper out of his wallet. "Take me to this address." Junior Oglesby waited a moment for the cabby to open his door. When the driver first put Elder Oglesby's bag in the trunk, Junior opened his own door and climbed in and slammed the door. Then he glanced over at a dumbfounded Elder Prentice, flashed a smile, and waved.

Elder Prentice's choices were limited. He quickly weighed the benefits of taking the streetcar alone against the disadvantages of leaving his companion and decided he could not leave his golden alone, no matter how despicable he was. J.P. caught the cab just before it left the curb and climbed in the front next to the driver. "Sorry," he said to the driver. "I'm with him, but don't tell anybody."

The driver smiled appreciatively at Elder Prentice.

When they arrived at the apartment, the cabby told Elder Oglesby the amount of the fare. Elder Oglesby pulled a wad of bills from his wallet and hesitated. He had no idea what the cabby had said nor what his new Monopoly-like money was worth.

"Allow me," said Elder Prentice, still in German. He pulled a bill from Elder Oglesby's wad and handed it to the driver. It was twice the fare. "Thank you. My friend says he especially appreciated your service," he said.

Once inside the apartment, Elder Prentice tried to count to ten before unleashing on his golden in English. He only made it to five.

"Elder Oglesby, my name is Elder Prentice. In case they forgot to mention it to you at the mission home, I am your senior companion. In fact, I am called your trainer, suggesting I will train you."

Elder Oglesby sighed but said nothing. Elder Prentice continued. "In this mission we speak German unless we're in an apartment or in a meeting with other English-speaking missionaries. We do not speak English in public."

"That seems rather impractical, since I can't speak German," interjected Junior from the old armchair in which he had already made himself comfortable. "If you're done with your little lecture, would you mind getting me something cold to drink?"

"I am not done with my little lecture, and I will not get you anything to drink," retorted Elder Prentice, who was finding it increasingly difficult to hold his temper. "In this companionship, we will each carry our own weight . . ."—J.P. glanced over at Junior.—". . . whatever it may be."

"Oh, great, weight jokes, and we've only known each other ten minutes."

Under other circumstances, Elder Prentice might have apologized for the slur, but not with this boy. "Let me tell you how our companionship will operate. We will both keep the rules. We will have fun, but we will work hard. When we cannot agree on something and a decision needs to be made, you will follow my lead. And you will never, ever, pull a stunt like that with the taxi again. If you ever try to walk away from me again, I will go directly to a pay phone and call the mission president."

"Ooh, calling the mission president, that does sound important," mocked Junior. "Perhaps you'd like to call my parents directly instead."

Elder Oglesby pulled out his wallet again—something that seemed to come very naturally to him—and took out a business card. "Here. Just call my dad at work. Tell him the son he bribed to come on a mission is behaving poorly and would love to go home."

The gold embossed letters on the card read, "Ryan Oglesby, Sr., Owner, Oglesby Motors, Salt Lake City, Utah."

"Great," said Elder Prentice with an exasperated sigh of his own. "I'm babysitting some rich kid whose daddy gave him a car if he'd go on a mission."

"Oh, not just a car," corrected Junior. "I don't think that would have done it, unless maybe it was a Mercedes. No, Mr. Oglesby—as I call my father—made serving a mission a condition precedent to owning the dealership one day. So here I am."

By this time Elder Oglesby had pulled an orange juice carton out of the fridge and was struggling to open it. Doing so without scissors was an acquired skill.

"Here," offered Elder Prentice after watching his companion struggle for a minute with the carton. He quickly tore the corner off along the dotted line.

"Thanks." The heavyset elder was now sweating profusely and seemed genuinely grateful to be able to get a drink. He filled a glass and drank it down in what appeared to be three or four gulps.

"Look," explained Elder Oglesby as he returned to the armchair, "I'm sorry about all that with the taxi. It had been a long trip and a long day. Why don't we just agree to leave each other alone as much as we can? When we're in the apartment, you do your thing and I do mine, okay? And when you . . . ," Elder Oglesby interrupted himself with a drawn out yawn, "when you say it's time to go be a missionary, I'll come along and you, you do all the talking, okay?" He yawned again mightily, and within less than ten seconds he was asleep.

21
Fingernails Unfit for Baptism

Of the many responsibilities that fell upon Elder Wesley Hawthorne as district leader, none was more serious or challenging than interviewing baptismal candidates. If he approved a baptism of someone who wasn't truly prepared or worthy, Elder Hawthorne feared he was helping qualify the individual for greater condemnation than if he or she had never been baptized. Moreover, the members would hold it against him and the missionaries generally if the person didn't stick.

On the other hand, if Elder Hawthorne unnecessarily delayed the baptism of individuals who truly were prepared, he might derail their spiritual progress and prevent them from ever getting baptized. And he would not exactly earn the appreciation of the missionaries who had believed such investigators were ready for baptism.

Fortunately, the first two interviews Elder Hawthorne conducted with baptismal candidates went smoothly enough, even if he felt almost like he was playing house. It was difficult to believe that these Germans saw him as someone who was legitimately in a position to judge their worthiness to enter into this sacred covenant.

With his third baptismal interview, however, Elder Hawthorne got the kind of challenge he had dreaded. His first inkling that this one would be different was hardly subtle. The Neumuenster bishop called Elder Hawthorne before he even knew he had an interview.

"Elder Hawthorne, this is Bishop Schmidt from Neumuenster. I'm calling to express some concern about a young man you're going to be interviewing for baptism next week. His name is Leo, Leo Grunwald. He is a very unique individual. I am sure he has a good heart, but I worry that he's not truly ready for baptism."

Elder Hawthorne listened respectfully. "He's . . . well, I'm not quite sure how to say this. You'll understand when you see him."

"When I see him?" asked Elder Hawthorne.

"Yes," confirmed Bishop Schmidt. "I mean, just look at his finger nails." From the silence at the other end, Bishop Schmidt realized his comment must have sounded strange.

"Listen. I'm having a difficult time articulating my concerns. And I don't want to intrude upon your duties as district leader. I just want you to be aware that this is not your typical baptismal candidate. This boy has been walking all over the continent for the last year. He was eating out of garbage cans. And he still doesn't seem to shower, and he won't dress appropriately for church. I just ask you to consider prayerfully whether this boy is truly ready for baptism."

Elder Hawthorne promised to take the matter seriously, as he did every interview. Bishop Schmidt seemed satisfied.

Elder Hawthorne was unsure how the Neumuenster elders could have someone ready for baptism if he hadn't heard about him yet in the weekly interviews. He promptly called Elder Morrell, the senior companion in Neumuenster.

"Well, it's true, we do have someone ready for baptism," confirmed Elder Morrell. "How did you know?"

"Bishop Schmidt just called me," replied Elder Hawthorne. "He's concerned."

Elder Morrell laughed and shared the comment with his companion. "Let me guess—did he tell you about his fingernails?"

"Well, as a matter of fact, he did mention something about that."

"Look, this guy's wild, there's no question about it. But his story is incredible."

Elder Morrell proceeded to tell Leo's story, complete with his appearance at the Neumuenster building the previous week after having walked home from Minden.

"So has he been to church twice?" asked Elder Hawthorne. President Cook required that all investigators attend church twice before being baptized.

"He came last Sunday and he's coming again this Sunday," replied Elder Morrell.

"All right, I'll keep an open mind." The elders agreed Elder Hawthorne would interview Leo the next Monday at district meeting in Neumuenster if Leo attended church again Sunday.

Elder Hawthorne was secretly hoping Leo would disappear so that his difficult decision would do so as well. He was almost disappointed, then, when Leo showed up on Monday and Elder Morrell verified that he had attended church the day before.

The man did have very long, very dirty fingernails. Elder Hawthorne tried not to stare. And despite the best efforts of the Neumuenster elders, Leo still reminded Elder Hawthorne of Charlie Brown's friend, Pig Pen.

Both the Neumuenster missionaries and Bishop Schmidt were right about Leo: he was not the typical baptismal candidate. The interview lasted an hour—not because Elder Hawthorne was cleverly probing, but because Leo had so much to say and so many of his own questions.

At the end of the hour, Elder Hawthorne was convinced that there was something to Bishop Schmidt's concerns. Leo did seem to have some reservations about what Elder Hawthorne thought of as peripheral issues, such as Sunday dress. Yet none of these concerns went to the questions he had been given to ask baptismal candidates to measure their worthiness to be baptized.

As to the important questions, Leo's conviction and understanding clearly ran deeper than any of the other candidates Elder Hawthorne had interviewed. If forced to give odds, he would have concluded the other two candidates had a greater chance of remaining "active," while Leo had a greater chance of attaining exaltation. The district leader knew, of course, that Leo could not take a separate route to exaltation. But if he stayed on course, there would be nothing half-way about his commitment.

"Well?" asked Elder Morrell when Elder Hawthorne and Leo finally emerged from the interview and Leo had gone into the restroom.

"He is something," responded Elder Hawthorne with a shake of his head. "But he answered all the questions correctly. I don't see how I can do anything but approve him for baptism. I don't want his sins on my shoulders."

Being a Hawthorne, though, it wasn't that simple. That night and many others, he wondered whether he'd make the right decision.

✦ ✦ ✦

A city about the same size as Tacoma, Washington, Bielefeld had one ward and four missionaries. Each Sunday morning the full-time missionaries met together with the stake missionaries and Brother Herbst, the ward mission leader.

"All right, brothers and sisters, let's review the progress the investigators are making," said Brother Herbst as he opened his briefcase and pulled out a stack of forms. This brother presided over this meeting—a fact lost on no one.

Brother Herbst took notes on a computer-generated chart as each of the three senior companions discussed the progress of their investigators. The leader peppered each reporting missionary with questions, many of which were questions much more appropriately asked by the zone leader or mission president. But Elder Roberts saw no point in fighting with the ward mission leader over turf, and Brother Herbst clearly enjoyed acting as a mini-mission president. Elder Roberts listened passively as the missionaries were grilled.

These meetings provided a good opportunity for coordinating the work with the members. Joint teaching experiences were arranged, and investigators' needs and interests were matched with those of members. Having finally witnessed for himself the remarkable difference members made when they actually found and fellowshipped investigators, Elder Roberts had also begun suggesting activities or programs to encourage members to share the gospel with their own friends.

Brother Herbst clearly preferred designing, distributing, and filling in charts he created on his computer. He had charts that tracked the missionaries' mastery of discussions, scriptures, and German; the number of new investigators, investigators attending church, investigators challenged, investigators committed to baptism, and investigators baptized; the number of missionaries sent out from the ward, the number of young men and young women eligible to serve missions, and even the number of letters sent by ward members to missionaries in the field. The only statistic Brother Herbst did not seem to track was the number of referrals the members had given to the missionaries.

Today will be different, thought Elder Roberts. The mission office had just sent out a new member-missionary manual for a course to be taught by a member to fellow members. The manual came from Salt Lake and was part of a new church-wide program. Elder Roberts was confident that it could not be taken lightly nor ignored.

Elder Roberts waited patiently as Brother Herbst took the meeting's participants carefully through each item of the agenda, of which everyone had been given a copy. Finally the mission leader asked whether the missionaries had any additional matters to discuss.

"Actually, I do have one item," said Elder Roberts. He tried not to grin as he pulled a set of the new manuals out of his bag and passed them around. "We just received these from Salt Lake. They're the manuals for a new member-missionary course to be offered during Sunday School. The course is nine weeks long, and it's supposed to be taught by a member rather than a missionary. The idea is to teach members how to share the gospel with their friends and neighbors."

Fortunately, Elder Roberts didn't know how to say "I told you so" in German. This was precisely the kind of thing he had been urging the ward to do for some time. He tried to show restraint as he waited for Brother Herbst and the stake missionaries to thumb through the manuals, but it was difficult.

"We thought perhaps Brother and Sister Schumann would be ideal teachers," suggested Elder Roberts. Brother Herbst grunted slightly and turned the page.

"Listen to this," said Brother Herbst—apparently not to Elder Roberts—as he leafed through the manual. "'During the first lesson, the members will be encouraged to select a family with whom they can share the gospel. By the second lesson, the members will have had some positive contact with their non-member friends, such as sharing a loaf of home-made bread or inviting them over to dinner.'"

The stake missionaries picked up on Brother Herbst's tone of voice as he read, and they began to chuckle. Brother Herbst continued flipping through the pages and reading selected excerpts.

"'By the third lesson the members will have invited their non-member friends to church. By the fourth lesson, the members' friends will be taking the discussions.'"

Brother Herbst chortled heartily. "I'll give you one guess as to where the people who wrote this manual live."

The stake missionaries joined in the fun. "Sounds good for Utah," they agreed.

"Wait, wait," exclaimed Brother Herbst with excitement. "Let's see what the members' task is for the ninth lesson. Yes, here it is. I knew it. 'By the ninth lesson, members should be identifying friends to invite to the baptism of the family selected at the outset of this course.'"

Brother Herbst and the stake missionaries erupted in laughter. Elder Roberts waited for the noise to subside before trying to salvage the course that had brought him so much hope.

"I realize that the goals in the manual might be, well, optimistic."

"Optimistic?" interjected Brother Herbst. "Try outlandish."

"Whatever you might think of the wisdom of those who wrote the manual," continued Elder Roberts with frustration, "I believe the ward should try teaching the class. It would be a wonderful way to teach members about sharing the gospel. With the Schumanns teaching it, it could be a powerful tool."

Brother Herbst bristled at this second mention of the Schumanns as possible teachers of the course. "The Schumanns have not been charged with responsibility for leading the missionary work in this ward," said Brother Herbst slowly, enunciating each word clearly as if speaking to people who had difficulty understanding the language. "I have. I will review the manual at greater length and determine whether it is appropriate for . . . for our culture." He then placed the manuals under a stack of forms, dropped them into his briefcase, and snapped it shut for effect.

✦ ✦ ✦

"You know Elders, sometimes I just don't understand," said Brother Schumann in a rare moment of exasperation after dinner later that day. "I can't understand why the members of the ward don't share the gospel with their friends and acquaintances."

"I have that same question," agreed Elder Roberts. "It seems at times as if members think of missionary work as feeding the missionaries, doing laundry for missionaries, supporting missionaries financially, or raising missionaries. We appreciate all the help people give us, but the most important thing they can do is share the gospel with their friends."

"People seem to view us a spiritual soldiers in the war," interjected Elder Keil. "And their job is to cheer us on while we fight."

"That's true, Elder Keil," nodded Brother Schumann. "What I'm going to say is harsh, Elders, but I believe it firmly. I think it's a matter of testimony. If you really believe or know that the only way back to Father is through believing in Jesus Christ and his atoning sacrifice, repentance, and baptism by one with the proper authority, I don't see how you can refrain from sharing that belief or knowledge with others."

"Oh, honey," offered Sister Schumann mildly. "I think most members of the ward have a testimony. They're just afraid, that's all. I can understand that."

"I suppose," replied Brother Schumann. "It just seems that true love will overcome that fear. But I guess I don't know what's in everyone else's heart. You're right—it's not my place to judge them."

Whether it was Brother Schumann's place to judge others or not, Elder Roberts had found his outburst very satisfying. It was good to hear someone with this brother's experience articulate the matter so clearly. On the way home in the subway, Elder Roberts was trying to remember Brother Schumann's words when Elder Keil interrupted his thoughts.

"Say, Elder Roberts, about what Brother Schumann said . . ."

"Yeah, that was great, wasn't it?"

"Well, I was just thinking about my friends back home, about what kind of job I've done sharing the gospel with them. They know about the Church and everything—even quite a bit about what we believe. But I'm not sure that I've ever really told them how I feel about it. I mean, listening to Brother Schumann, I can imagine my friends coming to me in the next life and saying, 'Why didn't you tell us about this—tell us that you actually knew these things?'"

Elder Roberts reflected for a moment on what he had told his own friends. They had discussed religion a lot—in a way. All of his friends could give a decent encyclopedia-like description of the Church and its doctrines. But had he ever told them from the heart what he knew? Elder Roberts didn't think so. And he was sure that he hadn't told them of his convictions since he had been on his mission, where his knowledge of the truthfulness of the gospel had deepened dramatically.

"Ouch," said Elder Roberts. "Maybe I'd better go easier on Brother Herbst."

"Or maybe we'd better write some letters," suggested Elder Keil. "Then you can still slam Brother Herbst, but with more credibility." Ralf Keil smiled, showing he was mostly joking.

The next P-day, the two missionaries spent most of their discretionary time writing letters to friends who hadn't heard from them since before their missions.

22
Going AP

"So, how's it going, Elder?" asked President Cook during Elder Prentice's zone conference interview in late September.

Elder Prentice was struggling to describe his problem in diplomatic terms when he noticed President Cook grinning broadly.

"You know just what I'm going through, don't you?"

"Oh, I think I might have some idea," ventured President Cook. "You're going nuts, aren't you?"

"Well, as a matter of fact, yes I am," admitted Elder Prentice. "This guy is here for all the wrong reasons, and he's got no desire to work or even to be here. Why don't you just send him home to his dad?"

"It's tempting," confessed the president. "But if I sent home everybody who came out for the wrong reasons or didn't want to work hard enough, I wouldn't have very many missionaries left. And more importantly, I would have sent home some of my best missionaries . . . before they had a chance to come around."

J.P. was a bit embarrassed at what he took to be a reminder about his past. "Okay, so what am I supposed to do while we wait for Elder Oglesby to come around?"

"Maybe you could help move the process along," suggested President Cook kindly.

"Oh, believe me, I've been tempted to help move things along mightily on more than one occasion."

"Tell me, Elder Prentice, what helped bring you around?"

"I suppose it was Uwe, the guy with cerebral palsy who we baptized in Bremerhaven," Elder Prentice replied after pondering the question for a few moments. "Yeah, I think that was the beginning of it—when I started actually caring about him."

"There you have it, then," declared President Cook as he slapped Elder Prentice on the knee. "Go find yourself someone for Elder Oglesby to care about, someone who will make him lose himself. . . . Oh, and one more thing, if you're anything like me, you've been keeping a mental portfolio on all the wacky things your companion does, and you probably share it with other missionaries when the opportunity arises. Erase it. Do everything you can to stop keeping track of his idiosyncrasies, and start looking for his strengths."

"That's a tall order, you know, President."

"I know," conceded the president, who reflected for a moment and then chuckled. The president's acknowledgment of this reality made his advice much more palatable to Elder Prentice. "Do what you can. Pray. The Lord can change our weaknesses into strengths."

With that, President Cook stood up, signaling the end of the interview. As always, he embraced Elder Prentice. "The Lord loves you, Elder."

❖ ❖ ❖

With each district meeting that passed, Elder Hawthorne felt a little less like an imposter. He certainly didn't enjoy serving as district leader, and he would never aspire to the calling, but he had come to realize that other missionaries struggled as much as or even more than he did. As he interviewed each companionship in conjunction with the weekly district meeting, he was pleasantly surprised to discover that he had some suggestions that proved helpful to other missionaries.

It helped that the work was going well for Elder Hawthorne and Elder Sampson in their own area. Elder Hawthorne felt the success they were having was mostly a function of having stumbled across a couple of golden investigators. Still, since he and Elder Sampson had witnessed only a couple of baptisms in their area since Elder Roberts left, Elder Hawthorne felt he would appear hypocritical to the missionaries in his district when he talked about striving for baptisms.

Unbeknown to Elder Hawthorne, none of the missionaries in his district sensed even the slightest trace of hypocrisy in their district leader. On the contrary, they found his candor and genuine humility refreshing for a leader.

✦ ✦ ✦

In Hannover the work was going well too. In fact, for Elder Roberts the work had never gone as well as it had with Elder Keil. The Schumanns provided the nucleus of the work with a steady stream of one or two serious investigators at any given time. In addition, Elder Keil and Elder Roberts managed to find several new people each week, and many of the people seemed to be progressing toward baptism.

The only leadership position Elder Roberts had not held in the mission was assistant to the president. As one of only four zone leaders in the mission, he was a natural candidate to become an assistant any time one went home, but that thought had not really occurred to him until he overheard two of the elders in his zone talking just before a district meeting.

"Elder Bradley's going home at the end of the month. Who do you think'll be the new AP?"

"Elder Roberts must have a good shot at it. I hear he's baptized fourteen people. And he's a great zone leader. I'd give him the best odds."

Elder Roberts wondered whether he really had baptized fourteen people. He certainly hadn't been the one to perform the actual ordinance that many times. He didn't even really know how to count baptisms, since many times he'd left a city before an investigator was baptized or he had only followed an investigator through to baptism who had been found by another set of missionaries before he had arrived in an area.

Working with the president would be a remarkable experience. Elder Roberts had envied the opportunity the assistants had to travel with President Cook and be tutored by someone like him. Elder Bradley had told him on a split once that when they traveled to zone conferences with the president, the assistants would spend the whole trip with their scriptures open asking the president all the questions they had stored up during their missions. Elder Bradley called it a once-in-a-lifetime opportunity. And teaching other missionaries at zone conferences and on splits was rewarding, Elder Bradley said, because it gave you an opportunity to influence many lives.

Nevertheless, there was one major drawback to being an assistant, according to Elder Bradley. You didn't get to continue working with your own investigators and seeing them through to baptism.

✧ ✧ ✧

During their first month together, Elder Prentice had essentially taken Elder Oglesby up on his offer. Whenever the companionship tracted, GQ-ed, or taught, Junior came along but Elder Prentice did all the talking. After his talk with President Cook, he struggled to change that, but change came slowly.

Elder Prentice coached, coaxed, and begged, until Elder Oglesby agreed to try taking every third door. Of course, the junior companion's inability to speak much German severely limited his options of what he could say. His lack of testimony severely limited his enthusiasm.

More than once, Elder Prentice took over a door approach or discussion for his faltering, disinterested junior companion, reasoning that the collective lives of the investigators were more important than the spiritual progress of his babied, arrogant companion. Yet something inside always prompted him to give his companion another attempt at taking some responsibility.

Nothing seemed to take. Thanks exclusively to Elder Prentice's efforts, the companionship continued to teach quality investigators and see them progress, but Elder Oglesby remained emotionally aloof from the work.

Two weeks after his interview with President Cook, Elder Prentice decided he'd had enough of the indirect approach. He could no longer restrain himself.

"Excuse me," Elder Prentice said with measured courtesy to his companion, who was sprawled on his bed reading a Tom Clancy novel. "I'd like to talk with you for a while."

Junior grunted and continued reading.

Elder Prentice decided to press ahead anyway. "The way I see it, you're throwing a two-year tantrum to spite your father, or something like that. Problem is, you're hurting yourself instead of your father. I know it's hard to believe, but throwing yourself into this work really does make you happy. It turns out all the things we're saying in the discussions are true. Believe me, I squandered away most of my mission, and I regret it."

Elder Prentice thought he caught Elder Oglesby glancing up from his book for a moment. "I'm happier now than I've ever been. A year ago you couldn't have convinced me that working hard as a missionary really would make me happy, or that all these things we teach people matter much. And I don't know how to convince you. Trust me enough to give it a try and see for yourself if I'm right. If nothing else, read the Book of Mormon and pray about it. Then you'll start to see. End of sermon."

Elder Oglesby didn't acknowledge that his senior companion had said anything, but Elder Prentice felt much better about having unloaded his feelings. He volunteered to make his companion breakfast, and Junior accepted.

For the next day or two, Elder Oglesby seemed unusually irritable. Even when exerting all his energy to see the good in his companion, it was hard for Elder Prentice to find anything positive in his companion. But with some intense prayer, Elder Prentice managed to refrain from making any of the sharp comments that had marked the companionship's first month together. After a couple of days, Junior's irritability subsided. In fact, Elder Prentice thought his companion was a bit friendlier than usual.

While tracting a few days later, Elder Oglesby made a comment to his senior—in German—with an idea about one of their investigators. The idea was a good one, but more significantly, the remark was the first comment that Junior had made to his companion, other than a complaint, since their first day together. Moreover, it was the first he'd ever made in German. Elder Prentice was flabbergasted.

Later that week, Elder Prentice was stunned when Elder Oglesby said something that resembled a testimony during a part of the discussion that called for a testimony. That night in the apartment, Elder Prentice decided to find out what had happened.

"So, how are things?"

"Oh, they're okay, you know," replied Elder Oglesby, who was preparing a snack for himself.

"I, um, I appreciated your testimony in that discussion tonight," said Elder Prentice as he took off his shoes and socks. "It really added something."

"Thanks." Elder Oglesby didn't seem interested in discussing the subject any further. Elder Prentice sensed it was best not to bring any more attention to the matter than he had.

✦ ✦ ✦

"Well Elder, the zone looks like it's doing very well," said President Cook in his October interview with Elder Roberts. "Your own companionship is remarkably successful, and that's the key."

"You'd have to be a pretty lousy missionary not to do well with the Schumanns in your area," replied the missionary.

"There's some truth to that," acknowledged President Cook with a chuckle. "But you and Elder Keil have been finding on your own as well as teaching the investigators the Schumanns have brought you. And most of the zone is doing well."

President Cook and Elder Roberts then discussed virtually every companionship in the zone, reviewing concerns and commenting on progress. Finally they came to Celle.

"I don't know what to do about Celle," confessed President Cook. "The work there is slower than anywhere in the mission. In fact, it's at a complete standstill. It's been that way for months now. Elder Wilson claims that the city has been tracted out four or five times within the last two years, and the people are angry about being disturbed so often by the missionaries. The members seem to agree, and they're not bringing in any contacts of their own. Elder Wilson and Elder Johnston have sent me a letter asking me to take the missionaries out of Celle and send them somewhere that they're more needed." President Cook shook his head slightly and let out a sigh. "What do you think, Elder Roberts?"

"I think Elder Wilson and Elder Johnston are right about one thing. It's probably time for them to move on," replied Elder Roberts. "But I think we should give the city one last chance before we close it."

"What are you suggesting?"

"How about sending in two real missionaries and letting them go at it hard. Who knows, maybe Elder Wilson's right. But I think we should let two dedicated missionaries take a crack at it before we close the door on those people."

President Cook smiled and slapped his thighs with both hands. "I was hoping you'd think that, Elder, but I wanted to get your opinion. The Lord loves you, and so do I. Keep up the good work."

✦ ✦ ✦

When the telephone rang the Tuesday night before transfers, Elder Keil jumped up to get it. "Will you still remember me and the little people when you're an assistant, Elduh?" teased the junior companion on his way to the phone.

"Assistant, schmistant," rejoined Elder Roberts. "I may be getting transferred, but I don't think it's to the office."

In the days approaching the transfer, Elder Roberts had thought about the possibility of becoming an assistant. He knew he would love the association with the president, but he also knew he would miss the opportunity to nurture investigators along the trail to baptism. In his heart, Chris silently prayed and hoped he could continue to work in the field.

"It's for you, Elduh," said Elder Keil as he handed his companion the phone. Elder Roberts' heart skipped a beat, and he wasn't sure whether it was because of disappointment or excitement.

"Elder Roberts, have I got an opportunity for you," began President Cook warmly. "I'd like you to finish out your mission in a way that few good missionaries can. I've prayed long and hard about this, and I think it's right. I'd like to free you up from your responsibilities as zone leader and send you out into the field with a great companion. I'd like you to revitalize Celle."

News of Elder Roberts' transfer spread rapidly through the Hannover Zone and even some of the other areas of the mission. It marked the first time one of President Cook's zone leaders had not finished his mission as a zone leader or an assistant.

"So instead of going AP, he's getting shipped to the boonies," Elder Roberts overheard one missionary in his district exclaiming to another just before he entered the room for his last district meeting in Hannover. "I bet he told the president off or something."

The missionary was embarrassed when Elder Roberts entered the room. Elder Roberts was tempted to set the record straight, but instead he just smiled. "The president found out my father's a lawyer, so I guess he decided to take it out on me."

✧ ✧ ✧

As Elder Prentice finished packing his bags for the November transfer, Elder Oglesby cleared his throat. "Um, would it be all right if . . . you know . . . as sort of a favor to you, I paid for a cab ride to the train station?"

Elder Prentice looked up from his luggage and took in his golden. He hesitated for only a moment. "Sure, why not."

The missionaries had a couple of minutes to spare after Elder Oglesby telephoned for a cab. His German was still terrible, but now it was at least no worse than an average missionary in Germany for two months. Elder Prentice was proud of his junior companion for speaking the language the last couple of weeks.

Elder Oglesby sat at the missionaries' makeshift desk, nervously drumming his fingers. Finally, he cleared his throat again. "Um, Elder, I just wanted to say, you know . . . well . . . you know . . . thanks, thanks for everything. You were right about the Book of Mormon and stuff."

Elder Prentice didn't know what to say, so he shook his companion's hand. To his surprise, the junior companion pulled his senior to him. "Good luck in Celle," Elder Oglesby said. "I'll, um, I'll miss you."

23
Going It Alone

On the train ride to Bielefeld, Elder Hawthorne still could not believe that he had been asked to serve as a zone leader. The fact that he had been asked to serve in that capacity was the most puzzling development yet of his mission. This is unquestionably one of those calls made for the benefit of the individual being called, not those whom he will serve, Elder Hawthorne thought.

As Elder Hawthorne wondered how someone like him could possibly lead a zone, his thoughts turned to one of his favorite assistants, Elder Ruttiger. An unlikely assistant, Elder Ruttiger's German was not as polished as most assistants', nor was his manner. Many assistants miraculously produced a fresh wool suit and a pair of sharp dress shoes for the end of their missions, but Elder Ruttiger still wore his steel radial suit, mailman shoes, and a rumpled overcoat.

Elder Hawthorne had worked with Elder Ruttiger once on a split, and he noticed that in his very unassuming way, Elder Ruttiger reached the hearts of the people at the doors and in the streets. His dialogues were not novel or particularly clever, but they were always genuine. Somehow he was able to get investigators, people at the doors, and missionaries alike to open up. He did a lot of listening.

What impressed Elder Hawthorne most about Elder Ruttiger was that Elder Ruttiger seemed to present the same face to companions, missionaries he was leading, and investigators. His tone of voice and mannerisms were consistent, regardless of his audience.

Elder Hawthorne's meditation was interrupted when the conductor's voice came over the intercom. "Bielefeld."

Elder Hawthorne scrambled wildly with his heavy suitcases and nearly fell as he stumbled from the train. Wesley feared his inauspicious entrance was an omen of things to come in Bielefeld.

✧ ✧ ✧

As with the start of a new baseball season, hope abounded at the start of the new Celle companionship. Although he hadn't particularly hit it off with Elder Roberts in the MTC, now that Elder Prentice had changed his ways, he was thrilled to be working with an elder as dedicated as Elder Roberts. His two months with Elder Oglesby had made him especially appreciative of a committed companion.

Elder Roberts relished the challenge Celle presented. The recently departed missionaries had left a list of three names of investigators, but none of the three were interested in talking with the new missionaries when they called. Each of them said their last meeting with the missionaries had been over a month ago.

Nor had their predecessors left much good will with the members. The ward mission leader had apparently drifted into inactivity three or four months earlier, and ward members seemed to view the missionaries largely as a burden—as Americans whose laundry they were obligated to wash every week. The setting was perfect for a miracle, unexpected by all but Elder Roberts and Elder Prentice.

❖ ❖ ❖

Every Monday Elder Hawthorne was to meet with his district and counsel with individual companionships. He had done this in Rendsburg as well, but two things were different about the job in Bielefeld.

First, he had a companionship of sisters in his district. To Elder Hawthorne, sisters seemed like grownups as compared to elders, and to him specifically. Trying to give them useful counsel was a daunting task.

Second, as the district leader of what President Cook called the model district in the zone, Elder Hawthorne was expected to set the standard for the other district leaders. If Elder Hawthorne could not have an impact on the missionaries in his district, he didn't see how he could expect the other district leaders to listen to him.

On Tuesdays, Elder Hawthorne received the weekly reports from every companionship in the zone. Among other things, the reports told Elder Hawthorne how many discussions had been taught, how many investigators had attended church, how many people had been challenged to baptism, and how many people had been baptized.

Because of what happened on Wednesdays, Elder Hawthorne felt personally responsible for the performance of each companionship in the zone. He opened his mail every Tuesday with the same trepidation he experienced in school when receiving grades.

On Tuesday evenings, Elder Hawthorne was to call the other three district leaders in his zone to discuss their reports. According to Elder Poulson, the assistant who oversaw the Bielefeld Zone, Elder Hawthorne was supposed to praise the district leaders for any improvements, ask them about any oddities, and suggest ways they could improve. "Don't be afraid to make 'em stretch, Elder," Elder Poulson had explained in a training session.

Of course, Elder Hawthorne was afraid to make anyone else stretch. His first phone call with the most senior district leader, Elder Cantor, did nothing to boost Elder Hawthorne's confidence.

"So, they brought in somebody from outside the zone to be zone leader. I see," noted Elder Cantor after the new zone leader introduced himself. "I guess they couldn't find anybody within the zone who was capable, huh?"

"Yes, well, um, no," stuttered Elder Hawthorne. "I mean, I'm sure a lot of other people could have done this job."

"Yeah, that's probably true," agreed Elder Cantor all too quickly. "So what's up?"

"Oh, I'm just making the weekly phone call, you know," answered Elder Hawthorne.

"Oh, that thing. Look, I've been a district leader for six months now," said Elder Cantor knowingly. "I think I've got the job down pretty well by now. So why don't you just save yourself the money and us both the time, okay? The reports pretty much say it all, anyway."

Elder Hawthorne finally convinced Elder Cantor to humor him and let him call every week, but the new zone leader did not have high hopes of "stretching" Elder Cantor or any of his other district leaders.

✦ ✦ ✦

Celle had never seen missionaries who worked as hard as Elder Prentice and Elder Roberts. They departed the apartment promptly each morning at nine a.m. After a few hours of morning tracting and GQ-ing, they returned to the apartment for lunch. While one elder prepared the meal, the other read scriptures or a Conference issue of the *Ensign* to his companion. During the meal, the elders discussed the morning's events and planned the rest of the day.

After no more than an hour in their apartment, the missionaries returned to the streets. When riding their bikes, the missionaries practically raced each other, and they never climbed stairs one at a time. Neither elder could have physically sustained such a pace at the beginning of his mission.

The first week, the missionaries taught only three discussions. In his entire mission Elder Roberts had never taught fewer than ten discussions in a week. He was surprised at how long the week seemed when so little teaching was involved.

Secretly, Elder Roberts hoped to turn the work around in Celle more quickly, but he refused to let the lack of immediate success dampen his spirit.

Neither did Elder Prentice show any sign of losing faith that the work in Celle would soon mushroom. From his Bremerhaven experience, he knew change took time. Working relentlessly with a missionary of Elder Roberts' caliber, he was sure they would soon find people prepared to accept the gospel.

✳ ✳ ✳

By late November, fall's pleasant crispness was giving way to bitter frost, reminding the missionaries of what a blessing summer had been. The only breaks in the pre-winter chill seemed to be for mist-filled days marked by steady, drizzling rain.

Darkness fell upon Celle before dinner, and evening tracting became markedly more difficult than it had been just a few weeks earlier. Signs of summer had lingered into October, but now summer was unquestionably and irretrievably gone.

After three weeks, Elder Roberts and Elder Prentice had only four investigators, none of whom showed much potential for progress. When the work went well, even tracting could be exciting, since it brought the continual promise of finding someone who was ready to listen to the gospel. Now, tracting was becoming drudgery.

For the first time since leaving Bremerhaven, Elder Prentice felt himself becoming numb to the work. Door after door, person after person curtly rejected the missionaries. An exchange of more than two sentences was beginning to feel like a success to Elder Prentice. He could find no good explanation for this turn of events. It was unthinkable that he had been able to find and teach several times as many people a week with Elder Oglesby as he was with Elder Roberts. Perhaps Elder Wilson had been right. Maybe all the wheat in Celle had been harvested.

Elder Roberts was just as perplexed at the companionship's lack of success. Although he had occasionally struggled to baptize, he had never had a problem finding new people to teach. In his mind, finding could be done through sheer obedience, faith, and hard work. His pace quickened a little more with each day that passed without success. He was determined not to spend the last two months of his mission languishing, without anyone to teach.

"Wait up, Elder," begged Elder Prentice between breaths one morning. Elder Roberts had arrived at the top of seven flights of stairs several steps ahead of his companion. Irked that his companion seemed to be slackening his pace, Elder Roberts had intentionally knocked on the first door without waiting for Elder Prentice to join him before knocking.

"Gotta keep moving," mumbled Elder Roberts as he stared at the door intently. He saw something move behind the peephole, but the door didn't open. He rapped hard three times right next to the peephole.

"Easy, Elder," urged Elder Prentice as he cleared the last stair.

"I'd rather be yelled at by someone than have them pretend not to be home," Elder Roberts said loudly in German, not caring if the person behind the door heard him. He moved to the next door and pounded on the door six times.

"C'mon, Elder, pounding like the police isn't going to get people to answer the door," reasoned Elder Prentice.

"If you figure out what will, let me know," retorted Elder Roberts rather sharply. "Right now nobody else is doing anything, so I've got to try anything I can."

"And just what is that supposed to mean?" demanded Elder Prentice, stepping squarely between Elder Roberts and the next door.

"Nothing," replied Elder Roberts. He placed his hand on Elder Prentice's shoulder to make some room as he walked to the next apartment.

Elder Prentice perceived Elder Roberts' gesture as a shove. Never one to let any sign of aggression pass unchallenged on the basketball court, J.P. pushed his companion toward the wall. "Don't mess with me!" J.P. was startled at the tone of his own voice, sounding like his voice from high school. Elder Roberts' scriptures had fallen to the ground, and he stood stunned against the wall.

The two missionaries eyed each other tensely. Finally, Elder Roberts muttered, "What's happening?"

Elder Prentice hung his head in embarrassment. "I don't know. I don't know." He leaned over and picked up his companion's scriptures. "I'm sorry, I don't know what came over me." Elder Prentice sat down on the top step.

"Me neither," said Elder Roberts uncharacteristically in English. "I could feel myself getting more and more wound up. I just . . . I mean . . . I don't how to deal with . . ." Elder Roberts searched for the right word. "With failure, I guess."

"I wish I could help you," offered Elder Prentice. "I'm not particularly keen on this myself."

The missionaries sat for a moment in silence. In desperation, Elder Roberts suggested that they pray.

"Right here?" questioned Elder Prentice.

"Why not?" Elder Roberts glanced around the top floor of the stairwell. There was no one in sight. He kneeled furtively, and Elder Prentice quickly joined him. "I'll say it," volunteered Elder Prentice.

No sooner had Elder Prentice begun the prayer than he heard a door hastily opened. Both missionaries looked up in time to see an old woman brandishing a broom, sweeping dust in their faces.

"Get out of here, you crazy men," the woman shouted hysterically. "Leave me alone, you hear! I've seen you snooping around up here, looking for people for your sect! Shoo!"

Elder Roberts and Elder Prentice needed no further encouragement. They raced briskly down all seven flights, out of the apartment building, and around the corner before stopping for air. Safely out of the range of the woman and her broom, the elders doubled over in laughter.

24
Teaching Old Dogs New Tricks

"I'll confess, President, I'm frustrated," explained Elder Roberts shortly after his monthly interview began with the president. "We're doing everything we can, but we don't seem to be making any progress."

"Well, it didn't come quickly for Ammon and his brothers, either," answered President Cook.

"But I've only got two months, not fourteen years," retorted Elder Roberts. He wanted a solution, or at least an explanation.

President Cook tried unsuccessfully to suppress a yawn, not from boredom, but from lack of sleep. After resisting for a moment, he gave in to the urge and opened wide while stretching out his arms. Then he clasped his hands behind his head, crossed his legs, and leaned back. Elder Roberts felt as if the president knew him well enough to be more casual around him than he would be with most missionaries. He also knew the president was winding up to give some advice.

"So Elder," he began, "why didn't the Lord let Lehi and his family have fire when they were in the wilderness?"

The question strained Elder Roberts' knowledge, but he finally remembered the answer. "The Lord wanted them to know they had been led by his power to the promised land."

"That's right," nodded the president with a smile, proud of his pupil. "And with Gideon, why wouldn't the Lord let him use all thirty-two thousand soldiers, or even ten thousand? Why did Gideon get only three hundred soldiers to fight against an innumerable enemy?"

"Same thing," replied Elder Roberts. "He didn't want them to think they'd saved themselves. He wanted them to know that Israel had been saved through the power of Jehovah, not through the peoples' own might."

Elder Roberts drew in a deep breath and nodded slightly.

"I don't know, it's just a thought," offered President Cook. He stood up and pulled the missionary to him as he did every month. "I love you, Elder. Keep up the good work. The Lord loves you and he's mindful of how hard you're trying."

The next day Elder Roberts and Elder Prentice fasted—the first time in several months that Elder Roberts had fasted on a day other than Fast Sunday. With each hour that passed, he was reminded more of his own frailty and nothingness—of his dependence on God for everything that mattered in life. At the conclusion of the fast, the elders knelt in prayer on the hard, threadbare carpet in their apartment. Elder Roberts acted as voice.

"Dear Heavenly Father, please forgive us if we have relied too much on our own strength. We know that we are unworthy servants and that we can do nothing of ourselves. We acknowledge thy hand in all our blessings. Please help us. Help us find the people in this city who are ready to change. If we need to do something different, please show us, please inspire us.

"We don't mean to complain. We know that we've been richly blessed, even if we may not get to teach another discussion for the rest of our missions. But if there are people in this city who will still embrace the gospel, please help us find them. We thank thee for the opportunity to serve thee. We ask that thy will be done, in the name of Jesus Christ. Amen."

❖ ❖ ❖

At least the work in his own area was going well, thought Elder Hawthorne. Elder Keil was the perfect companion, always trying to bolster Elder Hawthorne's confidence. And with the Familie Schumann fueling them with investigators and spiritual nourishment, the work was flourishing.

Except for the three companionships of sisters, the rest of the zone was not doing very well. Elder Hawthorne was made acutely aware of this every Wednesday night when Elder Poulson called, presumably to "stretch" Elder Hawthorne. Although the tone of each phone call was pleasant enough, Elder Hawthorne definitely felt stretched.

Elder Poulson always followed up on suggestions he had made and questions he had asked the previous week. He asked plenty of questions about what had been done to improve the problem areas he identified. Elder Hawthorne dreaded Wednesday nights.

A particularly troublesome spot in the zone was Elder Cantor's district. None of its companionships, including Elder Cantor's, seemed to be able to have any success in finding new people to teach.

"Oh, you know how it is in December," explained Elder Cantor when Elder Hawthorne gently broached the subject of finding.

Elder Hawthorne did not know. He and Elder Keil were seeing a fair amount of success in using the Christmas season as a reason to discuss religion with people.

"You can't get in anywhere," continued Elder Cantor. "People are too busy with the holidays."

"You might try emphasizing the importance of discussing Christ with people at Christmas," suggested Elder Hawthorne.

"Nice idea, but it doesn't work," Elder Cantor assured Elder Hawthorne. "Look, this is my second Christmas in Deutschland, and I know. Germans don't want to be bothered in December, okay?"

Elder Hawthorne bristled at Elder Cantor's arrogance, but the fact that his own experience proved Elder Cantor wrong enabled Elder Hawthorne to be gracious. Rather than cite the success he and Elder Keil had enjoyed so far in December, Elder Hawthorne decided to work on tracting with Elder Cantor during their next split.

✦ ✦ ✦

"Good day—we're missionaries from The Church of Jesus Christ of Latter-day Saints," began Elder Roberts before pausing to sneak a breath. As they had every day of their five weeks together, he and Elder Prentice had climbed the seven flights of stairs two at a time.

"Are you here to convert me?" quipped the tiny, elderly woman suspiciously. "And why are you panting?"

"The answer to the first question is yes," replied Elder Roberts with a smile and without hesitation.

Initially, like many other missionaries, Elder Roberts had responded to this question with a simple no, based on the technicality that the Holy Ghost rather than the missionary does the converting. But he had come to feel that this approach was rather misleading—Germans didn't buy it anyway. If nothing else, they were astute. Why were these young men knocking on their door and going through this effort, if not to convert them?

"But we're not here to brainwash you. We are messengers of Jesus Christ. We want you to listen to our message and ask God if it's true," Elder Roberts added. "We hope you will learn for yourself through the Holy Ghost that our message is true and that you will embrace it."

The gray-haired, physically frail woman seemed startled, yet slightly taken with the candor of the young American.

"And the answer to the second question is that we climb stairs fast so that we can share our message with as many people as possible," interjected Elder Prentice. "Also, he is panting because he's not quite as fit as I am." Elder Prentice winked to show this last comment was a joke, but the gesture puzzled Frau Trobitius even more than the joke.

"So, may we come in to share our message with you?" asked Elder Roberts hopefully.

"How old are you, anyway?" demanded the old lady.

"We're twenty," replied Elder Roberts.

"But that's one hundred and forty in dog years," added Elder Prentice.

Frau Trobitius ignored Elder Prentice's comment. "I'm too old to be converted to anything," she chortled. "You need to find someone younger to convert."

"You may have fewer years left on this earth than we do, but we all have the same amount of time left in eternity. Our message will change your life not just now, but for eternity. May we come in?"

Frau Trobitius could not explain away the earnestness in the young men's eyes. But she needed to be sure about one more thing before letting these strangers into her house. "Does it cost any money?" she asked.

"No," responded Elder Roberts. "Our message is free."

With that, the Oma (German for "grandma" and missionary slang for "elderly woman") invited the missionaries in and prepared them the usual bitter herbal tea.

✦ ✦ ✦

It had been over two months since Elder Roberts and Elder Keil had written their friends. Their letters were each several pages long, spilling out their testimonies and explaining why they were on missions. Elder Roberts had nearly written off hope of receiving any responses when he finally received a letter from Ted Woodson, one of the three friends he'd written. The missionary was surprised at the amount of anxiety he experienced as he opened the letter.

"Dear Chris," the letter began. "If I'd gotten your letter from somebody I didn't know, I'd say they were nuts. But for you to say the things you did, it makes me wonder. I'm amazed at what you're doing, at your commitment to this thing. You must really believe in what you're doing. When you get home, I'd like to talk to you about some of the things you said in your letter.

"I'm not ready to convert or anything like that, but I've got a lot of questions. Anyway, thanks for sharing your feelings with me. Once in a while I think about these kinds of things, but nobody ever really discusses them, so it was kind of nice to get your letter.

"I look forward to talking with you about these things when you get home." There was another page of the letter updating Elder Roberts on developments in the lives of their mutual friends.

Elder Roberts was elated. He'd laid it on the line for one of his best friends, and their friendship had survived. What's more, Ted actually seemed interested in learning more about the gospel. Elder Roberts floated through the rest of the day.

After watching the remarkable effect a personal missionary experience had on his companion, Elder Prentice finally asked a question that changed the work in Celle for months. "Elder, why don't we work more with the members?"

Elder Roberts reflected for a moment on the question. "Well, we do work with part-member families, and we try to bring members along to discussions when we can." His answer satisfied neither himself nor his companion.

"But why not work directly with the members?" continued Elder Prentice. "I mean, politely, boldly, sweetly, directly ask them to share the gospel with their friends. They all know they're supposed to do it. But so did you, and you didn't do it until Brother Schumann reminded you."

Elder Prentice encountered no resistance from Elder Roberts. "That's a great idea. Elder Thomas taught me just to work hard and let the members come to us, but I think you're right. Let's do it. Let's visit the members."

After some prayer, the Celle missionaries decided on a plan. They would visit each family in the ward in the next two weeks. After sharing Elder Roberts' own experience about writing the letter to his friend and reading a couple of scriptures about the importance of declaring the gospel, the missionaries would challenge and commit the family to invite one friend to church on Christmas, which fell on a Sunday.

❖ ❖ ❖

Elder Hawthorne scheduled his split with Elder Cantor for two weeks before Christmas. Elder Hawthorne wasn't sure he could tolerate a whole day with a district leader who seemed confident he had little to learn about missionary work, so he scheduled the split for a Monday. He asked Elder Cantor to meet him at the church at noon, just after district meeting. He and Elder Keil had plenty of investigators to teach, but they purposefully did not schedule any appointments for that afternoon or evening.

"So, a split on district meeting day," said Elder Cantor as he approached Elder Hawthorne when he walked into church just after district meeting ended. "Whatever."

Elder Hawthorne realized the idea was impractical, but Elder Cantor's sneering attitude confirmed that he'd been wise to schedule only half a day with this district leader.

"I hope you've at least got some discussions scheduled."

Elder Hawthorne couldn't tell whether Elder Cantor really hoped this, or whether he was challenging him to see if he had been able to schedule discussions during December himself. The zone leader had a tremendous urge to tell Elder Cantor that he and Elder Keil already had ten appointments scheduled for the week, but he wanted the Lord's help, so he refrained.

"No," responded Elder Hawthorne slowly. "No, we don't have any appointments for tonight. But I'd like to shoot for teaching two new investigators."

"Great," snorted Elder Cantor. "Checking call backs for splits with a district leader." Elder Hawthorne was surprised at how little effort his district leader made to conceal his lack of enthusiasm for his first split with the new zone leader.

"No, we won't be checking call backs," said Elder Hawthorne.

When tracting, the missionaries made notes in a book to keep track of which people had no interest, which ones said to come back some other time (usually because they didn't have the heart to turn the missionaries down cold), and which ones weren't home. A favorite activity of missionaries who wanted to avoid real tracting was to spend most of their time traveling around the city repeatedly visiting the "call backs."

Since these people hadn't slammed the door on the missionaries the first time, they weren't likely to be rude. It was an easy way to burn up a lot of time without actually knocking on very many doors.

"We're going to tract out a new street today," announced Elder Hawthorne.

"Whatever," said Elder Cantor, shaking his head slightly.

Elder Hawthorne was very tempted to ask Elder Cantor what activity was scheduled for their companions in Hannover, but he again held his tongue. "Let me just talk to a few more people and we'll get outta here," said Elder Hawthorne.

"I understand," replied Elder Cantor with sarcastic warmth, slapping Elder Hawthorne on the back. "Gotta get in a little zone leader schmoozin'."

After talking with the sisters briefly about the logistics for next week's baptismal service, Elder Hawthorne slipped unnoticed into a vacant room. He knelt and offered a fervent prayer, asking the Lord to fill his heart with love for Elder Cantor and to open the hearts of the people they would speak with that night.

Elder Hawthorne was not a big fan of "Spirit tracting," which he had often seen used as an excuse to pick some remote area to tract that would guarantee lots of travel time. But as he prayed, he felt prompted to pray together with Elder Cantor and seek the Lord's direction in deciding where to tract that evening.

A few minutes later, Elder Hawthorne and Elder Cantor returned to the same room. The zone leader offered the prayer, saying much the same thing as when he had prayed alone. This time he also asked for the Lord to help them know where they should go tracting.

As Elder Hawthorne prayed, he recalled a street of stair houses near the church that he had passed many times. He assumed that the street had been tracted out regularly since it was located so close to the church. But since those stair houses came to mind during the prayer, Elder Hawthorne decided to take the thought as inspiration.

When they reached the street Elder Hawthorne planned to tract, Elder Cantor sized it up and hesitated. I bet it's been a while since he's done some real tracting, thought Elder Hawthorne as he headed for the door of the first stair house.

"Say Elder," called Elder Cantor.

"What?"

"I thought we could, um, we could maybe start on the other side of the street."

"Whatever," said Elder Hawthorne in English, borrowing a line from Elder Cantor. Elder Cantor laughed, and they started on the other side of the street.

Elder Hawthorne made a conscious effort to keep a fervent prayer in his heart as they tracted. The success they saw made him wonder why he didn't always pray so fervently.

The first door was answered by a student who appeared to come from an Islamic country. Elder Hawthorne didn't even ask if he could come in. Instead he asked if the missionaries could return at six p.m. on Christmas Eve with a special message about Jesus Christ. The man agreed.

At Elder Hawthorne's next three doors he scheduled two appointments for Monday, the third day of Christmas. He had heard rumors that Bruder Herbst, the ward mission leader, might invite the missionaries to spend the entire day at his house. Appointments were the only sure way to be able to work.

At Elder Hawthorne's fourth door, he asked if he and his companion could come in and share a special message about Christ during this season in which the Savior is so often forgotten. The man invited the missionaries in as if he'd been expecting them.

The discussion went reasonably well. When it was over and the elders had left the apartment of their new investigator, Elder Hawthorne knocked on the next door. Elder Cantor seemed caught off guard, so the zone leader gave the door approach.

"We're missionaries from The Church of Jesus Christ of Latter-day Saints. Are you so busy in December preparing for the holiday that you're going crazy?" Elder Hawthorne asked a middle aged woman who appeared beleaguered.

"As a matter of fact, I am," replied the woman, placing one hand on her hip and holding the door with the other.

"Does it seem odd to you that life should be so hectic when we're celebrating the birth of the Prince of Peace?" continued Elder Hawthorne.

"The birth of who?"

"Jesus—the Prince of Peace," answered Elder Hawthorne.

"Oh, him. Well, I suppose. Yes."

"We are his messengers," represented Elder Hawthorne. "We have a message of peace to share with you, to help you remember what Christmas is all about. May we come in?"

Elder Hawthorne had never been let in two doors in a row before, but the woman decided she deserved a break from her housework and invited the missionaries in. This woman, too, agreed to a return appointment.

It was four-thirty, and Elder Hawthorne realized they hadn't stopped for lunch yet, so they took the subway to his apartment. By six o'clock they returned to the street where they already found two new investigators and set up a few appointments.

This time the missionaries tracted for nearly an hour without success. But then a young father agreed to let them come in and teach a discussion.

Elder Hawthorne, who had never taught three unscheduled discussions in a single day, was elated.

It was eight p.m. by the time they finished the discussion. "So, shall we go back to the apartment to discuss my district?" asked Elder Cantor.

"Not yet," replied Elder Hawthorne. "I like to work as late as I can—until at least nine whenever possible."

"Really?" asked Elder Cantor in dismay, but with much less disdain than before the split had begun. "We find it very difficult to tract after eight o'clock in the winter. People don't seem too happy about the idea of us knocking on their door so late in the dark."

"I know what you mean," agreed Elder Hawthorne. "We try to teach instead of tract after eight whenever we can. We always set our evening appointments for eight so that we can teach until nine or nine-fifteen. We try not to set appointments for earlier in the evening until we've filled the late slots for the entire week."

Elder Hawthorne was tempted to peek at Elder Cantor's weekly calendar, but the district leader's silence was evidence enough that the zone leader's suggestion was something Elder Cantor hadn't tried yet.

After setting one more appointment with a widower for Christmas Day, Elder Hawthorne and Elder Cantor were invited in to teach yet another discussion—this one off of Elder Cantor's door approach about Christ and Christmas.

On the way back to the apartment after the discussion, Elder Cantor told Elder Hawthorne he liked his Christmas door approach.

"I'm gonna have to come up with some door approaches like that for all those religious holidays the Germans celebrate in the spring."

The two missionaries spent the rest of the ride home trying to remember the names of all the religious holidays the Germans celebrated, as well as what New Testament event the holidays were commemorating. The split had gone better than Elder Hawthorne had ever imagined it could. That night, Elder Hawthorne earnestly thanked the Lord, since he had no question that the Lord was behind the day's success.

✧ ✧ ✧

It was easy to teach an *Oma* a first discussion, since they had nothing better to do than talk with missionaries. Elders and sisters who watered down the discussions could get invited back for innumerable visits with tea and cake or cookies, which were preferable to tracting outside on a cold day. But missionaries who testified of the truths they had been called to preach rarely got a second or third appointment. Senior citizens feared change more than anyone, so they were rarely willing to do anything more than talk.

Frau Trobitius was different. At the end of the second discussion, Elder Prentice had invited her to church.

"It's marvelous," he said. "Everyone sings there. Do you sing?"

"Not on key," she replied.

"You'll fit right in," continued Elder Prentice without missing a beat. "One of the things I like best is that members of the congregation speak, not just some minister who gets paid to think up sermons."

"They don't . . . they don't . . . um . . . ask visitors to speak, do they?" tested Frau Trobitius.

"No, but they make them sing a solo," said Elder Prentice with a wink. By now Frau Trobitius had figured out that Elder Prentice was joking when he winked, so she cast him a dirty look, then laughed.

"But seriously, it's wonderful to hear a variety of people with different backgrounds and experiences share their feelings and insights about the Savior and his gospel."

Elder Prentice went on to describe the entire three-hour block without apology and with great enthusiasm. Elder Roberts much preferred this energetic invitation to the subdued and almost embarrassed request offered by most missionaries.

To the missionaries' delight, the seventy-eight-year-old Frau Trobitius accepted the invitation.

"Well, I guess it can't hurt to see what your people are like," she said.

The missionaries arrived at Oma Trobitius's doorstep at eight forty-five on Sunday morning. Although they had no car to give her a ride, they knew their moral support might be just the extra boost she needed to take the radical step of visiting a strange church for the first time.

Oma Trobitius was ready when the missionaries knocked, and soon she was walking down the street with Elder Prentice on one side and Elder Roberts on the other. After about a block, the trio encountered one of Oma Trobitius's snoopy neighbors on her way back from her Sunday morning walk.

"Good morning, Frau Trobitius," the neighbor sang out with feigned sincerity. "And who are these two handsome young men?" she asked with a note of suspicion in her voice.

"My nephew's boys," lied Oma Trobitius. "They're just visiting. Have a nice Sunday morning," she added curtly, continuing on her way before the neighbor could ask any more questions.

When they were well out of the neighbor's earshot, Elder Prentice laughed. "Frau Trobitius, you really shouldn't lie," he admonished kindly. "You know, Elder Roberts and I don't look at all like brothers."

"I guess you're right," she conceded. "You don't look like brothers. I'll have to think of something better next time. But my neighbor is right about one thing. You are handsome young men." With that, she squeezed on the missionaries' arms and quickened her step toward the church.

25
Reap While the Day Lasts

Elder Hawthorne and Elder Keil spent Christmas Eve with the Familie Leben, and it was a wonderfully Christ-centered experience. Fortunately, Christmas Day itself fell on a Sunday, so the missionaries spent the morning in church. As feared, at church Bruder Herbst invited all the missionaries to spend most of Monday at his house. He wanted to provide dinner, show videotapes he had found of old BYU football games, and perhaps play some American football at a park.

"I'm sorry," replied Elder Hawthorne. "We're not permitted to watch or play football. And we have to work most of the day. But we can come for a couple of hours for dinner."

"What?" erupted Bruder Herbst. "Are you crazy? You can't work on the third day of Christmas. Nobody will talk with you on a holiday like that."

"We've got district meeting in the morning and appointments at one, three-thirty and seven-thirty," answered Elder Keil calmly.

They had spread out the appointments strategically. Bruder Herbst was irritated but unable to respond to the fact that the missionaries actually had appointments. He arranged for the missionaries to come for dinner at five-thirty.

After church on Christmas Day, Elder Hawthorne and Elder Keil enjoyed a longer dinner appointment than usual at the Schumanns. Then they spent a few hours street contacting in the pedestrian zone, which was almost, but not completely empty. The missionaries doubted anyone who was wandering around in the pedestrian zone would be any more offended by being approached by missionaries on Christmas than they were any other day. In fact, Elder Hawthorne found that most people they talked to had no family around for the holidays and were rather lonely.

* * *

In what both missionaries would later call a miracle, ten nonmembers attended church in Celle on Christmas Sunday. Elder Prentice and Elder Roberts had prayed intently for the Lord's blessings since the day they had received the idea, but neither of them had anticipated such a response.

One family had brought a young family of four, one older couple had brought a couple their age, one priest had brought one of his friends, and friends of two other members of various ages had come as well. And Oma

Trobitius had enjoyed the service sitting sandwiched between her two adopted grandnephews.

Elder Prentice and Elder Roberts split up at church and introduced themselves to all but one visitor whose member friend had ushered her quickly out of the building so the missionaries wouldn't be able to harass her. Of the remaining eight, five agreed to let the missionaries visit them that week, including the promising young family of four.

The members seemed even more surprised and elated than the missionaries. An almost palpable enthusiasm permeated the ward as members talked about how wonderful it had been to have so many nonmembers attend the Christmas services. The work in Celle was finally reaching critical mass.

✧ ✧ ✧

For several months Elder Prentice had been contemplating what he would say to the president in this interview. Because of Christmas, the December zone conferences were postponed until the first week of January—less than four weeks from when the missionary was scheduled to return home.

"Congratulations, Elder," said the president at the start of the interview warmly. "It looks like the work is coming around in a big way in Celle. Great things will happen there."

"Funny you should mention that," Elder Prentice began, trying to muster his courage. "I was . . . um . . . you know . . . hoping to talk to you about that some."

"About what?"

"About the future of the work in Celle. I've been . . . well . . . I've been thinking that . . . you know . . . with both Elder Roberts and me going home at the same time, there won't be any continuity to the work there. And things are just starting to take off. I'd really hate to see anything get lost in the transition. So, well . . . I was thinking, maybe I could stay on a little longer." Elder Prentice swallowed hard. "What I'd really like is a six-month extension."

President Cook was visibly surprised. After absorbing the news, he smiled. "I'm glad you want to stay. I wish every missionary wanted to stay. It shows your heart's in the right place. But the work will be fine in Celle. Don't tell anyone besides Elder Roberts, but we're going to move a set of sisters in there. They'll make you elders look like slackers," said the president with a smile.

Elder Prentice hung his head and said nothing for a moment. The fact that Elder Roberts and he were headed home at the same time had given him a good excuse to ask for an extension, and he had hoped it would suffice.

"President," Elder Prentice said softly without looking up, "I'm . . . uh . . . I'm just hitting my stride. I've peaked late, you know. I wasted a lot of time early on in my mission . . . ."

Elder Prentice paused because his voice was starting to quiver. He took a couple of deep breaths before resuming. "I let the Lord down, and . . . and I . . . um . . . I want to make it up to Him."

The elder pulled a tissue from his pocket and wiped his nose. Finally, he looked the president in the eye. "Please, you gotta let me stay on, President. I'll never have another chance."

With his last plea finally out, Elder Prentice broke down in tears, something he'd never done before in front of another man.

President Cook hesitated a moment before pulling Elder Prentice to him and hugging him tightly. He said nothing for what seemed like two or three minutes as Elder Prentice wept. Finally he pulled back, still holding J.P. by the arms.

"Elder, the Lord loves you. But this is it. Two years is what you get as a full-time missionary. It's time for you to move on now. The Lord loves you, and he'll forgive you and all of us for our sins if we repent. But there's something you can do besides getting an extension."

Elder Prentice looked up hopefully. "What?"

"You can do everything in your power to help make sure other young men avoid doing what you did. Your brother, your friends' brothers, the young men in your ward. Whoever will listen, tell them how you feel now so they can learn from your mistakes."

Elder Prentice nodded as he pulled the tissue from his pocket again.

"And don't stop sharing the gospel. At the start of your mission, I told you to reap while the day lasts, and to consider your mission the day. In a way, it is the day. You'll never have a chance quite like this again, at least not until you retire. But your whole life is the day, too. Now I'm telling you to think of your whole life as the day. If you want to show the Lord you love him, don't stop reaping as long as you're alive."

Elder Prentice nodded silently. President Cook embraced him again. "I love you, Elder. You've come a long way. And your life's just starting. You've become a fine servant of the Lord, and he'll use you."

❖ ❖ ❖

Elder Hawthorne and Elder Keil taught Ahmed Abdullah the first discussion the day after Christmas, and he had come to church the following Sunday. A complete aberration from the society in which he lived, Ahmed was a twenty-three-year-old student who lived the law of chastity and kept most of the Word of Wisdom. He knelt daily in fervent prayer and seriously studied the word of God, as he understood it. He believed God had communicated his will to humankind through prophets, and he acknowledged Jesus Christ was a great prophet. Ahmed was intrigued by Joseph Smith's story and the Book of Mormon. Within two weeks of receiving it, Ahmed seemed to be well on his way to learning of its truthfulness.

As far as Elder Hawthorne could tell, the only thing standing between Ahmed and baptism was acknowledging Jesus Christ as his Savior and the Son of God.

"If we could just get him over that thing with Jesus Christ," Elder Hawthorne mumbled mostly to himself on the way home from the fourth discussion. "He's so close—he keeps the commandments, prays, studies the scriptures. He's ninety-five percent of the way there."

The usually gregarious Elder Keil seemed quiet for most of the subway ride home. In the apartment, too, he was more subdued than normal as the elders prepared an evening snack and prepared for bed. Finally, when the missionaries were on their knees for prayer, Elder Keil cleared his throat.

"Um, Elder Hawthorne, I've been thinking about what you said, you know, about Ahmed being ninety-five percent of the way there . . . ."

"Yes?"

"Well, do you really think that's true?"

"I've never met a non-member who's so religious," answered Elder Hawthorne. "Heck, he's more religious than many members of the Church."

"He is one of the most dedicated people I've ever met, it's true," agreed Elder Keil. "But I don't know, it's just that I've been reading in the Book of Mormon, and it seems to me believing in Jesus Christ is the foundation, the whole thing. The Word of Wisdom, the law of chastity, none of that matters without Jesus Christ."

Elder Hawthorne reflected on his companion's comment for a moment, but said nothing.

"I just think maybe we need to discuss the whole idea of the atonement with him again, you know, really bear down with testimony about Jesus Christ. What do you think?"

"I can't argue with that," said Elder Hawthorne with a yawn. "There's no doubt that he's got to come around on the point of Jesus Christ."

The next morning and every other morning that week, Elder Keil and Elder Hawthorne decided to study the atonement in preparation of their special discussion for Ahmed. None of the scriptures were new to Elder Hawthorne, but by the third day he had come to view them in a new light.

"This is remarkable, Elder," exclaimed Elder Hawthorne as he and Elder Keil reread Luke twenty-four. "He actually asks the Father to let the cup pass from Him. Yet he knew what would happen if there were no atonement and no resurrection. And he asked to let the cup pass from Him."

"Maybe he hoped there was some other way, you know, like the ram caught in the thicket for Abraham," speculated Elder Keil.

"What do you think would have happened if he hadn't told the Father to let his will be done? Would the Father have let him suffer anyway?" asked Elder Hawthorne.

"I don't know," replied Elder Keil softly. "I don't know. I'm just glad he added that part."

The missionaries reexamined the scriptures that talked about the devastating eternal effects sin would have on all men, if it were not for the atonement.

"You know, Elder," mused Elder Hawthorne. "I must admit I've often thought of the atonement as something that's critical for serious sinners. But for people like you and me and even Ahmed, I've kind of thought of it as being like spackle."

"Like what?" asked Elder Keil, who had never heard the English word before. Elder Hawthorne didn't know the German translation for it, so he described what it did.

"So I think of us as generally keeping the commandments but frequently making mistakes, which are like little holes in our wall, and then we need the atonement to fill them in," explained Elder Hawthorne. "But the more we study this, the more I feel like I've got the proportions wrong. It's by the grace of the Savior that we're saved, after all we can do, and all we can do isn't very much compared to the grace we need to be pure before God."

"Yes," nodded Elder Keil. "That is how I've been feeling as I read the Book of Mormon."

The elders were now ready to teach Ahmed about the atonement.

❖ ❖ ❖

"Ahmed, you are one of the most devout people we have ever met," began Elder Hawthorne. "We believe you have learned to communicate with God as you seek to understand his will in your life. Tonight we ask you to pay special attention to the feelings of your heart, to see for yourself if the things we teach you are true. We testify that they are, and that God will make that known to you through the power of the Holy Ghost." Elder Hawthorne had been teaching with Brother Schumann every week, and it was rubbing off on him.

Elder Keil began by explaining the Fall and its effects. He discussed physical and temporal death, as they had in an earlier discussion. But this time the missionaries spent more time reading scriptural passages with Ahmed about each point of doctrine in the discussion. Ahmed asked many heartfelt questions as he struggled to better understand the effects of the Fall.

Elder Hawthorne then spent nearly twenty minutes exploring Alma thirty-four with Ahmed. Ahmed seemed to grasp what was being said on an intellectual level, but his heart could not accept it.

Elder Keil came to the end of the planned discussion by reviewing selected passages from Second Nephi chapter two with Ahmed, but Ahmed still resisted. Elder Keil was out of ideas.

Elder Hawthorne was about to wrap things up rather than press the matter any further when he felt prompted to try one last approach.

"Ahmed, imagine for a moment that you were alive almost two thousand years ago, and you lived on the American continent. You see a storm coming, a terrible storm, and as it approaches the earth begins to shake. The lamps in your house, the lamps everywhere, are blown out by the storm. You can see nothing but lightning. But you can hear the sounds of rocks breaking, buildings collapsing, and people—people screaming, some in pain, some in fear.

"For three hours the earth shakes, and you huddle in a corner with your family. The storms rage on. You are afraid. You try to light candles, to build a fire, but nothing will light. You see no stars, no moon, nothing but darkness.

"After many, many hours, maybe even days, the noise stops. Then you hear a voice, like it's coming from heaven, and the voice tells you of all the cities that have been destroyed because the people were wicked."

Elder Hawthorne looked down at his Book of Mormon as he quoted Jesus Christ. "Finally, the voice says, 'O all ye that are spared because ye were more righteous than they, will ye not now return unto me, and repent of your sins, and be converted, that I may heal you? Yea, verily I say unto you, if you will come unto me ye shall have eternal life. Behold, mine arm of mercy is extended towards you, and whosoever will come, him will I receive; and blessed are those who come unto me. Behold, I am Jesus Christ the Son of God. I created the heavens and the earth, and all things that in them are.'"

Ahmed listened intently as Elder Hawthorne spoke. Elder Hawthorne felt as if he himself were listening to someone else speak.

"The voice stops, but so does the crying. You hear the voice again, telling you to repent, to come to him like chickens to a hen. Finally, after three days, the earth is finally still. Instead of crying, some people start to rejoice, to give thanks unto the Lord Jesus Christ. And the light of day comes at last."

Ahmed was listening now with his eyes closed, his head back in his chair.

"You are drawn to the temple near your house, and you take your family with you, still huddling close together. You begin to talk with people—some of the few who have survived the destruction. You begin to talk with them about this Jesus Christ. You marvel at what has happened.

"As you're talking, you hear a voice. It is a most unusual voice, a pleasant voice. It is not loud or ugly like the sound the rocks made when they broke in the earthquake. The voice is small, almost quiet, but it penetrates your heart and makes it burn. It even shakes your body. But you cannot understand the voice.

"You hear the voice a second time, and you notice that others around you seem to hear it too, but no one can understand it. And then you hear the voice again, a third time. This time you think the voice is coming from heaven, so you look up. You open your ears and your heart, and this time you understand the voice."

Elder Hawthorne's voice cracked as he read the Father's words. "The voice's message is simple: 'Behold my Beloved Son, in whom I am well pleased . . . hear ye him.'"

Elder Hawthorne drew in a deep breath before resuming the story. "As you look toward heaven, you see a man coming down, dressed in a bright white robe. You don't dare open your mouth as you watch him descend. You believe he is an angel. The entire crowd is silent as the man comes and stands among them."

Elder Hawthorne cleared his throat before reading from the Book of Mormon again. "The man stretches forth his hand and says, 'Behold, I am Jesus Christ, whom the prophets testified shall come into the world. And behold, I am the light and the life of the world; and I have drunk out of that bitter cup which the Father hath given me, and have glorified the Father in taking upon me the sins of the world, in the which I have suffered the will of the Father in all things from the beginning.'

"When you hear this, you fall to the ground. Your whole family falls to the ground. Everyone around—without exception—everyone kneels on the ground with you. And then Jesus tells you to rise, to come to him, to feel the prints of the nails in his hands . . . and his feet, where . . . where he was nailed to the cross, so that you can know that he is the God of Israel and of the whole earth, that he was crucified for the sins of the world." Elder Hawthorne spoke slowly, of necessity.

"So, one at a time . . . you do. Your turn finally comes, and you see for yourself with your own eyes . . . and feel with your own hands and know . . . this is the one all the prophets have spoken and written about. . . . This is the Messiah."

Elder Hawthorne stifled tears, and Ahmed finally opened his eyes. Elder Keil seized the moment. "Ahmed, what do you feel in your heart right now?"

"I . . . I feel in my heart . . . like a beautiful sunset looks," answered Ahmed.

"Do you know where this feeling comes from?" asked Elder Keil.

"I believe it comes from God."

"It does," confirmed Elder Keil. "Why do you think God is giving you these feelings now?"

Ahmed leaned forward, breathed out a sigh, and then looked up at Elder Keil. "Because he wants me to know that what you are teaching me is true."

"That is right. Brother Abdullah, do you believe what we have taught you tonight is true?"

"Yes," replied Ahmed. "Yes, I do."

"Do you believe Jesus Christ is the Son of God and that he died for our sins?" pressed Elder Keil.

Ahmed looked down at the floor for a moment before answering. "Yes. I believe Jesus Christ is the Son of God. I can't believe I'm saying it, but that is what I have felt tonight, and I cannot deny it. I will not deny it."

"Will you then follow his example and be baptized, so that through his atonement you might become clean and pure from all your sins?"

"Yes. If that is what he would have me do, then that is what I must do now. I will never be able to return to my family or country again. But my parents taught me to follow God's way, wherever it leads, and that is what I am doing. I hope they will understand . . . one day, anyway."

Elder Hawthorne, who had almost regained his composure, was moved to tears again as he contemplated Ahmed's courage. As he basked in the glory of Spirit that had borne witness to him and to Ahmed of the divine role of Jesus Christ, he wished he could preserve the moment forever.

* * *

In the month of January, Elder Prentice and Elder Roberts committed the family of four and a teenage investigator to baptism. The missionaries' joy over the progress of these individuals almost made up for their sorrow over Oma Trobitius, who had become dear to both missionaries.

Oma Trobitius simply saw no way she could obey the law of tithing and survive, given her fixed income. Elder Roberts had done his imitation of Brother Schumann, but to no avail. Oma Trobitius had even shown the missionaries the math, and her case was compelling. Four days before they were to leave Celle, Elder Roberts and Elder Prentice visited their elderly friend to make one last plea.

Oma Trobitius was pleased to see her two young friends again and sorry they would be leaving her. After they had some coffee cake, Elder Roberts decided to try a novel approach, since nothing else had worked. He asked if she would mind joining them in singing a hymn. The gray-haired woman consented, and Elder Prentice pulled out his hymnal. The missionaries and Oma Trobitius huddled together to read the words as they sang.

God be with you till we meet again;
By his counsels guide, uphold you;
With his sheep securely fold you.
God be with you till we meet again.

Till we meet, till we meet,
Till we meet at Jesus' feet,
Till we meet, till we meet,
God be with you till we meet again.

Oma Trobitius removed her wire-framed glasses, wiped her eyes with a tissue, and replaced the glasses. "Will I ever see you boys again?" she asked.

"Not in this life," answered Elder Roberts. "But we hope to see you again, in the next life, at Jesus' feet."

Oma Trobitius looked down at the table and swirled her spoon in what was left of her tea. Finally, she looked up and asked Elder Roberts the question that had been haunting her. "Do I have to pay my tithing to be there?"

Elder Roberts hesitated for a moment before giving the only truthful answer he knew. "Yes. To enter into the kingdom of God, we must be baptized, and to be baptized, we must commit to pay tithing."

Oma Trobitius reached one arm inside the kitchen and grabbed a towel. Before she could remove her glasses, she burst into tears. For a full minute she wept without saying anything. Finally, between stifled sobs, she muttered, "But you told me it was free. You told me it was free."

Elder Prentice explained as well as he could that listening was free, that the reason tithing mattered was because the Lord needed our obedience, not our money, and that the Lord would provide. It was no use.

Elder Roberts said nothing. Hunched forward with his forearms on his knees, he hung his head in sorrow. Elder Roberts could not remember ever hurting more.

* * *

Because Elder Roberts was not a district leader or problem elder, Elder Hawthorne, as zone leader, would not normally have gone on splits with him. But as a token of kindness to his old senior companion, Elder Hawthorne had called Elder Roberts and arranged for them to split on their next to last day in the field.

They worked hard all day long, reminiscing between discussions and doors about their time together in Rendsburg. Elder Roberts also pumped Elder Hawthorne for updates on a number of converts in different cities, since Elder Hawthorne was able to talk with district and zone leaders from around the mission at the monthly leadership meeting.

Sister Hildebrand was still coming to church faithfully, although apparently she had not lost her cantankerous manner altogether. When her home teachers failed to visit her one month, she called them and asked if she should take it personally or if they just didn't care about all of the people they home taught. They had not missed a month since.

Leo attended regularly in Neumuenster for two months but had then disappeared. No one knew where he was. Some members still second-guessed whether he should have been baptized.

Brother Krueger, of whom Elder Roberts knew only through Elder Hawthorne's stories, had died in October. Although there were signs that he might have continued to struggle with giving up snuff, there was no question about the intent of his heart: he had left his modest estate to the Church.

The best news of all was that two families whom Elder Roberts had taught, as well as Brother Kraft, had gone through the temple. Elder Roberts wished he could have been there, especially for the sealings.

For both missionaries, the highlight of their split was dinner with the Schumanns and Sister Lohsa. Both missionaries had come to enjoy being in the Schumanns' home more than being anywhere but in the temple or their own homes.

As Elder Roberts listened to Sister Lohsa ebulliently praise the Schumanns and tell about giving her first talk, Elder Roberts could not help but wonder whether Oma Trobitius might not have been in the same position, had the Schumanns been in Celle to befriend her and teach her about tithing.

❖ ❖ ❖

"Elders and Sisters, congratulations," said President Cook to begin the testimony meeting for the eight departing missionaries. "You have served the Lord well. You can be proud of that. I mean, you can take satisfaction in that," corrected the president with a glance toward his wife. Sister Cook frequently reminded him there was no such thing as righteous pride.

"Tonight we'd like to hear your testimonies and bask in the Spirit together, one last time," he continued. "We'll begin by singing 'I Know That My Redeemer Lives.'"

As Elder Hawthorne listened to the introduction, it finally dawned on him that President Cook requested this hymn be sung at every zone conference. With the memory of his discussion with Ahmed still fresh in his mind, Elder Hawthorne's heart swelled as he sang the hymn whose words he had mouthed dozens of times before.

As each missionary bore his or her testimony, it was evident that all had emerged as genuine servants of the Lord. Some wept as they told of the miracles they had witnessed and the transformations they had undergone in the last two years.

Finally, President Cook stood to impart his last words of wisdom. As he listened to his mission president speak, Elder Roberts said a silent prayer of thanks for the opportunity he'd had to be influenced by such a powerful teacher.

"Elders and Sisters, tomorrow you'll fly home." The president paused to glance around the room and look each of his missionaries in the eye. "It will be a strange experience. Most of you will never come back to this place, and most of you will never be full-time missionaries again. When your stake president releases you, your mission will be over, and there's not a thing you can do about it. You may wish you could have done some things differently, but you can't. It's too late. The mission you've lived, that's the memory you've created for yourself for the rest of your life."

Sister Cook shot President Cook a stern glance, wondering where he was going with this line of thinking. "I don't mean to depress you. What I wanted to say is I think death will kind of be like this." Sister Cook furrowed her brow.

"I mean, imagine what it must be like to leave your body behind, knowing your life's behind you and you can't change what you've done. What I'm trying to say is, if you've served the Lord with all your heart, and you've got a comfortable feeling in your heart right now, then you wanna work hard the rest of your life so you'll feel that way when it's your time to go.

"And if you're experiencing some regrets tonight, well, then build on what you've learned here and live so as you won't have any regrets when you die. That's what you wanna aim for, having no regrets. You wanna be able to stand next to Parley Pratt and Heber Kimball when you die and feel good about it, knowing you did everything you could. That's what you want.

"Elders and Sisters, if you don't remember anything else I tell you, remember that our Heavenly Father is real. Jesus Christ is his Son. He died for our sins, and there is no way we could ever hope to dwell in the presence of a perfect, pure, glorified God except by being washed completely clean through the Savior's atoning blood. He loves us more than we could ever imagine."

Elder Prentice didn't recall ever seeing President Cook become emotional, but he thought he heard the president's voice quiver as he spoke of the Savior. "Anyway, you've heard enough from me. Let's sing a song and get you to bed."

The missionaries sang "Come Ye Children of the Lord." Elder Roberts was overcome as he sang the words of the third verse and contemplated the baptisms he'd witnessed.

> All arrayed in spotless white,
> We will dwell 'mid truth and light,

We will sing the songs of praise;
We will shout in joyous lays.
Earth shall then be cleansed from sin.
Every living thing therein
Shall in love and beauty dwell;
Then with joy each heart will swell.

After the prayer, the elders retired to a room in the basement stuffed with bunk beds. Elder Roberts, Elder Prentice, and Elder Hawthorne, who had all been companions, talked about what the president said.

"So if you had it to do over, what would you do differently?" queried Elder Roberts.

"That's easy for me," answered Elder Prentice. "I would have taken it seriously from the first day."

"Well, you must have made up for about six months in the three months you worked with me," reassured Elder Roberts.

Elder Prentice smiled. "I'm okay with it now. It was hard for a while toward the end, coming to grips with the kinds of things the president was talking about tonight. But I feel like I'm at peace with myself now, 'cause I gave it everything I had once I finally figured things out. Don't get me wrong, I still regret how I wasted away a year of my mission. But I know forgiveness is real, too."

"What about you, Elder?" Elder Prentice asked Elder Roberts.

"Oh, there are a bunch of things. I'd look for more families. It seems like nearly every family we baptized is still active, and only about half of the other people are. And I'd work with the members more from the beginning, like we did in Celle at the end."

Elder Roberts felt more but didn't know how to express it. Somehow he knew that if he'd felt as much love for people as he had for Oma Trobitius, he might have been able to touch more lives.

Elder Roberts and Elder Prentice both looked to Elder Hawthorne, who was examining his shoes as he unlaced them. "So how about you?" asked Elder Roberts. "What would you change?"

True to form, Elder Hawthorne could think of few things he wouldn't change. "I would have challenged the Familie Ulrich on the second discussion, maybe the first. I would have tried harder to love Elder Greisel."

Elder Prentice laughed heartily. "I bet Parley P. Pratt never had a companion like him."

Elder Hawthorne nodded. "I don't know, I'm sure I could have done everything so much better. But I guess most of all, I wish I'd come to understand the atonement better earlier. As I look back on my mission now, I can't believe I didn't emphasize it more. I don't know."

Elder Roberts shook his head. "I'm going to have to visit your ward to tell them what a great missionary you were, because you certainly won't," teased Elder Roberts. "It's too bad you and I can't pool our self-confidence and then cut it in half. We'd both be better off."

Elder Hawthorne smiled. "I'm gonna miss both of you. It was great working with you."

Soon someone turned out the lights. After he was sure everyone was through with their prayers, Elder Roberts wished his friends that they would sleep well: "*Schlafen Sie wohl*, elders."

From a bunk in the corner someone replied, "At least you'll be able to." And within minutes, Elder Roberts, Elder Prentice and Elder Hawthorne were deep in satisfying slumber.

❖ ❖ ❖

Sister Hawthorne looked as if she were going to burst when her son finally walked through the gate at the airport. For the first time in his life, Wesley Hawthorne hugged his mother in public without embarrassment. They squeezed each other for a full minute while Sister Hawthorne repeated, "It's so good to have you home." A little brother and a sister attached themselves to his legs.

"Mom, I love you," said Elder Hawthorne. He didn't even mind that his glasses had gotten smudged.

His father smiled broadly. "Son, we're . . . we're proud of you."

Elder Hawthorne didn't wait to see if his father would embrace him. Instead, he hugged his father as President Cook had hugged him.

"Here, Dad," the returned missionary said after they separated. From his breast pocket he pulled a fine German pen. "You can never have enough good pens. It's good to be home."

✦ ✦ ✦

Try as he might not to think about coming home, Elder Roberts had often reflected on what it would be like when he saw his family for the first time. When he heard strains of accordion music as he walked down the tunnel, he feared the worst. It was Steve, shamelessly and terribly trying to play, "The Bluest Skies You've Ever Seen Are in Seattle." Elder Roberts' father beamed, but his mother kept asking Steve to stop playing.

After a round of hugs and many tears from Sister Roberts, Steve asked Elder Roberts if he'd like to try playing the accordion. "You could play some church songs, you know. You'd be more entertaining than the Hari Krishnas."

Elder Roberts shook his head and laughed. "So how was it?" Steve finally asked.

"It was everything you ever said it would be," answered Chris honestly. "Thanks. Thanks for teaching me what you knew."

✧ ✧ ✧

In his bedroom at last, Elder Prentice unzipped his bulging suitcase and began the mundane task of unpacking. Two minutes into the job, his younger brother, Brandon, appeared in the doorway with a huge grin and a hand behind his back. He was sixteen now and looked much different than when Jon left. Elder Prentice couldn't identify what else had changed about his brother, but he seemed to have a slight edge to him that wasn't there before.

"Hey, Brandon, come on in and help me unpack," invited Elder Prentice.

Brandon laughed. "Some things never change, huh? Hey, I'm not so gullible now." Elder Prentice had gotten his brother to do a lot of work for him over the years.

"So what are you smiling about?" asked J.P. "Some girl?"

"Nope," replied Brandon. "I'm just smiling about, let's say, the musical education I got while you were away." Brandon pulled a CD from behind his back. "The Mormon Tabernacle Choir sings 'Achtung Baby.'"

Elder Prentice had almost forgotten he'd made the switch. "It's good to see you got exposed to some more, well, refined music," he said, trying to downplay Brandon's discovery.

"I knew you wouldn't change," boasted Brandon. "So did ya pick up on any German women?"

"No," said Elder Prentice softly. "No, I didn't. Look," he began, but then caught himself. "Say, I'm dying for a milkshake and I can't go alone yet. Wanna come with me? I'm buyin'."

"Sure, why not?" agreed Brandon.

On the way to the car, Elder Prentice put his arm around his brother. "I gotta tell you about this wild-lookin' guy we met when we were GQ-ing one day. He looked like a bum but he'd been wandering all over Europe, telling everybody about Jesus and stuff, because he'd read in the Bible that we should declare Jesus in every nation. It was wild."

"Don't tell me you've gone spiritual on me, Bro," resisted Brandon. "Some guy in another stake told me something like, 'If you thrust in your sickle, you'd better watch your fingers.' He said if you're not careful, a mission will just suck all the normalness right out of your body. Before his mission, his brother was a great guy, but he came back a walking spiritual zombie. I told him there was no way a mission could do that to you." Brandon's voice trailed off as he looked up at his brother uncertainly.

For a moment, Jon was silent. He wondered how he could ever share with his brother what had happened to him, how the best in him had been discovered, not suppressed. He dropped to one knee and bowed his head.

Brandon rolled his eyes and sighed.

Then in one fluid motion, Jon Prentice sprang to his feet, threw Brandon Prentice to the floor, rolled on top of him, and pinned both Brandon's hands to the carpet with his left hand. "In case you've forgotten, this—" explained Jon like a gradeschool teacher as he held up his right hand, fingers bent at the knuckles, "—is Mr. Noogie. Each time you interrupt one of my wonderful mission stories, you will get a visit from Mr. Noogie."

Jon rubbed his knuckles furiously on Brandon's head. With delightful familiarity, Brandon squealed in protest and mock pain, just as he had when Jon had used Mr. Noogie for much less noble purposes.

About the Author

Rob Eaton lives in Kent, Washington, with his wife and four children. Rob has served in a variety of callings in the Church, including Gospel Doctrine teacher, stake Sunday School president, young men president, and elders quorum president. He currently serves as a counselor in a bishopric and is a frequent speaker at youth firesides in the Seattle area.

After serving in the Germany Hamburg Mission in 1983-1984, Rob taught at the MTC in Provo, Utah. Later he worked for any BYU political science professor who would pay him, including Stan Taylor, Dave Magleby, and Noel Reynolds. After graduating from BYU with a degree in International Relations, Rob stayed on at BYU for a year to teach a political science research and writing course to students who will now take perverse delight in finding usage and grammatical errors in Rob's writing. He also worked as a research associate at FARMS for John Welch.

Rob attended Stanford Law School, where he was named Outstanding Oralist in the school's moot court competition and was admitted to the Order of the Coif. After practicing law for seven years, Rob is now a recovering attorney. He is currently Vice President of Membership for The Regence Group, which has Blue Shield and Blue Cross companies in Utah, Idaho, Washington, and Oregon.